P9-CEE-143

PRAISE FOR REBECCA YORK

"Rebecca York delivers page-turning suspense."
—Nora Roberts

"Rebecca York's writing is fast-paced, suspenseful, and loaded with tension." —Jayne Ann Krentz

"York delivers exciting and suspenseful romance with paranormal themes that she gets just right." —*Booklist*

PRAISE FOR SUSAN KEARNEY

"Kearney is a master storyteller." —Virginia Henley

"Susan Kearney is a gifted storyteller with carefully woven plots and refreshing characterization. Her style is crisp, and keeps her readers hungrily turning the pages."
—*Tampa Tribune*

"Out of this world love scenes, pulse pounding action, and characters who come right off the page."
—Suzanne Forster on *The Dare*

PRAISE FOR JEANIE LONDON

"London is a fan-pleaser!"
—*Romantic Times BookClub Magazine*

"Intrigue, suspense, action, and a satisfying romance. Jeanie London's *In the Cold* has it all."
—Jasmine Cresswell, *USA Today* bestselling author

MIDNIGHT

A COLLECTION OF NOVELLAS

MAGIC

REBECCA YORK • SUSAN KEARNEY • JEANIE LONDON

tor romance

A TOM DOHERTY ASSOCIATES BOOK
NEW YORK

Copyright Acknowledgements

"Second Chance" copyright © 2006 by Ruth Glick writing as Rebecca York
"Ulterior Motives" copyright © 2006 by Susan Kearney
"Temptation" copyright © 2006 by Jeanie LeGendre

NOTE: If you purchased this book without a cover, you should be aware that this book is stolen property. It was reported as "unsold and destroyed" to the publisher, and neither the author nor the publisher has received any payment for this "stripped book."

This is a work of fiction. All the characters and events portrayed in this book are either products of the author's imagination or are used fictitiously.

MIDNIGHT MAGIC: A COLLECTION OF NOVELLAS

Copyright © 2006 by Tom Doherty Associates, LLC

All rights reserved, including the right to reproduce this book, or portions thereof, in any form.

Edited by Anna Genoese

A Tor Book
Published by Tom Doherty Associates, LLC
175 Fifth Avenue
New York, NY 10010

www.tor.com

Tor® is a registered trademark of Tom Doherty Associates, LLC.

ISBN 0-765-35485-3
EAN 978-0-765-35485-3

First edition: May 2006

Printed in the United States of America

0 9 8 7 6 5 4 3 2 1

CONTENTS

SECOND CHANCES

BY RUTH GLICK WRITING AS

REBECCA YORK

Sara Drimmon stared in horror at the Second Chance Gallery. The green-painted cinder-block building that stood by itself at the edge of town looked like it had been an auto repair shop—and not too long ago. Two closed garage doors spanned most of the front. The weed-strewn yard and former driveway held a strange collection of art objects—everything from a naked Venus standing in the middle of a concrete fountain to a collection of gnomes who looked like they'd emigrated straight from the Black Forest.

But the array of junk wasn't what made the hairs at the back of her neck stir. She couldn't shake the feeling that something was inside the building waiting for her. And if she went in, her life would never be the same.

Well, how much worse could it be than it was now?

And what was she going to do—turn around and go home, after she'd driven four hours to this Maryland beach town?

A blast of July heat washed over her as she climbed out of her pickup truck and started toward the front door. Marcus Garrison had said he was selling off some of his stock. She might as well find out if there was anything inside worth hauling back home.

The interior was blessedly air-conditioned and surprisingly upscale—with enormous skylights that flooded the former repair shop with sunlight. Separate displays showcased antique furniture and Oriental rugs and shelves of glassware and china.

She passed them up, drawn to the art gallery in the corner. Most of the pictures were reproductions, Maxfield Parrish and Icart prints. But an original oil painting on the wall to her left made her catch her breath.

It was abstract and colorful, filled with tiny dots of thick oil paint in primary colors. The technique was what she would call pointillism, although not in the classic style. And she took back her observation that it was abstract. As she stared at the canvas, she began to make out shapes. A lady's dressing table? A mirror in a gilt frame?

"It's interesting, isn't it?" a deep voice said.

Sara whirled around to find herself facing a man in a beige linen suit blocking the doorway to the gallery. He was tall—well over six feet—and looked to be in his mid-sixties. His wavy salt-and-pepper hair hung below his collar. His narrow mustache was neatly trimmed, and his piercing blue eyes held her gaze.

"I take it you're Mr. Garrison?"

"None other." He gestured with a ring-filled hand. "I was afraid you wouldn't accept my invitation, but here you are."

She tipped her head to one side. "Who were you expecting, exactly?"

"You are Sara Drimmon, aren't you?"

The way he said her name made her nerve endings tingle. "Yes . . . I'm Sara Drimmon, but how do you know that?"

"Before I sent you the letter, I looked you up on the Internet. You have a Web site with your picture. So very modern for a woman who deals in the treasures of the past."

She tried to work her way through what he'd just told her. "Did you check the Web site of every dealer on your mailing list?"

"There was no mailing list. You were the only recipient of my offer," he said in his deep voice.

"Oh," she answered, feeling a jolt of alarm. It sounded like he had deliberately lured her here.

He was still blocking the doorway, and she wondered if she could slip by him and make it out of the shop, if he hadn't already locked the door.

"I read about you," he continued, his tone confiding now. "About you and Matthew Tripplehorn."

She sucked in a sharp breath. Not a day went by that she didn't think of Matt. Of what she'd lost.

"That was such a tragedy."

"Yes," she said, her voice low.

"You loved each other very much. Then your happiness was snatched away," Garrison continued, his deep voice making it sound like he'd shared in her pain. "And I was thinking that you were the perfect candidate to come see the painting."

"I don't understand," she whispered.

"I know. But perhaps you will if you have the courage to reach out for what you want." He went on in even tone. "That painting is called 'Midnight Magic.' It's very old. I became its custodian several years ago, and that's a tremendous responsibility. It was painted by a sorcerer as an escape hatch."

"I still don't understand."

"He didn't get what he wanted out of this life. And he longed to escape to a venue with more favorable . . . conditions. So he used magical paint to create an environment where he could be happy. The legend claims that when he finished the painting, he traveled into the universe he'd created on canvas and never returned."

Sara's eyes narrowed. "That's impossible."

"Is it? Haven't you longed to escape the sadness of this world after Matthew was killed? Wouldn't you like a second chance? Or are you afraid to take that leap?"

She swallowed around the lump in her throat. "Nobody gets a second chance. Matthew is dead. And that's the end of it."

"Go look at the painting."

Feeling light-headed, she took a step forward, then another. As she crossed the room, she stared at the bright dots that made up the surface of the canvas. The colors danced before her eyes, making her feel dizzy and disoriented yet, at the same time, strangely energized.

And the shapes hidden in the pattern took on a more solid appearance. The lady's dressing table. A colorful Oriental rug. The mirror.

With a dreamy feeling, she moved toward them, right up to the glistening surface. She felt poised on a threshold, as if she could walk right into the painting. No, that was crazy! Impossible. Still, she tried to take another step forward and felt some kind of barrier holding her back.

"I can't," she whispered.

"Is your fear keeping you here? Are you too timid

to dare?" Garrison asked, his tone mocking her. It sounded like he was far behind her now, his voice miles away.

Timid? Nobody had ever accused the Drimmon women of that. Her dad had died when she was only three. Mom had worked hard to survive, first as a clerk in an antique shop on Main Street in Fredericksburg, then as the owner. Sara grew up knowing a Queen Anne chair from a Chippendale or a Sheraton, and how to tell a reproduction from the real thing.

When her mother had gotten too sick to run the business, she'd taken over and made a reputation for herself in the Fredericksburg area, which was how she'd met Matthew Tripplehorn.

Matt. Her heart ached when she thought about Matt. Her lost love. And maybe that was what pushed her forward, through the barrier and right into . . .

Into what?

"Mr. Garrison?"

There was dead silence behind her. Not just silence—the complete absence of sound. She felt goose bumps rising on her arm. When she looked behind her, the man and the gallery had disappeared as though they had never existed.

Sara caught her breath. What she saw now was a wall covered with peach silk. Against the silk were small gold frames holding antique pictures of flowers.

She couldn't believe it. She recognized that wall. It was in the house of Cornelia Ballenger, in the ladies' retiring room on the first floor. She'd sold Mrs. Ballenger the paintings, then arranged to have them matted and framed. She knew the door to the right led to the bathroom. The door to the left led back into the hallway.

Sara's hands flew to her face, and she pressed her palms against her cheeks. Making contact with own flesh helped reassure her that she still inhabited her own body. Or *was* this her body?

With a small sound, she pivoted in the other direction, toward the French dressing table and the mirror above it.

Her heart was pounding. Seconds ago she had been

at the Second Chance Gallery in St. Michaels, Maryland. Now, somehow, she was back at the Ballenger mansion outside Fredericksburg, Virginia. Unless she had gone insane. Or was this a dream?

Right. A dream.

Her gaze focused on the mirror, and she blinked as she saw herself the way she'd looked a year ago—happy, confident. Not the sad, worn-down woman she'd become in the months since Matthew had been snatched away from her.

The transformation was startling, even to her own eyes.

Had she ever looked that young? That vibrant? That full of confidence? Had she ever been this sure that a long and prosperous future was stretching out in front of her?

When she'd walked into the Second Chance Gallery, her blond hair had been limply hanging around her shoulders. Now it was fixed in a sophisticated upsweep. Her wide-set blue eyes stared back at her, the deep circles underneath magically erased.

As she stared in wonder at her reflection, her hand went to her throat. She was wearing an antique pearl necklace, a piece she'd borrowed from her own stock to wear with the black designer cocktail dress that had come from the consignment boutique down the block from her shop. Bonnie Harrison was a friend of hers, and she'd put the dress aside, then called to say she had something she knew Sara would want. Of course, Bonnie had tried to charge too much. But Sara had struck a bargain—the dress in exchange for fifty dollars in cash and the washstand bowl and pitcher that Bonnie had been admiring.

As those details came back to her, Sara gasped

again. She not only knew where she was. More important, she knew *when*.

A year ago. When everything had been different.

She'd worn the black dress to the party that Cornelia Ballenger had invited her to because Mrs. Ballenger wanted to show off the clever little antique dealer who was filling in some of the bare spaces in her mansion with artwork and furnishings she'd picked up at auctions around the area.

Sara's hands shook as she touched her hair, then looked down at her feet cushioned on the Oriental rug. She was wearing stylish black pumps with the pearl accents. They hurt her feet, but she'd worn them anyway because they went so well with the cocktail dress, and she wanted to blend in with the sophisticated crowd she knew Mrs. Ballenger had invited.

And she'd worn black stockings to hide the Celtic band tattooed around her left ankle, since she was pretty sure the people here wouldn't appreciate the personal statement.

She fought to remember exactly what had happened after she'd gone into the ladies' retiring room. She'd only been there a few minutes to check her makeup. Then she'd walked outside the door and . . .

Oh God—and met Matthew Tripplehorn.

She went perfectly still, hardly able to drag in a breath. Matt. She was going to meet Matt. He was alive and well. Unless she was dreaming. Or crazy. Those were still possibilities.

Her heart started to pound so hard that she felt dizzy. Putting out her hand, she steadied herself against the dressing table.

Her fingers clutched the cold marble top, helping to ground her. Her breath shallow, she stared into the mirror. Everything she saw told her she was back in the past, before the love of her life had been killed.

Or was this some cruel joke?

Not trusting the reflection of reality, she swung around, half expecting to see Marcus Garrison in the Second Chance Gallery, grinning at the clever illusion he'd created.

Thank the Lord he wasn't there. And when she directed her attention outward, she could hear the sounds of the party, the string quartet that Cornelia had hired for the evening. Chatter and laughter. Cutlery clinking against china.

Her heart was pounding, and it was impossible to hold her hand steady as she reached toward the doorknob. What was on the other side of that door? Heaven or hell? Or nothing?

Before she could chicken out, she turned the knob and stepped outside. It wasn't *nothing*. The illusion or whatever it was held steady. She was in the side hallway that led from the drawing room to the back of the mansion.

As she stood there blinking, a woman's voice called her name.

"Sara. There you are! I've been looking all over for you."

It was Cornelia Ballenger wearing a big smile and a gray silk dress that was perfect with her sparkling white hair. Sara fought another wave of disorientation. The last time she'd seen Mrs. Ballenger, the woman had been screaming at her.

"How dare you come to Matthew's funeral. How dare you show your face here? If he hadn't gotten mixed up with you, he would still be alive."

Sara had never quite understood the logic of the

accusation, and she could hardly ask about it now. Dragging in a steadying breath, she tried to act like her insides hadn't twisted into a painful knot.

"My dear, you look a little pale. Are you all right?"

"Yes, Mrs. Ballenger," she managed. Pulling herself together she added, "I'm just a bit overwhelmed to be at this party."

"Nonsense, my dear. I want my friends to meet the woman who did such a marvelous job supplying me with artwork and antiques. And please, I've asked you to call me Cornelia."

"Cornelia." She swallowed. "Thank you for giving me this opportunity."

She didn't stop you from meeting Matt. She's not going to stop you now. She's only going to get hostile later, Sara silently tried to reassure herself.

They walked down the hallway together toward the party. The first guests they encountered were two tuxedo-clad men.

They both looked up as Cornelia and Sara approached.

"Bradley, Travis," their hostess said, "This is the young woman I was telling you about."

Sara already knew who they were—Bradley Tripplehorn and Travis Norton.

Bradley was Matt's married older brother. He hadn't done as well in business, and he was jealous of his brother's success. After Matt's death, she'd done some research on him—and Travis Norton, too. Bradley had gotten caught in a cheating scandal in college and had had to change schools.

Travis Norton's bio had turned her stomach. He specialized in taking over companies in trouble, gutting them and selling off what was left. He and Bradley were working on some kind of deal. Sara didn't exactly know what.

"Charmed to meet you," Bradley said, using a voice that sounded strangely like Prince Charles.

Matt had told her his brother loved to imitate voices. His grandmother probably didn't like him doing it at the party, but she wasn't going to chastise him in public.

"Nice to meet you," Sara answered, hoping that her distaste for the two men didn't show on her face.

After a few minutes of polite conversation, Cornelia led her through the crowd again, stopping to talk to other friends and relatives. Her country club buddy, Martha Swinton, talked about setting up a meeting with Sara to discuss some artwork. And so did Patrick O'Hara, Cornelia's financial adviser. Sara gave them both her business card, and suggested that they call her on Monday, even though she knew that O'Hara wanted to make a pass at her. She also knew from her research that he was sometimes careless about his accounting practices.

But all the time she was talking to the people in the room and remembering what she'd discovered about their backgrounds, her antennae were out, and her pulse was pounding.

Maybe Matt wasn't even here this time around. She knew he'd been out of town until right before the party. Maybe he'd changed his mind and decided he was too tired to put in an appearance.

She wanted to ask his grandmother, but she didn't dare. She hadn't met him yet. And there would be no reason why she would be interested in him, unless she was going to make a play for the family money. At least that was the way Cornelia would see it.

Finally, when she felt like she was going to jump out of her skin, she saw him across the room. Just that glimpse made her sway on her feet.

Cornelia didn't even notice. She was too busy telling another one of her friends about the paintings and furnishings Sara had sold her.

Sara struggled to pay attention to the conversation. But all the time she was watching Matt from the corner of her eye. He had spotted his grandmother and started across the room to greet her, just like it had happened the last time.

And just like the last time, his gaze found Sara, and his expression changed. She'd seen it a year ago. She saw it now—that rush of interest that she had been afraid to return because he was the grandson of Cornelia Ballenger, and she was the hired help.

This time, she allowed herself the luxury of smiling and of admiring him as he moved toward her through the crowd.

He was just under six feet tall with his wavy dark hair worn just over the ears and brushed to the side across his forehead.

His eyes were large and brown, his nose straight, his chin firm. He'd minored in drama at Florida State, much to his grandmother's disapproval. And he'd often won the leading-man role in department productions. He always looked great to her, but in a tuxedo he was positively devastating.

As he walked toward them, she struggled to breathe normally.

"Who's this lovely woman you're keeping to yourself?" Matt asked.

Cornelia gave him a startled look. "Why, Matthew, I didn't expect to see you here."

"I caught an earlier flight from Boston, so I decided to stop by," he said. "Lucky for me."

Sara listened to the familiar words.

"So who is this woman I came here to meet?" he asked again.

Cornelia could hardly refuse an introduction, so she graciously said, "Matthew Tripplehorn. Sara Drimmon. Sara is the antique dealer I've been working with."

"Oh, yes. You mentioned her. But you didn't tell me she was so young and lovely."

Sara flushed. She'd been embarrassed by Matt's words the first time. Déjà vu didn't help.

"Well, I'm sure Grandmother wants to mingle with her other guests." Keeping his focus firmly on Sara, he asked, "Have you eaten?"

She shook her head.

"Then let's go see what's on the buffet table."

"Matt, I wanted to introduce Sara to some of my associates."

He turned back to Cornelia. "This is a party. She doesn't have to work tonight," Matt pointed out.

"We both know that a party is a marvelous place to make connections for potential clients."

"Well, then, I've decided to change my office decor, and Sara is the perfect consultant."

The last time she'd played out this scene, Sara had felt caught between Matt and his grandmother. She was still caught. But she had no doubt about what she wanted.

"I'd be glad to discuss your office," she said to Matt.

Cornelia gave her a disapproving look. Sara knew that Mrs. Ballenger hadn't counted on her meeting Matt tonight. And her relationship with her patron had gone downhill after that. But she didn't care—not when she was getting to spend the rest of the evening with Matt.

The rest of the evening? And more? Lord, she'd take as much as she could get.

"Let's go check out the food," Matt said.

"OK." She gave Cornelia an apologetic look, then walked across the room with Matt toward the gallery where the buffet table was set up.

"Are you really interested in redoing your office?" she asked.

"I wasn't. But you could change my mind."

"I'm not supposed to be working tonight," she reminded him, struggling to keep her tone light when her head was spinning.

He grinned. "Right. So how did you meet my grandmother?"

"She was browsing in my antique shop. She liked my merchandise and bought a painting."

"And bargained your price down first, I assume?"

She laughed, remembering the conversation. "Yes."

"And everything she's bought from you has been below what you wanted to get for it."

"I . . ."

"You're paying for the opportunity to sell to the Ballengers and the Tripplehorns."

"I've made out okay on the transactions," she said, although she certainly hadn't done as well as she would have liked.

Before they reached the buffet line, another man came up to Matt. It was Josh Hemingway, who was a vice president of Matt's company.

"So how was Boston?" Josh asked.

"Good."

"Did you get those contracts?"

"Yeah."

"Great. You asked me to keep tabs on the building. You wanted a progress report?"

Sara struggled not to betray a sudden surge of fear. The building. Oh Lord. He must be talking about the construction project out near one of the shopping malls, where Matt had died.

Sara tried to listen to the men talking, but the buzzing in her ears and the thumping of her heart made it almost impossible to take in the words.

Had Josh brought up the project in the first version of this scene? Or was this something different?

A warning?

From whom? Fate?

Last time around, Matt had left the project almost entirely to Josh. Was this different? Was Josh going to drag Matt over there tonight to meet with Dave Olson, the contractor? Was everything going to be snatched away from her before it even happened?

She felt like she was swaying on a high wire as she waited to hear Matt's next words.

"Why don't we talk about it in the morning?" Matt said. Josh looked disappointed, but Matt remained firm. "At the office tomorrow."

It's all right. The office. Not the building site.

The other man strode off, and Matt turned back to Sara. "Sorry."

"That's okay," she managed to say.

"Let's eat."

He led her to the buffet line, and she stared at the food. Roasted vegetable salad, marinated Kalamata olives and artichoke hearts, bruschetta, thin-sliced fillet of beef with horseradish sauce, poached salmon with

dill marinade. She hadn't wanted to look greedy last
time. This time she wondered if she could swallow anything. But she put food onto her plate because she
wanted to have dinner with Matt, and he'd think it was
strange if she just sat there and watched him, which
was what she really longed to do.

They reached the end of the table, and she held her
breath, waiting to find out what would happen next,
because this time could be different. It was already
different.

Matt looked around the room. "Unless you like eating with a plate on your lap while trying to juggle a drink at the same time, we could go find somewhere more comfortable."

She let out the breath she'd been holding. "That sounds like a good idea."

They stopped at the bar in the main room. She got a Coke. Matt asked for a glass of red wine.

Drinks and plates in hand, they walked down a back hall, through a door and into one of the estate's private rooms, the same room where they'd eaten dinner the last time.

It was outfitted for the men in the family with a tartan rug, a leather sofa and matching chair, a coffee table made from an old cobbler's bench, and a television concealed by an antique armoire. The pictures on the walls were of hunting birds that she had supplied to Cornelia.

Matt set his plate on the coffee table. She did the same. Last time, she had settled into the armchair. Tonight she sat down on the sofa and waited to see what Matt would do. He sat on the other end of the sofa.

She struggled to keep her hand from shaking as she carefully cut a piece of fillet. As far as Matt knew, they had just met. But she was sitting here alone with the man she loved, the man she had thought she would never see again.

It felt like there wasn't enough oxygen in the room for her to draw a full breath. But she knew that had to be an illusion because she didn't fall over and slump to the rug.

Matt took a bite of salmon and swallowed. "So where have you been hiding all my life?"

"I've lived in Fredericksburg since I was a little kid. But you probably don't do much cruising through antique shops."

"Right. You have your own shop?"

"Yes."

"How did you get into the antique business?"

"I learned it from my mom. When she retired, I took over the business from her."

"Um."

Although the conversation might not be deep, she had the feeling something important was happening between them. She'd felt it the first time, but it carried more weight now that she knew where they were headed.

"What do you do for fun?" he asked.

"Fun?"

"You know, drinking at the Lamplighter Pub. Riding the roller coaster at Busch Gardens. Sea kayaking. The old fishing hole. The carnival that's in town this week. What's your pleasure?"

She laughed. "There's not much opportunity for sea kayaking in downtown Fredericksburg."

"No, but I've looked forward to the carnival every year since I was a kid."

She pushed a bit of salmon around her plate, remembering that they'd gone there together the last time around.

"We went sometimes. Not every year. But I liked it, too."

They kept chatting, talking about their lives. She knew all the information Matt was giving her—and more. It was a pleasure to hear him tell her again, about how he'd been into polo as a teenager, how he'd majored in art history and minored in drama, then buckled down and gotten an MBA. They shared a passionate interest in art and design, although he kept that side of himself hidden from most people.

The whole time they were talking and eating, she ached to set their plates aside and reach for him. He was so close. She caught his familiar scent and tried not to watch his lips as he ate. Or his hands.

He finished eating and looked over at her half-full plate. "Are you still working on that?" he asked.

She'd forgotten he'd said that. Even as she remembered, she burst out laughing.

"What?"

"Waiters use that phrase all the time, and it always gives me such an odd image."

"Yeah."

"I'm finished."

He stood, picked up the plates, and took them outside, where he set them on the sideboard near the door.

Then he turned toward her. "Do you want some dessert?"

"No, thanks."

He came back inside and closed the door.

Unable to sit still, she stood, too, and they walked toward each other, right into each other's arms.

Thank God. Finally.

"Sara?"

She couldn't speak because her heart was blocking her windpipe. Slowly, giving her time to change her mind, he lowered his head, and she raised her mouth to meet his.

The kiss started out sweet, even tender. But it took only seconds for it to change from sweet to sweltering.

Their first kiss, as far as he knew. Yet she had done this before, and that made it all the more achingly intense.

Part of her stood outside herself watching, marveling at the reality of being in Matthew Tripplehorn's arms again. But the actual living, breathing Sara Drimmon was engulfed by the sensation of his lips moving urgently against hers, his hands gliding up and down her back, the rich scent of his body.

She remembered that the kiss had been intense. This time it melted her bones, made her cling to him to stay on her feet.

Matt's mouth moved over hers, speaking to her in a secret language that only the two of them shared. The intimate contact brought with it the hint of the wine he'd drunk with his dinner and the essence of the man.

Matthew Tripplehorn. Her lover. The man she thought she would never kiss again.

She clung to him as his tongue explored the inside of her lips, her teeth. She was so aroused that she could barely think coherently.

She felt his erection pressing against her middle, and she wanted to reach down and clasp him there. And more. She wanted to lower his zipper and free him, then tear off her panty hose and pull him down to the rug.

She recognized the impulse as madness. She might yearn to make love with him again, but as far as he was concerned, they had just met.

Still, she ached to feel him inside her. She wanted everything before it vanished into thin air.

He lifted his head and looked down at her, and she watched his eyes come into focus. "Are we under a magic spell?"

"Yes," she whispered, because that was pretty close to the truth. A sorcerer had dotted magic paint over a canvas. And she was reaping the rewards.

"I think you were destined to be in my arms."

He had said that the first time they had disappeared into this room together. Now it meant so much more. She ached to tell him that they had kissed before, and a whole lot more. But she didn't want to come across as a nutcase.

So all she did was cling to him.

Laughter drifted toward them from down the hall, reminding her that they were not really alone.

"Do you want to get out of here?" he asked.

"Yes."

"Where do you want to go?"

"The boat dock," she said. That's what they'd done before. Gone down to the dock and made out.

"That's what I was thinking."

"Your grandmother is going to be upset if she sees us leaving."

"Then we'll make sure she doesn't." He opened the door and looked out. "The coast is clear."

Taking her hand, he led her away from the chatter and music of the party and toward the side of the house. They slipped into the kitchen, where a catering service had set up a command center. Behind the scenes, the staff filled trays and serving dishes with second helpings of the food already on the table. More workers readied trays of crème brûlée that would be passed among the guests.

Another team stacked dirty dishes in carrying cases to take back to the catering kitchen, where they would be washed.

Sara and Matt slipped out the side door into the humid summer night, then walked around the catering truck pulled up to the kitchen door.

It was dark outside except for the floodlights illuminating the grounds. The shrubbery and trees were a shadowy mass in the background. Once they'd cleared the house, she giggled. "I guess we made it."

"Yeah."

He took her hand and led her down the driveway, where he leaned over and gave her another kiss. They were both so wrapped up in each other that almost nothing else registered.

But a shivery feeling danced at the back of Sara's neck.

Then she thought she heard someone shout to Matt.

"Did you hear that?" she asked.

"No. What?"

This was something new. Something that hadn't happened when they'd been here the last time. She'd read books about time travel, and she'd thought it was supposed to be difficult to change the past.

But this wasn't exactly time travel. This was magic travel, she reminded herself.

Suddenly, all her senses were on alert. Turning, she looked up the driveway and what she saw brought a gasp to her lips.

"Oh Lord."

Hearing the panic in Sara's voice, Matt whirled, and an icy wave swept over his skin.

A car was rolling toward them along the driveway, picking up speed as it came down the hill.

His grip firm on her arm, he pulled her out of the way of the vehicle. It was a Lexus SUV, probably one of the largest and heaviest cars on the estate grounds tonight.

They jumped into a flower bed, and the massive car lumbered past, missing them by inches.

He turned to Sara. She looked dazed. "Are you OK?" he asked urgently.

"How did that happen?" she whispered, sounding bewildered.

"I'd like to know."

Matt turned back to the vehicle. It was still moving, but as far as he could see, no one was in the driver's seat. All on its own, it careened down the driveway.

"Jesus!"

He watched the SUV reach a curve in the driveway, climb the curb, and mow down a stand of hundred-year-old boxwood bushes before finally coming to a rest.

One of the parking attendants his grandmother had hired for the night came pounding after it, his eyes wide with shock.

Matt approached the young man, trying not to shout in the guy's face. "We could have gotten killed. What the hell happened?"

The attendant looked like he wished he could sink into the ground. "I don't know, sir. I was getting Mrs. Wellsburg's car and when I turned around, I saw the SUV fifty yards from where I'd left it."

"Did you see anyone in it?"

"No, sir."

Other people had appeared outside the house. Patrick O'Hara, his grandmother's financial adviser. Josh Hemingway, his vice president for development.

Josh stared at the car, which had stopped only a few feet from the wall of the house.

Matt strode to the SUV, threw the door open, and looked into the passenger seat. When he started to get in, Sara put a hand on his shoulder.

"Don't. You'll mess up any fingerprints."

He turned to face her. "Fingerprints? You think we should call the police?"

She lifted one shoulder. "It looked like . . . like somebody tried to hurt you."

"It was an accident," he said because he couldn't believe anything else. If someone had tried to injure him, they would have had to see him and Sara leave, then hurry out here after them and make a quick decision to act. All pretty far-fetched.

"Did you hear someone call you?" she asked.

"No. Did you?"

"I thought I did."

"I guess to warn us," he suggested.

Sara looked like she wanted to argue about that, but she only took her lower lip between her teeth. He climbed into the car and pressed the emergency brake with his foot. He'd owned a Lexus, and he knew how it worked. The same pedal turned the brake on and off. In this case, it was off. No surprise. And the gearshift was in neutral.

He glanced back at the attendant, who was watching him with a sick look on his face.

"Didn't you have the brake engaged?"

"I thought I did." The attendant shifted his weight from one foot to the other, then backed up a couple of steps. "That car was parked at the edge of the drive, pointing downhill because the man who left it said he wanted to go home early. Maybe somebody was fiddling with it."

"Who?"

"Kids might have been attracted by the party. They could have thought it would be funny to send one of the big expensive cars rolling down the hill."

Matt nodded. He remembered in his younger days fooling around with the cars parked for an event like this. "And somebody took the brake off and put it into neutral," he mused.

He examined the front end of the car. It had come through the accident virtually unscathed. Too bad he couldn't say the same for his grandmother's boxwoods.

"What should I do?" the attendant asked.

"Move it out of the bushes. Then tell the owner what happened when he comes back."

The man looked relieved that someone else was making the decisions.

"Shouldn't we tell your grandmother?" Sara asked.

Matt thought for a moment. "There's nothing she can do about damage to her landscaping tonight. Let's not spoil the party for her."

"That's probably best."

He gave Sara a critical inspection. "You look pretty shaken up. Let me take you home."

"My car . . ."

"Grandmother can have somebody drive it over to your place in the morning."

"Okay," she agreed. But she didn't sound entirely convinced.

"She's got enough people working here, so that won't be a problem."

They walked down the driveway to where he'd parked his own Mercedes.

In the front seat, he glanced across at her. Her hands were tightly clasped in her lap, as though she were trying to keep them from shaking.

"Everything's fine," he murmured.

Still he saw that her large blue eyes were troubled.

"I guess that really spooked you."

"That car could have . . . could have . . ." She shuddered.

He covered her small hands with his much larger ones. Her hands were icy cold.

"You take things very seriously," he said.

"Well, I had a lot of responsibilities from an early age." She gave him the ghost of a smile. "But I'll try to lighten up."

He headed toward town. "I should have asked. Where to?"

"Princess Anne Street."

"You're not going back to the shop, are you? I was going to take you home."

As they passed under a street light, he saw her cheeks turn pink. "I live in back of the shop. It's . . . convenient." She raised her chin. "And it saves a lot of money."

"Good idea," he replied, focusing on the road ahead. Her answer was a reminder that she lived in a different world from the one he inhabited. She was saving money by living and working in the town's business district. And he could buy property anywhere he chose. But what did their status matter? He was attracted to her, and he wanted to get to know her better. Actually, there was more to it. He couldn't shake the feeling that he had known her very well in the past, and that he'd been given a chance to get to know her again.

"What?" she asked.

He could have lied. Instead, he tried out his thoughts on her. "Just playing with a little fantasy."

"Oh?"

He swallowed. "It feels like we've known each other for longer than a few hours."

"Yes," she breathed.

"You feel it, too?"

"Very much." She reached out and pressed her hand over his where it rested on the steering wheel. He took his hand from the wheel so he could knit his fingers with hers.

Sara closed her eyes, clinging to Matt's hand. Words clamored behind her closed lips. There were so many things she ached to say to him now that she had the chance. She wanted to prove that they did know each other well. She could tell him she knew about the time he and Bradley had gone swimming in the creek, and how he'd cut his foot on a piece of glass and been afraid to tell his parents because he wasn't supposed to swim there in the first place. She wanted to say she knew how upset he'd been when his parents had divorced, and his mom had moved to France. His dad was still in the area, but he was too wrapped up in his new wife to pay much attention to his sons.

She longed to tell him about the problems with her own mother, to get that out in the open because she was sure somebody had used that against her the last time around. But revealing Mom's secrets would certainly be going too far for her first evening with Matt. She settled for hanging on to him and telling him how she'd helped arrange knickknacks in the shop when she was in kindergarten.

"You got an early start," he commented.

"Yes. I could tell sterling silver from silver plate before I was in first grade."

As they drove onto Princess Anne Street, he slowed. "Where to?"

"My shop's called Peggy's Fancy."

"Who's Peggy?"

"My mom. I kept the name when she retired."

"Is she still in the area?"

"She died."

"I'm sorry."

"That's OK," she murmured, since she never knew quite what to say under the circumstances.

At the end of the block, she gave him directions again. "There's an alley and a parking area in back.

Take the first right. Then it's the third building from the corner."

He made the turn, then found the back of her shop and pulled into the parking space.

She should thank him politely for driving her home, then exit the car and go inside. But she remained silent as she slowly opened her door.

He did the same. As if they'd made a mutual agreement, he followed her around a vine-covered trellis into the small patio area she'd made with used bricks she'd carted home from a house being demolished.

A light shone down beside the back door, and she tried to see the patio through Matt's eyes. It was small and screened from the businesses on either side by a stockade fence. Her neighbors used the back area for a shipping dock. She wanted a place to unwind in the evenings.

Along the fence were planter boxes filled with impatiens, which gave her color in the shade. The wrought aluminum patio chairs, side tables, and classic statuary were items she'd picked up at estate sales.

"This is charming," he said.

"I like to come out here and relax."

She unlocked the back door and led him into her little apartment. The tiny bedroom was in the back. Between the bedroom and the shop was a sitting room with a small kitchen area on the left and a storage closet on the right. The bathroom was off the bedroom.

When she turned on a tabletop Tiffany-style lamp, Matt looked around. She saw him eye her brass bed with its antique quilt. To put a little space between them, she crossed the rag rug and stood beside a Victorian dressing table that she'd acquired a few months ago. Or was it a year and a half ago? She wasn't sure how to keep time.

"You could moonlight as an interior decorator," he said.

"I have my pick of the pieces that I get at auctions or from estate sales. I keep what I like best and put the rest into the shop. So I rotate things in and out of here," she said, feeling like she was babbling.

Matt crossed to her. "I don't usually . . ." He trailed off.

"Neither do I," she answered. "But we can go with your fantasy. You and I are long-lost lovers."

"And somebody wiped out our memory, so we don't remember what we were to each other in the past."

She couldn't tell him that she still had those precious memories or that her heart was bursting with love for him. Instead, she whispered, "But we can find out what we are to each other now."

"Lord, yes." In the supercharged atmosphere of the bedroom, he reached for her, and she came into his arms. She had vowed that she wouldn't allow herself to get intimate with him too quickly. But it was impossible for her to keep that silent promise.

Not when fate had given her a second chance. And even if he didn't remember what they had been to each other, she sensed the same urgency in him.

His mouth swooped to take possession of hers, and she moaned in surrender.

He had sent heat coursing through her blood when they'd kissed at his grandmother's house. Now that heat came rushing back as though someone had opened a furnace door.

He angled his head to take more complete possession, his tongue sweeping into her mouth, conquering and yet, at the same time, soothing.

All her senses were tuned to him. His wonderful

taste, the hard muscles of his body, the erection straining behind the fly of his tuxedo pants. Greedy for physical contact, she twisted her fingers into his dark hair.

She broke the kiss so she could look into his eyes and say, "This isn't just a one-night stand."

"No. Never."

White-hot need sprang between them like a forest fire out of control, sweeping everything away but the drive to be close to him, then closer still.

He brought his mouth back to hers for a long drugging kiss, pushing her farther and farther into the inferno of their own making.

His hands were at her back, lowering the zipper of her designer dress. She helped him pull it off her shoulders, then stepped out of the expensive frock, kicking it out of the way as though it were no more important than a beach blanket.

He kept his mouth on hers, exchanging hot greedy kisses as his hands found the catch of her bra. She helped him send it after the dress, then reached for the studs at the front of his tuxedo. His fingers tangled with hers as they both hurried to open his shirt. His tuxedo jacket joined her dress on the floor, then his shirt, until finally, finally they were both naked to the waist, and he could pull her into his arms again, swaying her upper body against his.

The sensation of her nipples sliding against his hair-roughened chest made her cry out.

Then he angled himself away so that he could take her breasts in his hands, cupping and squeezing them, his fingers moving over her heated flesh.

"More. Oh Lord, more," she managed to say.

"Like this?" he growled, his fingers cresting across

the hard, aching tips, then catching them between thumbs and forefingers to make her gasp with pleasure. It was what he knew she liked. And now he was doing it again, as though he were reading her mind—or remembering.

She didn't have to tell him what she wanted next. His hands were at the waistband of her panty hose, pushing them down her hips. She stepped out of her shoes and kicked them away along with the panty hose as she reached around him to unhook the cummerbund he still wore. Then her hands were at the fly of his pants.

Lowering the zipper, she reached inside, finding his penis and clasping it in her hand.

He made a strangled sound as she ran her hand up and down the length, then circled the tip, just at the edge where she knew he liked it best.

He kicked off his pants, and they moved together toward the bed. Luckily it wasn't too far because she couldn't have managed to stand up much longer.

They fell together onto the mattress in a tangle of arms and legs, their movements frantic as they rocked together, kissed, touched.

He bent to take one distended nipple into his mouth, sucking strongly, turning her molten.

She could only draw in panting little breaths as his hand moved down her body, sliding into her most sensitive flesh. When he took a gliding stroke from her vagina to her clit, she knew she was close to climax.

He took her up and up, until she was desperate for release. But not like this.

"Please. I want you inside me when I come. Please."

"God, yes."

He covered her body with his, and she reached down to guide his way.

When he was inside her, he went very still, looking down into her face, his expression registering the wonder of the moment.

She lifted her hand, touching his cheek, overwhelmed with emotion. She had thought she would never make love with him again, and tonight he was in her bed once more.

He kissed her on the mouth, and she stroked her hands down his back. Slowly, he began to move inside her, tuning her body to his.

She wanted it to last forever, but the tempo quickly picked up speed. Hot currents darted through her, making her frantic for release. She surged against him. Her heart hammered. Her body was drenched in sweat, vibrating with pleasure almost beyond bearing. And then an explosive climax took her.

As she felt her inner muscles spasm, she heard his shout of satisfaction.

They collapsed in a damp, tangled heap on the quilt. She held him to her, vowing she would never let him go.

Words she longed to speak burned behind her lips. She wanted to tell him she loved him. She wanted to say that having him back was the most tremendous thing that had ever happened to her. She wanted to vow that she would keep him safe this time.

But she could say none of that, so she stroked her hands over his broad back and kissed his cheek.

He cleared his throat. "I feel like a wanderer come home . . . from exile."

"Are you always that poetic?"

"No."

"You said it very well. I feel like you've come back to me. Finally."

She didn't want to move. She wanted to hold him like this all night. But the air-conditioning had dried the perspiration on their bodies and she began to shiver.

"We should get under the covers."

"Yes."

He stood so they could turn down the quilt and top sheet. When she slid her leg over the side of the bed, he looked at her ankle, then stroked his fingers over the Celtic design.

"That's a very sexy tattoo."

"A girlfriend and I did it on a dare a few years ago."

"What did she get?"

"A dragon on her butt."

Matt laughed. "You're kidding, right?"

"No she's the free-spirit type."

She pulled the spread aside, and they settled down again in the double bed. Snuggling against him, she stroked her lips over his shoulder. She was exhausted from the emotional reunion that only she really understood—although he seemed to have some inkling that they had known each other before.

"You look worn out," he murmured.

"I'm okay."

The sophisticated upsweep into which she'd pinned her hair was drooping badly. She felt him taking the pins out and setting them one by one on the night table before combing his hands through her hair.

"Your hair is like spun gold," he whispered.

"Um," she answered, drifting on his words and the wonderful feel of his hands touching her.

"I like it better down."

"It's a mess."

"Because of me." He continued to run his hands

possessively over her. "If I hadn't decided to come to Grandmother's party, I wouldn't have met you tonight. And that would have been a tragedy."

"We would have met some other time," she whispered. "Soon. Somehow fate would have brought us together."

"But I'm glad it's tonight."

"Yes."

She thought of second chances. Was fate cruel enough to snatch him away from her again?

She vowed not to let it happen! This time she knew what was ahead. This time she was prepared.

Matt turned and looked down at her, and she realized he must feel her tension.

"What?"

"I'm happy."

His eyebrows arched questioningly. "And that makes you tense?"

"Were you ever afraid to be happy because that would be . . . unlucky?"

He thought for a few moments. "No. But maybe that's the arrogance of my upbringing."

She nodded against his shoulder, struggling not to reveal anything about the future.

He stroked her eyebrows. "It's late. You should sleep. We'll continue the conversation in the morning."

"Okay," she whispered, then felt sudden panic. Would there be a morning? What if this were some kind of reverse dream, and it would be all over if she let go of consciousness?

She fought against sleep, but she was too tired to stay awake. Her eyes drifted closed. And for a while her slumber was blessedly peaceful. She was warm and safe and sleeping where she belonged, next to Matt.

Then a dream sunk its sharp claws into her flesh.

She was driving through a storm. Rain lashed her car, drumming on the roof above her head. Lightning crackled across the sky, and a clap of thunder sounded too close for comfort.

The wind seemed to hold her car back, and she cried out in frustration. She knew her destination. Matt had called to say he'd be late for dinner because Dave Olson, his contractor, needed him to stop by the building site.

She was supposed to meet him, and they could leave for dinner from there.

In reality, she remembered being late because she'd gotten stuck in traffic. But maybe that wasn't how it would happen in this replay of her life.

So she fought onward, trying to get to the construction site. In her past life, she'd had no idea that Matt was in danger. But this time she knew what was going to happen.

She had to get there first and stop him from going into the building. But as the agonizing seconds ticked by, she feared she would never make it in time.

Reaching into her purse, she found the cell phone she'd just bought and tried to call his number. But the storm must have cut off communications because she kept getting a message that she had reached his voicemail.

All she could do was keep driving, praying that she wasn't too late to save Matt.

Finally, after what seemed like hours, she pulled into the newly paved parking lot. Matt was ahead of her, and she saw him stop at the curb and climb out of his car, heading for the building, running to get out of the rain.

She kept racing toward him, lowering her window so she could shout at him. "Matt, no! Stop. Stay back."

The wind whipped the trees into a frenzy and carried her voice away.

Matt didn't hear her. He kept moving, hurrying toward his destruction. Or maybe the wind was pushing him toward his doom.

She leaped out of her car and ran after him, praying that she could catch him in time.

But it was already too late. As she watched in horror, the building exploded in flames.

"Matt, no!" She screamed as she watched a wall of fire engulf the structure.

Someone was shaking her. "Sara, wake up. Sara, it's all right. You were dreaming."

She fought whomever was trying to hold her in place. "No, get off of me. I have to save him."

"Save who? Sara, it's Matt. You were having a bad dream."

Her eyes blinked open. In the illumination coming in from outside the back door, she saw Matt was beside her in bed. His hand was cupped around her shoulder, gently shaking her.

"It's all right. It was just a dream."

She held back a sob. Just a dream! No, it was terribly real.

"Can you tell me what you were dreaming?" he murmured.

"I was there. I saw . . ." She gulped. "I saw the building catch fire again. And I couldn't do anything about it again," she whispered.

"Again? What are you talking about? What building?"

She struggled to bring herself under control. "Did I say 'again'?"

"Yes."

For long seconds she debated telling him the truth.

A deep, abiding fear kept her from being honest. She struggled to hold back a sob, but it burst from her lips. Reaching for Matt, she clung tightly, marveling at his solid muscles, his warm skin. He was here. He was alive. He hadn't vanished. And he hadn't been caught in the burning building—not yet, anyway.

He stroked her back while she fought to bring herself under control. Finally, she pulled a tissue from the box on the bedside table and blew her nose.

"Can you remember any more of the dream?" he asked gently.

"No," she lied. Lifting her head, she stared up at him. "Do you believe in magic?"

"Real magic?"

"Uh huh."

He laughed. "I'm too down-to-earth for that."

She nodded, pretty sure it was true.

"What does magic have to do with your dream?"

"What if it was a warning?"

"From whom?"

She shrugged. She could hardly explain about Marcus Garrison and the Second Chance antique shop.

"Fate?" she said in a small voice.

She ached to share her terrible burden with Matt. Really, she wanted desperately to lay it all out for him. But she didn't dare. Not until he knew her better and knew that her feet were firmly on the ground. Or were they?

Unable to cope with her own fear and uncertainty, she clasped her hand around the back of his head and brought his mouth down to hers.

The sensuality of the night before surged to life again. And this time was better than the last. They had satisfied each other only a few hours earlier, so there was no need to hurry. Matt made love to her slowly and tenderly. And when he entered her, his movements were smooth and even until she reached the point where the languid pace drove her toward madness.

"Please," she gasped, "I can't wait any longer."

He picked up the tempo, and she plunged into a long, shuddering climax, then felt him join her.

Afterward he kept her close, stroking and kissing her until she fell asleep again. And this time her dreams were warm and safe.

Around seven, she felt him stirring beside her. She would have hung a Closed sign on the door and kept him in her bed all day, except that she knew he had to go to work.

He got up and started collecting the clothing that they'd scattered on the floor. Then he pulled on his tuxedo pants and slipped out the back door. He returned with a gym bag, then stopped and stared at the ankle she'd thrust out from under the covers.

"I never knew a tattoo could be arousing. I was wrong."

She grinned. "Arousing enough to keep you here?"

He looked regretful. "There are things that need attention at the office."

She nodded, thinking about the construction project, but she didn't mention it.

"Do you mind if I take a quick shower?" he asked.

"Be my guest."

While he was in the bathroom, she put on a robe, straightened up, and made the bed.

When he came out, he was wearing shorts and a T-shirt.

"I keep gym clothes in the car. Better than driving home in my tux."

"Right."

After her own quick shower, she dressed in an outfit that was similar to Matt's.

"Do you want to use my razor?" she asked when she emerged from the bathroom.

He rubbed his face. "I guess I look a little grim."

"I'd say masculine."

He gestured toward his casual outfit. "Since I can't go to the office like this, I'll shave when I get home."

"Let me see what I have for breakfast."

"You don't need to go to any bother for me."

"I might not be able to."

She truly had no idea what was in the refrigerator, but to her delight, she found an abundance of ingredients. After starting a pot of coffee, she took out a carton of eggs.

"How about a ham and cheese omelette?"

"Sounds good, if you don't mind cooking."

She might have said she'd make any excuse to keep him here. Instead she said, "I like having the excuse to cook breakfast."

"Okay. If you let me help you."

She remembered that he enjoyed cooking, so she set him to work chopping onions and peppers, while she mixed the eggs and cut up part of a ham slice. Then she made one big omelette and cut it in half.

They ate out on her deck, enjoying the food and each other's company. And she wished life could be as simple and as satisfying as it seemed that morning.

But she felt time ticking away. She only had three weeks to make things come out differently.

And she didn't even know where Matt thought they were going from here. Maybe this time he didn't want to get involved with her. It was hard to believe that. But she felt her throat close when she thought about how the rules had changed. She was back in her own past— sort of. Yet too many details were already coming out differently.

When he spoke, she tried to listen above the buzzing in her ears.

"So, do you want to go out tonight?" he asked.

She vividly remembered what they'd done last time. "Have you ever been to a country auction?" she asked.

"No."

"It's fun. This one is at an auction gallery about ten miles from here. I got a notice that they have consignments from two couples who are moving to Florida."

"What about dinner?"

"We can buy food there. Maybe pork barbecue, coleslaw, cherry pie. That kind of thing."

"Sounds good."

Last time they'd had a fun evening. This time she felt a small nagging worry. But she managed to smile and say, "I'd like to get there by seven."

"I'll pick you up at six thirty, after you close."

"I'm looking forward to it."

Matt kissed her good-bye before nine, which was lucky because two men from Elmwood delivered her car fifteen minutes later to the parking space at the back of the shop. She gave them a ten-dollar tip, then waited nervously for the phone to ring. When it did, she jumped.

As she had expected, the caller ID told her it was Cornelia Ballenger.

Sara dragged in a breath and let it out before answering. "Mrs. Ballenger, I was just going to call you and tell you what a good time I had last night."

"You disappeared rather early," the older woman said in a disapproving voice, and Sara could picture the sour look on her face.

"Yes. Thank you for having my car brought home. That was very thoughtful of you."

Mrs. Ballenger's voice dropped a few degrees in warmth. "We're trying to clean up the lawn."

"Oh." She couldn't make herself say she was sorry to have caused any inconvenience.

"You don't happen to know about some ruined box-woods, do you?"

"Yes. A car rolled down the driveway and hit them."

"You saw it?" Mrs. Ballenger asked, like it had been Sara's fault.

She had tried to avoid speaking of Matt. Now she was forced to admit out loud that she'd been with him. "Matt and I saw it. But the parking lot attendant had the situation under control," she answered.

"Why didn't you inform me about the bushes?"

"We didn't want to spoil the party for you."

"Yes, well I'm afraid I have to cancel our meeting today. I have a lot of cleanup to attend to. And I'm quite worn out from last night."

"I understand. Do you want to reschedule?" she heard herself ask because it was the logical question, even when she knew the answer was going to be no.

"Let me get back to you later."

"That would be fine," she said, trying not to sound stiff when she understood that she was getting fired from the biggest freelance job she'd ever landed. And most of the people she'd met at the party would turn away from her, too, when they realized she wasn't working with Cornelia anymore.

Well, she'd survived last time without a high-profile patron. And she would do it again.

She looked at her watch. It was almost time to open the shop. But she wanted to think about last night while she had a few moments alone.

While she changed into work clothes—a silk blouse and dark slacks—she thought about the differences between this time around and last. Matt hadn't come home with her in her past life.

So that was definitely different. But all of the key players had been at the party. A year ago she'd been too overwhelmed to study them. Last night, although she'd paid attention to Matt's associates, she still didn't know who might want to hurt him.

Previously, the fire inspector had discovered evidence of arson. But nobody knew why Matt had been in the building.

He'd told her that he was meeting Dave Olson. But Olson claimed he hadn't contacted Matt. And his phone records confirmed that. There had been a call to Matt from a prepaid cell phone, however. Unfortunately, no records showed who had purchased it.

There had always been one other key question in her mind. If someone were plotting murder, was Matt the real target?

Because he wasn't the only one who'd been summoned to the construction site. She'd gotten a call, too. And she'd gone to meet him. Only she'd been late, and he was the one who had gotten trapped inside the burning building.

She felt a shiver travel over her skin. She couldn't dismiss the possibility that the fiery death had been meant for her, and Matt was supposed to get there after the tragedy.

Once she started thinking about that, she couldn't stop her mind from spinning out an elaborate fantasy. Martha Swinton had been at the party. And both Cornelia and Martha had very much wanted Martha's granddaughter, Lucy, to marry Matt. Only Matt and Lucy had broken up a couple of months before he'd met Sara.

What if Cornelia and her good friend had hatched a plot to get rid of the new and, in their eyes, unsuitable woman in Matt's life?

Sara pressed the heels of her hands against her eyes, wishing she hadn't thought of that scenario. Two nice old ladies plotting murder? That showed how desperate she was to pin the crime on *someone*. But not just *anyone* would do. She had to figure out who had really hatched the plot.

Which meant she needed to focus on what had happened last time and figure out how she could stop it. But it was so hard to separate the past from the present.

She remembered the past from a year ago, but she was finding out that she hadn't come back to quite the same world as the one she recalled.

And all she could do was pray that her knowledge of the past would make Matt's future come out differently.

Her big goals were to stop him from going to that building in three weeks. Or to figure out who had set the fire—and stop them.

But she had to deal with a million details along the way. Like, what about the car that had come lumbering down the driveway last night? Was someone trying to run her down? Or run Matt down?

Or was it really just an accident?

She made a frustrated sound. She didn't know, and she felt like she was trying to put together a puzzle when some of the pieces from another puzzle had gotten mixed in.

Maybe the first thing she should do was see if she could make some changes. And perhaps making Lucy Swinton a test case was a good idea.

In the old version of Sara's life, Lucy and Matt had broken up already. And judging from his behavior last night, that still must be true. But Sara knew about the previous relationship because—in the old version of her life—Lucy had come into the shop to say how sorry she was that Sara hadn't been allowed at the funeral.

Their relationships with Matt had given them a bond. And they'd cried together over his death. They'd started hanging out together because they shared a sorrow that nobody else could understand.

Then Lucy had met Peter McCall, and they'd started dating, and Lucy had told Sara that her world had opened up again.

So what if she could get Lucy together with Peter

months ahead of schedule? It would make a good test case. If Sara could do it, she'd know that her actions could affect this time line. And it might even help set up some kind of positive energy force to change everything for the better.

Feeling excited about the experiment, she looked around the shop. She'd gotten a partner's desk recently, and a few months ago, in the other time line, Peter had said he wanted one for the new house he was furnishing.

Going to her file, she found Peter's office number and dialed. His secretary put her through.

"I've gotten in a partner's desk that has your name written all over it," she said.

"How did you know I wanted one?"

"Intuition. Can you come by at lunchtime and take a look at the one I've gotten in?"

"You bet."

After snagging Peter, she called Lucy. They'd gone to high school together, but they weren't exactly best buddies—yet.

"It's Sara Drimmon," she started. "How are you doing?"

"Okay."

"I saw your grandmother at Cornelia Ballenger's last night, and I was thinking about your telling me that you never know what to buy her for a birthday present."

"That's right."

"Well, I think I have the perfect picture that you could give her—an original French painting that has a lot of charm. It's a scene in an old hill town, a view of a stone stairway leading to a shuttered doorway. Along the steps are potted plants."

"I'd like to see it."

"What about noon today?"

"That will work."

After hanging up, Sara got out the painting. She remembered that she'd been thinking about keeping it, but she had a more important goal now.

It was only a little after ten. Usually her assistant, Grace Plover, would have been in by now. She was about to pick up the phone and ask Grace if anything was wrong. Then she stopped and thought about the time period and remembered that she'd given Grace the week off, so she wouldn't be in until Monday.

She walked restlessly around the shop, checking her stock and rearranging some glassware. Many of the pieces were items she'd sold over the past year, and she distracted herself by trying to remember each buyer and what price they'd arrived at.

Buying from an antique shop wasn't like walking into a retail store where the price was firm. A lot of people wanted to bargain, so Sara was always prepared to take a slightly lower figure—particularly if they paid cash and saved her from having to pay the credit card fee.

It would be interesting to find out if she would sell these items to the same people. And would the price be the same?

Peter arrived just after noon, and she led him to the desk.

"This is gorgeous. When did you get it in?"

"A few days ago."

"Thanks for calling me."

He looked at the tag hanging from one of the drawers. "Are you sure you can't lower the price a little bit?"

"For you . . . fifteen percent."

"Then we have a deal."

The bell over the door tinkled and Sara looked up to see Lucy stepping into the shop. She spotted them right away and came over. And Sara was pleased to see both parties looking at each other with interest.

"Lucy Swinton, this is Peter McCall. Peter, this is my friend Lucy." To Lucy she added, "Peter has just built himself a gorgeous house, and he's looking for some special furnishings. Why don't you come give him an opinion on this desk."

"It's spectacular."

"And Lucy came to look at a painting for her grandmother. Let me get it."

Sara disappeared into her sitting room, where she'd stowed the painting. She stayed there for several minutes. When she came out, Lucy and Peter were deep in conversation, getting to know each other. She hated to interrupt, but she didn't want Lucy to feel embarrassed later when she realized she'd completely forgotten why she'd come to the shop.

"So here's the painting," Sara said brightly.

Both Peter and Lucy turned. After giving the picture a long look, Lucy smiled. "You're right. It is perfect. I should have driven over so I could take it home before I have to get back to work."

"I've got my car. I can give you a ride," Peter offered.

"I'd really appreciate it."

After Lucy paid for the picture, Peter carried it out of the shop for her. It looked like they were going to click. And why not? They'd clicked last time—only it had been months later.

Sara's success left her with a warm glow. Peter was a good catch. His family was almost as prominent in the area as Matt's, and Sara already knew from her other time line that Mrs. Swinton approved of him.

She was still congratulating herself when the shop bell rang again, and she looked up to see one of her regular customers, a middle-aged matron who collected antique snuffboxes, porcelain flowers, and glass cream pitchers, among other things. "Mrs. Lewis," she greeted her.

"I'm just browsing."

"Go right ahead."

Mrs. Lewis came in about once a month, and her browsing often led to big sales. But Sara suddenly remembered something else about the woman. Last time around, after Mrs. Lewis had returned home from one of her visits to the shop, she'd forgotten about the greasy pan in her oven and turned on the heating element. It had caught fire and done many thousands of dollars worth of damage in her kitchen.

Had it been this visit? Sara thought that was a good bet.

"You must remember to take that pan out of the oven," she said.

The woman looked up, startled. "Why, I do have a pan in the oven. I'd forgotten all about it. How did you know?"

Sara shrugged. "I'm not sure. When you walked in the door, a picture of your oven catching on fire came into my mind."

"I never knew you were psychic."

"Sometimes I get these insights," Sara answered.

"Well, I'm going to go right home and take care of it before I forget." Mrs. Lewis made a hasty exit. She came back a half hour later, thanked Sara profusely, and bought a very expensive snuffbox.

* * *

Matt looked up from his computer to see Josh Hemingway standing in his office doorway.

"You got in late this morning," his second in command said.

Matt kept his expression neutral. "Heavy date last night."

"With that Sara Drimmon?"

"Yeah."

"I went back inside after you left. Your grandma was pretty annoyed that you checked out."

"She doesn't run my life."

Josh nodded.

"Sometimes she gets a notion into her head, and you can't change her mind."

"You'd know that better than me."

"So did you come in to talk about my grandmother?"

"No. Like I said last night, I wanted to talk to you about the building."

"You might as well sit down. I sense this is going to take a while."

"Yeah. Olson's behind schedule."

"What's his excuse?"

"He says some materials were on back order. And he's having trouble getting enough men to work the job."

"You'd think he could get all the Mexicans he wants. And at cheap prices, too."

Josh laughed. "I think he's nervous about getting busted for immigration violations."

"Yeah."

"Do you want me to call him in, or go out there?"

"We can let it ride for a few days. If he can't get his act together, I guess you—or I—need to sit down for a chat with him."

They talked for a few more minutes. Then Josh left,

and Matt looked back at his computer screen. But after a few minutes, he gave up pretending to work.

Leaning back in his ergonomic chair, he closed his eyes and brought up an image of Sara Drimmon. He loved her silky blond hair, her wide blue eyes, her supple body, her quick mind. She was the most exciting woman he'd met in a long long time.

He really liked her. And he thought the attraction was mutual. It felt good to talk to her, to let her in on his thoughts. But it was also true that they could just sit together, not needing to speak, and he'd be happy.

So was his grandmother going to be a problem? Unfortunately, she had very proprietary feelings about family. And she had an excruciatingly well-developed opinion about the kind of woman Matthew Tripplehorn was supposed to marry. She probably thought Sara wasn't good enough for him because Sara hadn't been born with a silver spoon in her mouth.

Well, he'd just have to change her mind.

Sales at Sara's shop were brisk all day, aided by her memories of what had happened the first time around. She might have trusted that her good luck was holding if she hadn't been worried about the weeks ahead.

But she couldn't think that way, she told herself. Determined to be upbeat, she showered and changed into her favorite auction outfit—jeans, running shoes, and a comfortable knit top.

Matt came to the back door at six-thirty as promised. He was wearing a dark polo shirt and jeans. Every time she saw him, she marveled at how fit and relaxed he looked.

"I see I got the dress code right," he said as he eyed her outfit.

"Good guess."

She gave him a long hug, enjoying the luxury of having him in her arms again. It was tempting to suggest that they should just stay inside. She could keep him captive in her bedroom for the next three weeks, making love.

But then she'd be back in the same nightmare that she'd lived through before, unless she could change things.

"I know you said you'd pick me up, but it's better if we take my truck. Okay?"

"Fine."

She climbed into the driver's seat of the truck parked beside her car, and Matt took the passenger seat.

"Your grandmother canceled an appointment with me," she said when they were settled in the cab.

He sighed. "She gave me a lecture on disappearing in the middle of the party. I'm sorry she's taking my rudeness out on you."

"I wouldn't call it *your* rudeness. I was a willing participant. I guess I wasn't thinking about how your grandmother would react. I just wanted to be with you, so I accepted your invitation."

He reached over and pressed his hand over hers where it rested on the steering wheel. "And I'm really glad you did. I was supposed to be working today. Instead, I was thinking about you all day."

"Likewise."

He cleared his throat. "I'm usually cautious about relationships."

"So am I."

"But being with you seems so right."

"I'm glad it's not just me."

"I should say something important, I guess."

When tension spread through her and made her arm stiffen, he laughed. "Don't worry. It's nothing bad."

"Okay."

"I said I was cautious. But that doesn't mean I haven't dated a lot of women. Before, the relationship always stayed in the present. I mean, I just thought about what it was like with them as things existed now." He shook his head. "I'm getting this tangled up, but what I'm trying to say is that with you it's different. I can imagine the two of us together five years from now, ten years, twenty years. I can picture the two of us growing old together."

"Oh, Matt." She turned her hand up and laced her fingers with his, holding on for dear life. "I can, too," she whispered.

She wanted to say so much more. She wanted to tell him what they had to do to make the future come out the way they wanted. But she still didn't feel comfortable revealing that she'd come back in time—not when their relationship still was so new.

They arrived at the auction gallery a few minutes later.

"The way it works—you register and get a number. Then, if you win a bid, you give the number so you can't change your mind and slip out without paying."

The hall was already crowded with people and merchandise. She smiled as she watched Matt taking in the scene, eyeing the crowd and the collection of items that were going on the block—everything from a nineteenth-century armoire to a Victorian china cabinet. And lots of much smaller items.

Many of the people here were familiar to her—other dealers buying for their shops or home owners looking for interesting accent pieces.

"How old are those, do you think?" Matt asked, gesturing toward a set of Lenox china.

"Sixties."

"How do you know?"

"By the cups. They're very wide and scooped out. You'd never see that shape in Lenox cups now."

"So what about that?" he asked, pointing to a school desk that looked like it had taken some hard wear.

"Fifties. You can peg it by the plain, square shape—and there's no inkwell."

"I'm impressed."

They each got a number, and Sara looked at more of the merchandise. She saw a marble-topped washstand she knew would be snapped up quickly in her shop.

The bidding on an old Victrola had already started. Some people held up their numbers to indicate a bid. Some raised a hand or nodded. She smiled as she watched Matt studying their behavior. He was here to have fun, but he couldn't just sit back and relax. He had to analyze the players and the moves.

He sat out the bidding on several pieces, then jumped into the competition for a lawyer's bookcase.

"How high should I go?" he whispered.

"They're pretty pricey. If you want it, you're going to have to top the competition."

"Okay."

Everybody but Matt and another man dropped out. When Matt got the bookcase for six hundred and twenty-five dollars, the other guy gave him a dirty look.

But Matt was obviously too exhilarated by the thrill of victory to care.

The washstand came up, and Sara entered the fray. At the end, she found herself in a contest against the same guy who had challenged Matt. Once again, he looked angry when he had to drop out.

Smaller pieces were up next, so they took a break and

got some food—pulled pork barbecue, baked beans, and coleslaw, which they ate at the back of the room.

After that, Matt jumped into the auction again and got a fireplace set.

"You did great for a first-timer," she told him.

"When can we come again?"

"Next week," she answered, feeling good about setting a date that far in advance. But at the same time, it made her conscious that time was ticking by—and she had to change Matt's future.

After paying for the purchases, she drove the truck to the large doors at the back of the hall. They put the washstand in first, then worked their way through the rest of the purchases. The bookcase came apart in sections, so they loaded them separately. They'd just gotten the last piece into the truck, when the guy who'd lost the auction to Matt came outside.

"So are you pleased with yourself?" he asked.

Matt turned to face him. "Yeah." His voice was even, but his arms and shoulders were stiff.

"You've got your family's money coming out of your ears. So why do you have to butt in and spoil it for the guys looking for a bargain?"

"You were free to outbid me."

"Oh, sure! I can't outspend a guy like you. But I should have bid you up to a thousand dollars, then let you have the damn thing!"

As Sara watched the two men facing each other, she felt her heart start to pound. The sore loser looked like he was spoiling to beat up somebody, and Matt was the target. Nothing like this had happened last time they'd been at the auction. The guy hadn't even been here, and Matt had bid against someone else—a woman. So why this nasty little change?

Because this time around Matt was in more danger? Why? It seemed like her coming back had changed the balance of the equation of his life—and not for the better.

Sara stepped quickly toward the man. "I've got a lawyer's bookcase at my shop that you can have for the same price we just paid," she said.

"Who asked you to stick your honker in?"

Matt's expression hardened. "Don't speak to the lady that way."

For a long, tense moment she was afraid one of the two men was going to throw a punch.

Then the other guy backed off. "Forget it," he muttered and walked away.

Sara sagged against the side of the truck.

"That happen often?" Matt asked in a casual voice.

"Not often. Do you know that guy?"

"Yeah, actually. His name is Wagner. He used to work for my grandmother. She fired him because he was a slacker."

"So he had a grudge against you."

"Looks like it."

Wagner had dampened their good mood, and they rode home in silence.

"We should drop the bookcase and the fireplace set at your house," Sara finally said as they neared the turnoff to his place.

"Good idea."

She started to slow for the turn, then realized she wasn't supposed to know where he lived.

"Which way?" she asked.

"Turn right."

She did, then paused to ask for directions again. He took her to a quiet street where the lots were large and so were the houses. Matt's house was set well back from the road and hidden by trees.

Previously, she'd admired the location. Now it made her nervous. Someone could get murdered up here, and nobody would know about it.

As she pulled up at the garage, a floodlight came on. She cut the engine, opened her door, and walked around to the back of the truck. But as she fumbled with the latch on the tailgate, her hand trembled.

"What's wrong?" Matt asked.

"That guy spooked me. You don't think he'd come after you, do you?"

"Nah. He's a coward."

While they carried the sections of the bookcase to the mudroom door, she looked around at the trees that blocked the view of the neighbors. "This is a perfect location for an ambush."

"But we're not living in the Old West."

She nodded.

"You could come in and protect me. Spend the night." He wiggled his eyebrows.

"That's a tempting offer."

It was almost beyond her power to refuse. But she couldn't spend the night with him—not now. She had to think about what was happening. Maybe just by being near him, she was drawing danger to him. And she had another problem, too. She knew his house very well, and she was afraid she'd give that away.

"But I'd better not," she added.

"Tired of me already?" he asked in a low voice.

"Lord no!" She gathered him close and hugged him tightly as she struggled to frame an explanation. "This is happening so fast. I need us to slow down a little."

"OK. I understand."

She knew he really didn't. Things had gone pretty fast the last time, and neither one of them had wanted to put on the brakes.

Raising her head, she pressed her lips to his, trying to tell him without words that her feelings for him ran deep. The kiss turned more passionate. When he finally lifted his head, they were both out of breath.

"Have you changed your mind?"

"Don't tempt me beyond endurance."

"Will you go out with me tomorrow night?"

The only answer was yes.

"How about the carnival? We can have hot dogs and french fries for dinner."

"It's a date."

"I'll pick you up." He stopped short and laughed. "No wait—I left my car at the shop."

She laughed with him. "I guess we both forgot about that."

They finished unloading his purchases, then drove back to the shop.

She knew he wanted to come in, but she said, "I'm sticking to my guns."

"I'm pretty sure I could change your mind."

"I know you could, but I'm going to prove my willpower."

She spent a restless night second-guessing herself. She'd been afraid to stay at Matt's house. Or let him stay with her. Finally she decided she'd been a fool to pass up a chance to make love with him again. And as she waited on customers the next day, she kept willing the time to pass quickly.

When Matt arrived at six-thirty, she was wearing a pretty flowered sundress that she knew he liked. And she'd exchanged her work shoes for sandals.

He had on jeans again, and a black T-shirt.

"I was thinking about you all day," he said as he folded her into his arms and gave her a long kiss. "Are you sure you don't want to skip the fair?"

"Why don't we let the anticipation build?"

"I can go along with that."

As they drove toward the fairground, she asked about his day, listening carefully for any signs of stress. But unless he was hiding something from her, it all sounded normal.

The carnival was pitched on a broad field outside the city limits. Several men were directing traffic. Matt paid his five dollars and got into the line of cars parking on the grass.

As they joined the crowd strolling toward the midway entrance, he took her hand again, and she held on tightly, still wondering how to play the part she'd been thrust into.

Ahead of her she could see the Ferris wheel. And a merry-go-round.

"It sounds like, with your business, you have a lot of different irons in the fire."

"Right. I do a little of this and a little of that."

"Give me an example."

"The Tripplehorn Corporation has a lot of far flung enterprises. We do everything from making tools to importing coffee from Jamaica."

"Why so diverse?"

"Because the success of a business fluctuates according to what's hot and what's working at the moment. Suppose I'd focused on providing computer support to US users? I'd be out of luck right now, because it's cheaper to send the business to India—and Ireland."

She nodded, then asked, "Does your brother, Bradley, work with you?"

"He wanted to build his own empire. Now he acts like we're rivals," he said in a tight voice.

"And you're winning the race, even when you didn't want to play 'can you top this' with him?"

"Yeah."

She'd known that, of course. Now she was wondering how far Bradley would go to beat out his brother.

Matt switched back to his own business. She knew he was good at what he did, and she enjoyed listening to him talk.

"I'm getting ready to invest in a company that provides security services to local customers. So I'm studying their operation, and I'm putting up an office building near the Martha Washington Mall."

She struggled not to tense up again when he mentioned the project. "That sounds interesting. Are you going to move your office there?"

"That's the plan, but there will be lots of other tenants. The ground floor will have a restaurant and some shops."

"So you never have to go out of the building to get a good lunch?"

"Good guess."

It wasn't a guess. He'd told her about that plan last time.

As they walked down the midway, she took in the sights and sounds of the carnival—barkers touting their attractions, kids begging their parents for rides or cotton candy, groups of teenagers showing themselves off to the opposite sex.

"My nose tells me the food is over this way," Matt

said. "I promised you a hot dog. But it looks like you could have a more exalted Polish sausage with peppers and onions. Or a taco or shish kebab or funnel cake."

"Funnel cake for dinner?"

"We can share one for dessert."

She looked at the offerings from the various food booths, then opted for shish kebab. Last time, she'd taken him up on the Polish sausage.

They ate at picnic tables set up near the concessions, then munched on funnel cake as they walked around looking at the booths.

After wiping powdered sugar off her fingers, she gestured at a stand where fairgoers threw wooden balls at stacks of "milk bottles." "Can you win me a teddy bear?"

"I think the bottles are filled with lead."

"Well, we can have that guy guess your weight," she said, pointing to another attraction.

"Or yours."

"Forget it."

They walked farther into the fair, past a fortune-teller's tent. She didn't remember seeing the tent the first time, but maybe she had been too focused on Matt to notice it.

A middle-aged woman wearing a blue and gold dress and a blue bandanna around her hair was sitting outside. She called out to them. "Have your fortune read. Find out if you're going to grow old together."

Matt stopped, and the woman took advantage of his interest.

"Come over and learn your future," she said.

Sara felt a wave of cold sweep over her. "Let's get out of here," she said, taking a step back.

"Are you afraid?" Matt whispered.

"Yes."

"You should face your fears."

She wanted to tell him this wasn't the way to do it. But he tugged on her arm, and she reluctantly followed him to the tent.

"I am Madame Raina. Come inside. Make yourself comfortable. I usually charge twenty-five dollars for a reading. But I'll give you a special price—fifteen dollars."

"A bargain," Matt answered.

Madame Raina ushered them inside. To Sara's surprise, the floor was covered with a very high-quality Oriental rug. Brightly colored hangings formed the ceiling of the tent. There were several chairs draped with flowered fabric and a table covered in a heavy throw. A clear crystal ball sat on an ornate silver stand in the middle of the table.

"You see the future in that ball?" Sara asked, hear-ing the shaky quality of her own voice as she gestured toward the orb.

"And the past, as well." She sat down in one of the chairs and pointed to the two seats across from her. "Make yourselves comfortable."

Sara fought the impulse to run out of the tent. She didn't want this woman poking into her past—or her future. But she couldn't explain why she was nervous, so she sat down next to Matt, clasping her own hands tightly in her lap and hoping for the best.

"Which one of you should I do?" Madame Raina asked looking to Sara, then Matt, then back again.

"Start with Sara."

The woman held out her hand.

Sara gulped. "I thought you used the crystal ball."

"I can get more if I connect with you physically."

Matt and Madame Raina were both watching her, so she offered her hand.

The woman took it and held it for a moment before letting go and looking down into her clear glass ball.

She didn't speak for several moments, and Sara fought to breathe normally.

"You came from a long distance," the woman finally said.

"Yes," Sara whispered.

"You have great courage."

"I'm just . . ." Her voice trailed off as she looked to-ward Matt. He was watching the transaction intensely.

Madame Raina looked toward him, then back to Sara. "The outcome depends on you."

She hadn't wanted to come in here. Now she leaned forward. "What can I do?"

"The things you are already doing."

"I need to know more."

"Trust yourself."

She felt as though this woman had dipped into her mind, and the two of them knew exactly what they were talking about. As they sat across the table, they spoke in a kind of shorthand that made perfect sense to both of them. But Sara couldn't help wondering what Matt was thinking. She wanted to ask for more specific advice, but not in front of him.

Maybe if she came back later?

"Can you tell me anything about my future?" Matt suddenly asked.

Madame Raina gave Sara a long look, then swung her gaze toward Matt. "I can't reveal your future," she said in a low voice.

"You don't know it?"

"You have two possible outcomes," she said.

Sara struggled to keep breathing normally.

"The way it turns out depends on you—and on her."

Matt laughed, but it sounded forced. "You mean she has to decide whether she's going to stick with me?"

"Something like that," the woman answered, a slight edge in her voice. "It will all be clear next month."

Of course it would. The unreality of the conversation made Sara's stomach knot. This woman *knew*.

"The carnival travels around. Where would I find you next month?" Matt asked.

"I'll be in St. Michaels, Maryland, visiting my daughter. She has a house right off Main Street. Her name is Traymore. The only one in the phone book."

"St. Michaels," Sara whispered. "Do you know Mr. Garrison?"

"I do."

"What about him?" Matt demanded.

"He owns an antique shop and art gallery. He was selling off some of his stock, so I went there to have a look."

He nodded. "Did you buy anything?"

"No," she managed to say, then stood abruptly. "I think there's something in here that I'm allergic to. I'm feeling a little dizzy. I need to leave."

"I understand," Madame Raina answered.

Sara rushed outside and stood dragging in deep drafts of air. The interior of the tent had been dimly lit. Outside, the sun was just setting, painting streaks of pink and orange across the sky.

Sara stood staring at the midway, trying to come to grips with what had just happened. While she'd been in the tent, it had sounded like Madame Raina had known her recent past—and her two possible futures. Or maybe Madame Raina had a bureau drawer full of bits of generic wisdom, and the customer could draw any conclusions she wanted.

But it hadn't seemed generic when it was happening. It had seemed too real. And the St. Michaels connection was just too weird.

Matt followed Sara onto the midway. She looked pale and shaken, like she'd come face to face with a ghost during her session with the medium. "Are you all right?"

She looked toward him, then away. "I'm feeling a little . . . strange," she whispered.

He wasn't sure what to say and finally settled on, "That was a pretty outré exchange the two of you had."

"Yes."

She wasn't giving him much information, so he

tried another tack. "You sounded like you knew what she was talking about. Did you?"

"Well . . . it could have meant a lot of things," she said evasively. "I'd rather not get into it until I get a chance to think about it."

He pressed his lips together. So much for imagining that they were going to share all their thoughts with each other. Obviously, he'd started forming a picture of her before he had all the facts. She began walking rapidly down the midway, and he followed.

"I'm sorry I suggested going to the fortune-teller."

She kept walking with her head down. "That's OK."

"Where are you going?"

She stopped and turned toward him, and he thought he saw tears in her eyes. "Sorry. Can we go home?"

He was still trying to figure out what had happened in that tent, but he said, "Sure."

She made directly for the exit, then hurried through the parking lot and back to his car. He clicked the lock as she reached the door.

When she'd settled in the passenger seat, he turned on the ignition so he could cool the interior with the air-conditioning.

Before he could put the car in gear, she turned to him and pulled him close.

"Oh, Matt. Oh." To his surprise, she started to sob.

He cradled her against himself, stroking her back and shoulders the way he'd done after her nightmare. "Sweetheart, tell me what's wrong. Please tell me."

She kept her face down, soaking the front of his shirt with her tears.

"What did that woman do to you?"

"She knows!"

"About what?"

She pulled away and fumbled in her purse. When she found a tissue, she wiped her eyes, then blew her nose.

Struggling to keep the frustration out of his voice, he said, "Please don't keep me in the dark."

She kept her head down. He saw her lick her lips. "Something . . . bad happened to me . . . and she knows about it."

"What?"

"I . . . I can't tell you."

"Why?"

"It's too upsetting."

"You don't trust me enough to tell me about it?"

She looked up, her eyes pleading. "I trust you. I'm sorry I started crying."

"Were you raped?" he asked urgently.

Her expression grew apologetic. "No . . . oh, no. Nothing like that."

"What?"

Her fingers clamped on his arm. "Someone I loved was killed."

"Who?"

"Please, don't make me talk about it anymore."

"Does it have something to do with that guy in St. Michaels?"

"No."

"Then why did you mention him?"

"I don't know," she insisted, but her voice didn't ring true.

"Does it have something to do with the nightmare you had last night?"

She didn't speak, but he knew from her expression that they were connected.

She looked away, and he wanted to press the advantage, make her level with him. A little kernel of fear stopped him. Did he really want to find out something he wasn't meant to know?

Before he could work his way through that logic, she reached out and pulled him into her arms again, clasping him close.

"This is what matters," she whispered.

Everything else faded from his mind as his senses reacted on a dozen different levels. He felt her very feminine, fine-boned body, inhaled her delicious scent. As he cradled her close, he was vividly conscious of the way her breasts pressed against his chest and her hands stroked through his hair. Heat spread through him. Heat and something deeper.

"Matt," she sighed out, her hands moving over his face, touching him as though she were blind and that was the only way she could find out what he looked like.

She raised her face to him, and his breath hitched. As he stared down into the depths of her eyes, he felt the intensity of the moment, felt it vibrating between them.

He knew that if he didn't have more of her, he would go mad. He traced the line of her lips, and she opened at his touch, sucking his finger into her mouth, stroking it with her tongue.

That erotic touch made him dizzy, and he gathered her closer, overwhelmed by the feel of her body against his.

She had spoken of anticipation, and he knew he had been waiting for this moment since the morning he had awakened in her bed.

That was his last coherent thought as she tangled her fingers in his hair and brought his mouth down to hers.

He felt need spiraling out of control. And as his

mouth moved against hers, she made a small whimpering sound that only added fuel to the fire. On a surge of desire, he dipped into her mouth with his tongue. Her tongue leaped to meet his, stroking and sparring, telling him she felt the same desperation.

"Matt," she gasped into his mouth.

A hot current of desire wrapped them together. He rocked her against himself, feasting on her mouth like a starving man invited to a banquet.

They were in his car. In a parking lot. But the windows were tinted. And nobody was coming back to the vehicles in this area because the people who had arrived when they did were still at the carnival.

Those thoughts flashed through his mind as he reached to unzip the back of her sundress and pull it away from her shoulders so he could reach inside and cup one of her breasts, then stroke his fingers back and forth across the hardened tip.

She made a moaning sound. "Move the car seat back," she said in a frantic voice.

He knew she was thinking the same thing as he. He did as she asked, using the button on the side of his seat to give them as much room as possible.

While he did that, he watched her pull her dress to her waist and drag her panties off. He reached under her dress, stroking her bottom, then dipping into her folds.

She was incredibly wet and swollen. And when he eased his finger inside her delicious warmth, she whimpered, then bent to work the snap at the top of his jeans, then his zipper.

When she reached inside and clasped her hand around his erection, he made a strangled sound of pleasure. She freed him from his pants, and he thought she would climb into his lap. Instead she leaned down, stroking her tongue around the head of his cock as though she knew exactly what he liked.

He watched her intently as she took him into her mouth, moving slowly up and down in a motion of such sensuality that he was afraid he would go off like a Fourth of July rocket.

"Don't," he gasped. "I don't want to come like this. I want you with me."

She raised her head, and the intensity of her gaze blew him away. "I needed to taste you."

His hand was still under her skirt. And he drew his finger out of her, stroking up to her clit before angling downward again.

She was so hot and ready for him. And he thanked God for that, because he didn't think he could wait another moment.

"Come here."

He lifted her up, and she straddled his lap, then came down on his erection, crying out as he entered her.

Immediately she began to move in a frantic rhythm, and he thrust deep inside her as he found her mouth again with his, and they exchanged hot, deep kisses.

Somehow he held back until he felt her inner muscles start to contract. Then he let himself go in a blinding climax. She followed him over the edge, crying out in pleasure.

When she collapsed against him, he wrapped her tightly in his arms, kissing her cheek, her hair, and then her lips.

For long moments, neither of them moved. Then she looked up and made a strangled sound.

"Oh, Lord, I forgot where we were!" Scooting off his lap, she pulled her dress down to cover her hips while he put himself back together.

He looked over, seeing her blush.

"We're okay. Nobody else is in this part of the lot."

"But they could be! We should leave."

He reached to start the engine, and it made a terrible screeching sound, reminding him that he'd already done that. Now it was his turn to blush.

He drove her home. He'd been thinking about spending the night with her, but he made the excuse that he had to be up early in the morning. Then he kissed her good-bye. It wasn't a passionate kiss. Drawing back, she gave him a shaky smile.

But as he watched her walk to her back door, he saw her shoulders slump.

He almost changed his mind then. He felt bad about dropping her off after their passionate tryst in the car. The sex had been fantastic. But what about the rest of the package? He knew she didn't trust him, and she'd used sex as a way to get him off a subject she didn't want to discuss.

And her behavior had started him thinking about whether he really wanted to get more involved with a woman who was hiding something from him.

CHAPTER 9

Sara unlocked the door, walked into her bedroom and
threw herself on the bed.

She had cried after she and Matt visited the fortune-
teller. She cried again, great racking sobs.

She was messing everything up. Just by knowing the
future, she was changing the whole equation between
herself and Matt. She could see it in the way he had
looked at her. Feel it in the wall that had suddenly
risen between them. But there was nothing she could
do about it except tell him what was driving her crazy.
And she was pretty sure he wouldn't believe her. He'd
just think she was a candidate for the funny farm.

She winced, then lay in the dark, staring at the
ceiling.

From out in the shop she heard several clocks chim-
ing. It was only nine.

She reached for the phone and dialed information.

"What city. What listing."

"St. Michaels, Maryland. Second Chance."

She held her breath, hoping that she hadn't made the place up. But the operator came on the line with the number, and she scribbled it on a notepad.

With shaky fingers, she dialed, wondering if Garrison was even going to be at his shop this late in the evening.

After three rings, a man answered.

"Is this Marcus Garrison?" she asked.

"Yes it is."

"This is Sara Drimmon."

"Who?"

"Sara Drimmon. You wrote me a letter about some pieces you wanted to sell."

"I'm sorry. I don't know what you're talking about."

"You sent me into the painting. 'Midnight Magic.' I need your help."

Someone else might have hung up then. He only said, "Ah . . ."

"You remember?"

"No. Perhaps that's still in my future."

"Oh, Lord, you're right." Desperately, she asked, "But you believe me?"

"Yes."

The relief was enormous but short-lived. "What should I do? Everything's a mess. This can't be what you intended."

"I'm sorry. I didn't paint the picture. And I don't know why the painting chose you."

She struggled for calm. "Does it always send people into the past?"

"Oh, no. It sends them where they need to go." He sighed. "I can't help you. The painting gave you a second chance, but you have to work out the details on your own."

She struggled to hold back a sob. She wanted to plead with him because she was pretty sure she couldn't do this by herself.

Instead she said good-bye and hung up, then lay staring at the crack on the ceiling over her bed.

What about Madame Raina?

Feeling frantic, she wanted to dash out of the house and drive back to the carnival. But this was the busy time of the evening. Madame Raina was probably seeing other customers. Tomorrow in the early afternoon was better. Madame Raina wouldn't be busy, and it would be more likely that they could sit and talk. The least she'd get was a sympathetic ear.

All night, Matt kept thinking he would have slept better in Sara's bed. But when he'd dropped her off, he'd been uneasy about the way their relationship was developing.

By morning, he knew he couldn't just walk away. They'd connected in a very fundamental way. Not just with the fast and furious sex. He'd sensed they could have something important together, and he didn't want to toss it away.

He wanted to talk to her. Maybe if he told her how vital honesty was in their relationship, she'd level with him.

At eight, he reached for the phone to call her. But before he could pick up the receiver, the phone rang.

Sara! She was on the same wavelength as he was. She was calling to say she wanted to talk.

Without looking at the caller ID, he picked up the receiver.

"Hello."

"Matthew, I was hoping you could come have breakfast with me this morning."

It wasn't Sara. It was his grandmother. He started to say he was sorry, but her voice sounded grave. "We need to talk."

That's what he'd been thinking about Sara, but it was Grandmother who had reached out to him.

He wanted to decline. Instead, he said, "How about nine o'clock?"

"That would be fine," she said, then hung up.

He showered and dressed in the shirt, slacks, and sport coat he was planning to wear to the office. Then he drove over to Elmwood. The old homestead, he thought with a wry smile. The house was one of his earliest memories. As a little boy, he'd thought it looked like a castle. And when he'd gotten older, he'd wondered why his grandmother wanted to rattle around in a house that big.

She'd told him she was saving it for future generations. Of course, he and Bradley couldn't live in the mansion together. So was she planning to leave it to one of them and cut the other one out?

Really, he didn't need a mansion. Bradley was welcome to it. They could negotiate something, he was pretty sure. Something that would leave Bradley feeling good about himself.

Philips opened the door before Matt could knock. "Mrs. Ballenger is in the conservatory," he said in the stiff, formal way that Grandmother appreciated. She liked servants to know their place, even if they'd been with the family for fifteen years.

Matt strode down the hall to the Victorian conservatory that was Grandmother's pride and joy. It was full of the orchids that she cultivated, with ficus and other

tropical trees providing the filtered shade that the delicate flowers required.

Grandmother was sitting at an ornate, glass-topped
patio table. When Matt saw the two other people in the
room, he stopped short.

His brother, Bradley, and Patrick O'Hara were sitting at the table. Matt walked to the remaining chair,
but he didn't sit down. They all had coffee mugs and
plates with the remains of scrambled eggs, fruit, bacon, and Danish pastries sat in front of them.

"Are we having a party?" he asked.

"Patrick stopped by to talk about some financial matters with me. He was just leaving," Cornelia said.

"Good to see you," Patrick said.

Because he couldn't bring himself to say anything so
positive, Matt made a noncommittal sound. He had
never liked O'Hara, although the man seemed to be doing all right by his grandmother's investments. Maybe
because Matt checked up on him.

The financial adviser and Cornelia exchanged
glances, and Matt had the feeling that they'd been talking about him before he arrived.

On his way out, O'Hara carried his plate to a service
cart near the door to the hallway.

Matt kept his face bland as he walked to the buffet
table and helped himself to eggs, bacon, and fruit. Then
he poured coffee and took his breakfast to the table.
He'd asked if they were having a party. It felt more like
an ambush.

He carefully pulled out his chair, sat down, and
picked up a strip of bacon because he knew his grandmother hated to see him eat it with his fingers.

"You're forgetting your manners," she said.

He shrugged and kept eating. When he'd finished

the bacon strip, he asked, "Did you ask me here for an etiquette lecture?"

"No."

He looked at Bradley. "What's going on?"

"Grandmama asked me to join us," he said, doing a good job of imitating an old-school Southern gentleman.

"Cut out the funny voices," Cornelia snapped. "This isn't a situation comedy."

"Sorry," Bradley apologized.

"So, why do we need a family conference?" Matt asked.

"We need to talk about continuing the Tripplehorn name in a suitable fashion."

Matt inclined his head toward his brother. "You all are trying to get pregnant, right?"

"Yes," Bradley muttered. He and his wife had had trouble conceiving, and they were currently undergoing fertility treatments.

His grandmother gave Matt a direct look. "Sara Drimmon is not a suitable match for you."

"I just met her a few nights ago. What makes you think I'm contemplating marriage?"

"I saw you together. You were thick as thieves."

"An interesting way to put it. You trusted her enough to help you pick out some furnishings for the family shrine."

"It's not a shrine! And those were purely business transactions. I allowed her to sell me some paintings and furnishings at too high a price because I thought she deserved a chance."

"She doesn't need your patronage to succeed. And I'd say that you took advantage of her services because you knew you could manipulate her into selling you artwork and furnishings cheaper than you could get them elsewhere."

"I resent the implications of that statement," his grandmother said.

Bradley shifted in his seat. "We should get to the point," he murmured.

"What's that?" Matt snapped.

"Did Sara Drimmon tell you that her mother died in a mental institution?" Bradley asked.

Matt's fork clanked against his plate. Turning toward his grandmother, he asked, "Is that true?"

"Yes."

"How do you know?"

"Because I did a background check on her. Her mother became seriously depressed, and the business began to suffer. Sara was forced to seek medical help for her mother. And after she got Peggy Drimmon out of the picture, she had to bring the business back from the brink. I found all that out when I considered working with her. Her mother's illness didn't stop me from buying from her. But it makes her unsuitable for a daughter-in-law. Has she told you about the mother?"

"We've only known each other for a few days. We didn't get into family histories. I didn't tell her about Great Uncle Sedgwick, who sold the Confederacy guns and ammunition at inflated prices. And I didn't tell her about cousin Barbara who got pregnant out of wedlock and was forced to give the baby away for adoption. And . . ."

His grandmother held up her hand. "All families have dirty laundry they keep to themselves."

"Exactly. But I would have told her the family

secrets—if we were going to get serious about our relationship."

"Would have?" his grandmother asked, catching the way he'd put the comment into past tense.

"I'm not going to sit here and allow you to dictate my personal life," Matt said, then stood up.

His grandmother also stood. "If you marry someone I consider unsuitable, you can be sure that the family mansion will go to your brother," she said in an even tone.

"Do you think I care about that?"

"You should."

"Well, I don't. I don't need your mansion or your money. I'm doing very nicely on my own. And when I build a house, it will be what I want, not what my grandmother thinks is suitable."

"I will not have you speaking to me with such disrespect."

"I'm sorry. You're the one who started the conversation." Facing his grandmother squarely, he said, "Sara has all the qualities you should admire in a woman. She's strong. You just told me she's resilient. She's an excellent businesswoman. And a lot more."

He strode out of the room before he could say something that he'd be sorry about later.

As he climbed into his car, he knew where he was going—to Sara's shop to speak to her. He'd defended her to his grandmother. But he couldn't let go of the feeling that she was keeping something important from him. She'd said someone she cared about had died. Was she talking about her mother? Was she ashamed about the way Peggy Drimmon had died? Was that the secret she was hiding?

Or was she cracking up herself? That session with

the fortune-teller had sent her into a tailspin. Why? Was she superstitious? Was she embarrassed that Matt had witnessed the strange session?

He couldn't answer any of those questions on his own. But he knew he was going to ask her.

Sara had intended to wait until the afternoon to go to the carnival. But as she climbed out of bed, she knew she was too jumpy to wait.

As she was about to exit the back door, she heard a knock on the shop door.

Oh, Lord, could that be Matt?

When she hurried through the shop, she saw two customers peering through the glass. Even though she hadn't intended to open, her hours said otherwise.

She unlocked the front door, then let a couple who were touring the East Coast look over her merchandise.

They ended up buying a very nice painting done in the Pre-Raphaelite style.

As soon as the couple left, she shut the door again, put out the closed sign and drove to the carnival grounds.

But as she approached the field where the booths and tents had been set up, she saw that men were taking down the rides, and most of the more easily disassembled units were already gone.

She pulled up near the entrance to where the midway had been and got out. All the men she saw looked busy, so she walked across the trampled grass, hoping to spot the fortune-teller.

But she'd taken only a dozen steps when a loud voice called out, "Hey, you can't go down there."

She turned to face a short man who looked to be in

his fifties. He was wearing overalls and a baseball cap turned backward, a style she had never understood.

"You can't go in there," he repeated. "We're breaking camp, and you could get hurt and sue us."

"I'm not going to sue anyone. I'm looking for Madame Raina," she said.

"She ain't here. Her son took her in the trailer."

"To the next carnival grounds?"

"That ain't none of your bee's wax."

Sara stood there with her chest tightening, making it difficult to breathe. "I . . . I need to talk to her."

"Come back next year," he said, then followed the advice with a cackling laugh, like he thought the world was going to end before that.

For her, it might.

After a silent debate, she asked, "Would twenty dollars help you remember where I could find her?"

"No. 'Cause I don't know where she went. Not to the next carnival setup, anyway."

Sara nodded and turned away, clenching and unclenching her fists. Was the woman hiding out? From her? Or had Marcus Garrison called her and told her to get out of the picture until things broke one way or the other?

No. Garrison claimed he didn't know who she was because they hadn't met yet. Or was he lying?

She recognized the thoughts as paranoid. The medium and the antique dealer didn't have a conspiracy going, did they?

Feeling defeated, she headed back to the shop. When she pulled around back, a car was sitting in the parking space next to hers.

CHAPTER 10

It was Matt's car. As soon as she rushed past her privacy fence, she found him sitting in one of her lawn chairs. He looked up when she came barreling onto the patio.

He took in her agitated appearance and stood, but he didn't approach her. "Sara, what's wrong?"

"I . . . I went out to the carnival grounds to talk to the fortune-teller. But they're packing up. And she's gone."

"Why was it important to talk to her?" he asked in an even voice. Still, she could see tension around his eyes and mouth as he spoke.

"Did something happen this morning?" she whispered.

"Yeah. My grandmother and my brother called me to Elmwood for a little chat."

The tone of his voice told her it hadn't been a chat about the weather. Oh, Lord, now what?

She felt her throat clog, but she kept her gaze steady. "What did they want?"

"They wanted to tell me that your mother had a nervous breakdown, and she died in a mental institution. Is that the truth?"

"Yes," she whispered.

"I can understand why you might not want to tell me about that."

"I would have. When we got to know each other a little better," she answered. "She suffered from depression all her life. After my father left us, it got worse. But she held things together so she could support herself and raise me. Finally, life just got to be too much for her." She hitched in a breath and let it out. "While she was in the hospital, she committed suicide."

"I'm sorry."

"It's not something I tell people the first time I meet them. Or the second," she said, knowing she sounded defensive.

"Fair enough." His gaze narrowed. "But you've been acting pretty strangely. Jumpy. Like you know something important, but you're not telling it to me. And then that business with the fortune-teller really freaked you out. Would you care to level with me about that?"

The edge in his voice made her feel as though a lead weight had settled onto her chest, crushing the life out of her.

"I can tell you, but I don't think you'll believe me," she answered.

"Try me."

She looked around the patio. There was a high fence on either side, but anybody could be out of sight, listening. "Let's go inside," she said, wondering what she was going to do now.

They stepped into her bedroom. Because she didn't feel comfortable there, she led him into the little sitting room. He stood in the center of her Oriental rug, his arms folded across his chest.

She walked to him and laid a hand on one arm, pulling it away from his body. "Hold me."

His arms came around her. But she felt the stiffness in his body.

"I haven't done anything wrong," she murmured. "The only thing I've done is tried to save your life."

"Jesus! That's a pretty loaded statement. Why is my life at risk, if you don't mind my asking?"

He pulled away from her and sat down on the Victorian love seat, and she figured he wanted to watch her face while she spoke to him.

She took the chair opposite, her own tension making her lean forward.

"I guess your grandmother and your brother convinced you that I'm suffering from paranoid delusions."

"Actually, you've been doing a pretty good job of that yourself."

"Suppose I told you I knew the future? And that what the fortune-teller said really spooked me."

"I can go with the spooked part."

She searched her mind for something to convince him. Could she tell him something else that was going to happen? Something they could verify?

Unfortunately, she hadn't paid a lot of attention to the news. And what would a prediction prove? Nothing right now. They'd have to wait for any event she mentioned to actually happen.

The hard look in his eyes made her throat clog.

"I don't know where to begin."

"Pick a jumping-off place," he suggested, his voice icy.

She laughed, and the sound grated in her ears. "I'm living part of my life over."

"What the hell does that mean?"

"I told you I went to St. Michaels, Maryland, to see an antique dealer named Marcus Garrison." As she looked at Matt's closed expression, she sensed that this interview was just an exercise in futility. Still, she forced herself to continue. "I didn't go last week. I went a year from now, when I was still trying to put my life back together."

His brow wrinkled. "A year from now? Come on!"

"It was next year. At least from my point of view. I went into his gallery. Maybe we can call him up and he can take a digital photo of the building and E-mail it to you. Then I can tell you what it looks like."

"What would that prove except that you'd been there?"

She sighed. "I guess you're right." Feeling like she was standing at the edge of a cliff in an icy wind, she wrapped her arms around her shoulders.

"Obviously, keeping secrets makes you uncomfortable. You'll feel better when you tell me."

"I doubt it." Keeping her gaze fixed on Matt, she said, "Mr. Garrison's gallery is called Second Chance. He named it that because he's got a painting called 'Midnight Magic.' It's made up of a bunch of dots—pointillism. Do you know what that is?"

"Yeah."

"I could see shapes in the dots. Things that looked familiar." She swallowed. "He told me it was painted by a magician using magic paint. The man disappeared inside the painting."

Matt snorted. "And you believe that?"

"I didn't. But I felt like the painting was drawing me to it, drawing me *into* it. I . . . I stepped up to it. Then *into* it. And when I came out the other side, I was in the lady's retiring room at Elmwood the night of the party."

"Go on," Matt said evenly.

She was sure he didn't believe her. But she couldn't stop now. "I came out and talked to Cornelia. She introduced me to some of her friends. Then I met you—again. I'd met you the same way a year ago. At the party. At least for me it's a year ago. And I came back. Only not everything is the same. Some things are different. Like the car rolling down the driveway toward us. That didn't happen last time. Instead, we ended up at the boat dock, making out. And we didn't go back to my place and make love. You didn't spend the night with me. At the auction, that man who picked a fight with you wasn't there. That didn't happen the first time. And the fortune-teller. We didn't meet up with her at the carnival." She stopped because she had run out of steam.

"That's quite a story."

She looked pleadingly at him. She didn't want to say the next part, but she had to. "Matt, that building you're having constructed is going to burn up. And you're going to be inside when it does. Someone is trying to kill you. Or they're trying to kill me—and you got caught in the trap."

"Jesus! You expect me to believe that?"

"It's the truth."

"Well, it sounds like . . . like . . ."

"Like I'm crazy?" she supplied helpfully.

"Yeah." His eyes narrowed. "Or you need to make up a story to cover up something bad."

"I swear it's the truth."

"And how did the building catch on fire?"

"Arson."

"When is this catastrophe supposed to happen?"

"Before . . . it was a little more than two weeks from now. But it could be different this time."

He stood. "Right now, I think I need to . . . uh . . . go away and think about what you've said."

She stayed where she was, her hands gripping her shoulders. "You don't believe me."

His gaze locked with hers. "Did you think I would?"

"No," she whispered. "That's why I didn't want to tell you. But I could see you reacting to the way I was acting. And I didn't know what to do about it!"

He walked toward the bedroom, toward the back door.

She leaped up and rushed after him and grabbed his shoulder. He went still, but he didn't turn.

In desperation, she began to speak quickly, almost stumbling over the words in her haste.

"Matt, don't you remember saying that it felt like we'd known each other a long time, that we belonged together? I think that's because it's true. We met a year ago. At least in my time line. That's why I came back here with you that first night. I never would have made love with you right after we met. But it wasn't the first time for me. I missed you so much. I wanted you back. I wanted to be with you again. Matt, please."

He turned to face her. "You're telling me I'm going to die in a fire."

"No! Don't you understand? I came back to save you."

He probably couldn't deal with any more of her crazy talk. He strode through the bedroom and out the back door.

Since they'd come inside, the sky had darkened and the wind was picking up. A storm was coming.

It was the perfect backdrop for her despair.

She was losing Matt—again. Because he didn't believe her. But who would credit such a wild story?

Lord, was there some way to prove it to him? Her mind scrambled for something—anything.

As Matt crossed the patio, he stopped and pulled out his cell phone, and she realized it had been ringing.

He spoke into the phone, then closed it again and started across the patio again.

Sara dashed outside. "Matt—wait. I thought of something."

He turned to look at her.

"I didn't go into your house the other night. But I've been there before. In . . . in that past life. I know you've got a mug that's got the face of a bearded man on the front. I know you have your parent's leather furniture in your den. I know your bed has a burgundy spread. I know you bought a big new refrigerator a couple of months ago—a Viking. I know you just saw your tailor and ordered a bunch of suits."

He waved his hand dismissivly. "My grandmother could have told you any of that."

"She didn't talk to me about you. Because she didn't want us to meet. I was good enough to work for her, but I wasn't good enough for you. And she was angry that we hooked up. Remember, she canceled the appointment she had with me on the morning after the party?"

He shook his head. "Like I said, I can't deal with this now. Dave Olson needs to see me."

She watched him walk away, watched the wind whipping at his hair.

When his car started, she pressed her fist against her mouth. He thought she was lying—or was crazy. And it *was* a pretty crazy story. She probably wouldn't believe it if it hadn't happened to her.

The sky was so dark that it looked like night. A bad storm was coming.

A bad storm. When the implications hit her, she made a moaning sound. She'd been so focused on what happened last time that she wasn't thinking about *now*. Today.

Dave Olson had called Matt. He was going to meet David Olson at the construction site. Just like the night he'd been killed. A night when there had been a bad storm. Not much rain, but enough wind to whip the fire up to inferno proportions.

She had no proof, but she was pretty sure the timetable had been moved up. It wasn't in two weeks. This was the fateful day.

"Oh, God. Oh, God."

Even as the fear grabbed her, she felt a pang of self-doubt. She couldn't be sure this was it. But she knew she had to go out to the construction site. Dashing back into the house, she grabbed her purse.

She'd gotten a few miles from the house when she thought about her cell phone. She could call Matt and warn him.

Wait—no she couldn't. In this reality, she hadn't bought the phone yet.

And even if she could call, Matt wouldn't believe her. He hadn't believed her wild story. And she had told him the danger was two weeks away. Now it would seem like she was changing things around.

Or maybe she really was caught in the grip of a delusion.

She clenched her hands around the wheel. It didn't feel like a delusion. It felt real. But that could be part of the mental illness—if that was what was going on with her.

Last time she'd taken the highway to the construction site and gotten there too late. This time she took the back road.

Matt had guessed wrong. He'd thought the highway would get him to the meeting faster. But two minutes after he'd taken the on-ramp, he ran into a massive traffic jam. The sky above him looked bruised. Up ahead, through the darkness, he could see lights flashing. Apparently someone had gotten into an accident.

Either people were slowing down to gawk, or the wreck was blocking one of the traffic lanes.

He pulled out his phone and punched in Dave's number to say he'd be late.

The phone rang and rang. Then Dave's voice mail picked up, which was strange because they'd just talked a few minutes ago.

When he felt the hairs at the back of his neck prickle, he tried to dismiss the creepy sensation.

Sara had told him a wild story about going through a painting and ending up finding herself back in time.

On the face of it that was impossible. But she'd seemed so desperate to make him believe her. And all he could think was that she needed psychiatric help. So what had he done about it? Walked out on her.

Because he couldn't deal with it—not after the session with his grandmother and Bradley. Not after he was half-thinking that she was trying to pull some scam on him.

But suppose what she'd told him was real? She'd come back to save him. She'd thrown in some stuff at the end of the conversation about his bedspread and the leather furniture. And she knew he'd just been to his tailor.

Grandmother could have told her about the leather furniture because she was glad he'd taken his parents' old set. She might have even mentioned that he'd been to the tailor or that he'd gotten a new refrigerator. But her sense of propriety would keep her from talking about his bedroom—wouldn't it?

Shit! Now he didn't know what to think. Only, he simply couldn't believe that Sara had walked through a picture and come back from a year in the future. That was impossible.

But she had said he was in danger.

He hadn't wanted to believe that, either. Yet the first night he'd met her, an SUV had come rolling down the driveway toward them. Then, at the auction, Wagner had threatened him. The jerk hadn't really been much of a menace. But he supposed the incident with the SUV could be considered a murder attempt.

One thing he did know. He shouldn't have simply walked out on Sara.

As the traffic inched along, he picked up his cell phone and dialed the number of her shop, but she didn't answer.

Like Dave, she'd vanished into thin air. Or she'd seen his name on the caller ID and decided not to pick up?

Uncertain now, he looked at the line of cars barely moving ahead of him. He could get off at the next exit and turn around, but what good would that do if Sara wasn't even at the store? He'd better find out what Dave wanted. Then he could go back to Sara's and try to have a coherent conversation.

As he sat in the car, he decided that maybe he shouldn't be stupid about this meeting. After a few moments' thought, he called another number, and this time he got through.

Sara sped along the two-lane highway, then turned onto the access road leading to the construction site. She drove slowly past the parking lot. There were only a couple of cars—not Matt's, thank God. None of the workmen were around. They'd probably been sent home because the storm made conditions unsafe.

She wanted to turn into the driveway and wait for him in the parking lot. But if someone was in the construction trailer or hiding in the woods, that person would see her. And she needed to find out what was going to happen.

The sky looked like nuclear night had descended over Fredericksburg. The wind was whipping the trees around, lashing at them as though administering punishment. And she imagined she saw the building swaying. Maybe it would fall down before Matt arrived. That would be the best thing. It would be all over, and he would be safe.

Only she didn't really believe that. They'd try to get him again, whoever they were.

She drove farther up the road where she found a place to turn around. She was heading back in the direction of the driveway when she saw Matt's car turn into the lot and speed toward the construction site. He stopped at the trailer and got out.

Gunning her own engine, she raced after him. But before she crossed the lot, he was out of his car and heading toward the building.

As she rolled down her window, she heard him shout, "Dave?"

The contractor answered. But not from the trailer—from the building. "Matt in here. Help me, my foot's caught. I can't get out."

"Dave?"

"Yes. Help me. Hurry."

As she watched Matt lean into the wind and sprint toward the building, she tried to figure out what was happening. Dave's voice sounded like it was coming from the interior. If he was in there, he could get caught in the fire, too.

She looked wildly around for help, and a flicker of movement in the woods caught her attention. As the wind blew low branches to the side, she saw someone watching the unfolding drama.

But Matt was facing in the wrong direction to see anything but the construction project, and too focused on the voice that sounded like it was coming from inside the unfinished structure. He was bent over, running toward the facade, preparing to duck under the partition that partially blocked the door. "Hang on. I'm coming."

Matt was on foot. She was still in the car. As he raced toward the building, she drove over the curb and onto the bare dirt, her tires crunching over construction debris.

Hearing the car, he whirled around, then gaped at her. "What the hell?"

Through the open passenger window, she shouted, "Stop! For God's sake, stop. He isn't in there. He's in the woods."

In the next second, she heard a popping sound, and the first floor of the building burst into flames.

Matt sprinted around the car, avoiding a tongue of fire that shot through the front door of the building. He reached the driver's door of her car as the blaze struck the vehicle.

Yanking the door open, he snapped the catch on her seat belt and hauled her away as flames leaped at her vehicle.

With his hand firmly in hers, he pulled her twenty yards away, then pushed her to the ground as the car turned into a giant torch.

Moments later, chunks of masonry started raining down from the burning building onto the car.

Matt sheltered her with his body, but smoke enveloped them, making them both cough. And heat crept toward them.

"Let's get out of here," Matt choked out.

They were halfway to his car when a shot rang out. Then another.

Looking up through reddened eyes, Sara saw the blurry shape of a man coming toward them. It wasn't Dave Olson. It was Bradley Tripplehorn, Matt's brother. And he was shooting at them.

"Get behind the dumpster," Matt whispered.

The smoke billowed up, obscuring Bradley again. And obscuring them, too, she hoped.

They both ducked around the end of the large metal container. Before Bradley could shoot again, she heard someone shout, "What the hell?"

But the smoke had distorted his voice, and she didn't see who it was—or whether it was friend or foe.

"Keep down." Matt looked around the side of the

dumpster, then picked up a two-foot piece of discarded lumber before charging into the roiling smoke.

As she watched him disappear, she knew she couldn't stay where she was when he was in danger. She found a similar club and followed him. At first she could see nothing, and her heart pounded in her chest.

Then she thought she heard the sounds of scuffling.

Another shot rang out, and her heart leaped into her throat.

"Matt!"

"I'm all right. Stay back."

She locked on the location where she'd heard his voice. As she ran forward, she picked up the sounds of a fight.

In the swirling smoke, she almost stumbled over Matt and Bradley—and another man.

Again, it wasn't Dave Olson, but Josh Hemingway, Matt's vice president. Together they subdued Bradley. Josh picked up the gun from the ground and held it on the older Tripplehorn brother.

"Thanks for getting here in time," Matt panted.

"You said it was urgent," Josh replied

Matt turned back to his brother. "What the hell is going on?" he demanded. "Are you and Dave working together?"

"I'm not talking."

Matt grabbed his brother's hair and tipped his face up. "Yeah, well, now that my head is on straight, I'm thinking that you imitated Dave's voice to get me here. Why?"

Bradley's eyes were defiant, as he pressed his lips together.

"What did you do? Set off a fire bomb by remote control? Only Sara's car blocked your line of sight, and you thought I was already inside, didn't you? Your mistake!"

Bradley glared at him.

"I guess I could have been in that burning building by accident, but do you think shooting me could possibly look like anything but murder?" Matt demanded.

"What does it matter with a crazy woman involved?" Bradley bit out.

Sara stared at him. "You were going to shoot us both and make it look like I did it?"

"I want a lawyer," he answered.

Matt glared at Bradley. "Killing your brother is a little over the top. But then you've been jealous of me for a long time, haven't you? What did you want? The house? All of Grandmother's money? Were you and that friend of yours—Travis Norton—going to take over my business?"

Again, Bradley declined to comment.

Turning to Sara, Matt added, "I would have been toast by now, if you hadn't had the guts to drive up to the building. Thank you. I know that sounds pretty inadequate," he added.

"I'm glad I got here in time," she choked out.

He looked like he wanted to say a lot more, and she wanted to hear what it was. But right now, they had to get Bradley into custody.

"We'd better call the police and the fire department," she said.

He pulled out his cell phone and punched in 911.

The police arrived ten minutes later, and the fire department was close behind, although there wasn't much of the building left for them to save.

Bradley started shouting that he'd been set up. But Josh, Matt, and Sara all told a very different story.

And when the cops walked into the woods, they found the transmitter that Bradley had used to set off the explosion. Presumably, his fingerprints were all over it since he had counted on taking the evidence away with him.

They hauled him to the station house in handcuffs. Sara, Matt, and Josh rode in another patrol car.

After lengthy and separate interviews, Bradley was charged with attempted murder. The rest of them were free to go, and a uniformed officer drove them back to the parking lot where they'd left their vehicles.

Sara stared at the burned hulk of her car and shuddered.

Matt followed her gaze. "The good news is that nobody was inside."

"Yes."

They climbed into his car, and she wondered what would happen next.

"You're covered in soot," he said softly, reaching to stroke his finger against her cheek and coming away with a blackened fingertip.

"So are you."

"Then I guess neither one of us is going to mind getting dirty." As he spoke, he reached for her and dragged her into his arms, where she clung to him.

"You could have gotten killed," he growled.

"So could you."

"But we're both fine, thanks to you. Sara, I'm so sorry I didn't listen to you."

She pulled back far enough to search his face. "Are you saying you believe what I told you about going into the picture and going back in time?"

"Yes, I am." He looked contrite. "Unfortunately, when you told me, it seemed like a lot to swallow."

She nodded. "I had a lot of trouble believing it myself."

"I should have known you'd never lie to me," he said, his voice thick.

Her vision blurred, but she kept her gaze steady on him. "Thank you. I know I was acting really strange. So many things had special meaning for me, and I couldn't explain them to you or anyone else."

"Your nightmare—you were dreaming about the fire, weren't you?" he asked.

"Yes."

"But you said it happened differently the last time?"

"Yes. I got a call from Dave—only it was really Bradley—to meet you at the construction site. I was caught in traffic, so I arrived after you did. And it was already too late."

"This time it was the other way around. I got caught in the traffic jam. And I would have been dead if you hadn't been waiting for me." His breath hitched. "Thank you for not giving up on me."

"I couldn't." She lifted her face, and he brought his mouth down on hers for a long, sweet kiss.

When the kiss finally broke, she said, "Let's go home."

"To my house."

"Okay. I was too nervous to go in last time. I mean—I was afraid I'd give away that I'd been there a lot of times before. But now you can fix me a cup of that cranberry tea you've got in the pantry." She dragged in a breath and let it out. "It was such a strain trying to pretend I didn't know stuff."

"I can imagine. I'm sorry."

"Not your fault."

"And it's all over now." He looked abashed. "Tell

me about the antique shop in—where was it—St. Michaels, Maryland?"

She told the story while they drove.

"You are so brave," he said as he pulled up the long drive and into the garage.

"I didn't have a choice. I had to save you. But I kept feeling like the ground was shifting out from under my feet."

"Sara, I'm so . . . so sorry."

"It came out all right."

"It will—if you say you'll marry me."

She couldn't hold back a small grin. "You're a week ahead of schedule on that."

"This time I already know you a hell of a lot better. There's nothing like sharing a near-death experience to put things into focus."

Again he reached for her, and she nestled against him. "I love you so much," he said, his voice strong.

"I love you. I've been aching to say that since I came back."

They hung on to each other for long moments. "We should go up to St. Michaels and thank Mr. Garrison," he said.

"Yes."

"But right now, I think we should go inside. And I'm hoping you'd like to try something a little more stimulating than a cup of tea."

She grinned at him. "I think we're on the same wavelength."

EPILOGUE

"What do you think?" Sara asked.

Matt was staring in fascination at the facade of the Second Chance Gallery.

"When you told me someone had turned an auto repair shop into an antique and art gallery, I couldn't quite picture it."

"Who could?"

He pulled into a parking space beside the green-painted cinder-block building just outside the prime business district of St. Michaels.

It was after dinner, but there were still customers in the gallery, judging from the four cars in the parking lot.

Matt reached for Sara's hand as they walked through the weed-strewn yard past a fountain featuring a dolphin. Apparently somebody had bought the Venus. No, wait. Garrison hadn't acquired it yet.

Inside, the air-conditioning kept out the August heat.

Matt looked around in wonder at the soaring

ceilings and the large display area crammed with antiques.

"I thought you had a lot of stuff in your shop. There's five times the space here."

As she led him into the picture gallery, her grip tightened on his hand. The magic painting was there, abstract and colorful, filled with tiny dots of thick oil paint in primary colors.

Sara studied the painting from across the room. Last time she'd seen the lady's dressing room at Elmwood. Now she saw only swirls of color. She was almost afraid to find out, but she asked Matt, "Do you see anything in it?"

"Just dots."

She let out the breath she'd been holding. "I guess you're not going to disappear on me."

"Happy people don't see anything but an abstract pattern," a voice from behind them said.

They turned to see the gallery owner.

"Actually, I don't need confirmation that I'm very happy." She smiled. "I'm Sara Drimmon . . ." She stopped and started again. "Well, actually, I'm Sara Tripplehorn, and this is my husband, Matt. I called you a few weeks ago."

"I remember." Garrison eyed Matt. "I take it that everything worked out well for you."

"Yes."

"Let me close up for the night, then come back to my office. We should celebrate with a glass of champagne."

"That would be lovely," Sara answered.

The office was in a room at the back of the building with walls made of bookcases. Garrison walked to the chair behind his desk. Sara and Matt settled on an antique love seat.

Their host got a bottle of Dom Perignon from a small refrigerator, then took flutes out from a closed cabinet.

After popping the cork, he poured some champagne for each of them.

"So what are your plans?" he asked, as they sipped their champagne.

"Well, I'm planning to leave Fredericksburg," Matt said. "My business doesn't require my staying there, and we'd like to move to a nice, comfortable town away from the family influence."

"So your wife would be looking for a new place to set up shop?"

"Yes," she acknowledged.

"Would you be interested in this property?" Garrison asked.

Sara stared at him in surprise. "Is it for sale?"

"I'm also looking to change my fortunes. Lately I've been seeing a very interesting city when I look at the painting. It's Italianate, but I don't think it's actually in Italy."

"Where?"

"Some other world, I imagine. I told you, the painting doesn't always send people into the past. It sends them where they need to go."

"You'd take a chance on another world?" she asked.

"I think I have to," he said, his voice grave. "But we aren't here to discuss me. I was worried about who could take over the gallery. But you're the perfect candidate."

"Why?"

"You're a success in the antique business." He looked from her to Matt and back again, grinning. "You could use your husband's money to fix up the place a bit. And you'd be a wonderful custodian for 'Midnight Magic.'"

"Why me?" she breathed.

"Because your personal experience has acquainted you with the painting's power, so you understand how important a second chance can be."

She felt a shiver of alarm. "What if I send the wrong people to the painting?"

"There are no 'wrong people.' If it's going to work for them, they select themselves."

"How many people have gone through?" Sara asked.

Garrison answered at once. "Not a lot. In the past ten years, maybe fifteen."

Sara felt Matt's hand tighten on hers, and she turned to him. Their eyes locked. "Thank God I was one of them."

Garrison smiled at them. "Wouldn't you like the chance to give that gift to others?"

"It's a big responsibility," she said. "If someone goes to another world then they won't come back here. And I won't get to find out what happened to them."

"Yes. But they choose to take the risk," Garrison said.

"Let me think about it. Maybe I should consult Madame Raina."

"She does have amazing insights. She came by and told me she'd met you, and that she wished she could affect your future. But that was beyond her power."

"She knows about the painting?"

"She's one of the few who knows the secret."

Sara nodded.

"Take a few days to think about my offer. Talk it over with your husband. Or Madame Raina, if you like. She's at her daughter's house. When you feel ready, come back and see me. Whatever you decide, I'm sure it will be the right thing for you."

They stood up and walked out of the shop, Sara's hand clasped tightly in Matt's.

"What do you think?" she asked when they were alone.

"Well, I like the town. This would be a good place to live—and bring up children."

"Yes."

"But maybe we should sleep on it."

"Sleep on it. Are we really going to get much sleep?"

He laughed. The sound filled her with joy. And she was pretty sure she knew what she was going to do with her future.

ULTERIOR MOTIVES

BY
SUSAN KEARNEY

CHAPTER 1

They'd found her.

Merline Sullivan tilted her rearview mirror, spied the zoom camera lens of the paparazzo in the car behind her, and pressed the gas pedal toward the floorboard. Her snazzy Corvette responded with a satisfying surge of acceleration over the Maryland highway and put distance between her car and the one pursuing.

Could she lose them before she ran out of gas? Her gauge registered almost empty.

She hung a left, then veered right, pulled behind a dry cleaner shop and parked. After taking a moment to wipe her sweaty palms on her faded jeans, she scratched the itchy skin beneath the cast on her wrist, broken during a Rollerblade fall, and wondered exactly how long she'd have to be out of the limelight before the press stopped hounding her.

As the white sedan in pursuit screeched to a stop behind her Corvette and the stench of burned tires filtered through her AC, she realized that, although the two months when she couldn't work had seemed an eternity to her, not enough time had passed for her adoring public to forget her—hence the stalkerazzi.

With a frown Merline pulled back into traffic, carefully and slowly, as if she didn't care that they'd found her. As if she didn't care that the one thing she was good at, the one thing she loved, the one thing that made her happy had been taken from her. Merline might have been born with her big voice, but she'd honed it with long hours of practice and discipline into a finely tuned instrument, and after years of performing in hick bars and rinky-dink towns, she'd hit the big time, becoming an "overnight success."

Along the way to becoming a superstar, she'd lost her last name. And her small-town midwestern accent. Madonna might have been her personal hero and Sheryl Crow a friend, but Merline's talent had soared her right to the top of the pop charts. And she'd stayed there. Platinum album after platinum album. Grammy Awards and movie offers. A-list parties, plus a bulging bank account—she'd had it all.

Her workaholic tendencies had been praised in the press. No one had understood that she worked to keep the fear at bay—the fear that one day, everything she'd struggled so hard to achieve would be gone. And now the worst had happened. Without her voice, she couldn't sing. And if she couldn't sing, she didn't know what to do. Singing was who Merline was. She needed to sing to be happy, needed to sing to remind herself she'd mastered at least one aspect of her life.

Knowing she wouldn't be able to lose the paparazzo and adhere to the speed limits within the small town of St. Michaels, Maryland, Merline resisted the urge to speed. Instead, she searched for opportunity and when she spied an empty parking spot, she signaled with her blinker and pulled over.

The sedan pulled right behind her, smashed her rear bumper. Her front passenger side tire slammed into the curb. Metal crunched. The air bag opened, and from the loud popping, she surmised her tire had just blown out. Damn. Luckily Merline hadn't yet removed her seat belt. She wasn't hurt.

She reached around the air bag, turned off the engine, and cracked open her door to spy a long camera lens aimed at her face. "Merline. Look over here."

Jerking back into her car seat, she slammed her door shut and gripped the wheel tightly. It wasn't enough Alfred Cusak had crashed into her. The sleazebag who'd been hounding her for a month wanted to take her picture, capture her at an embarrassing moment. Sheesh. A normal person would ask if she'd been hurt and apologize for crashing into her car. Damn parasite.

Breathe.

Perhaps she could drive away on the bad tire. The motor revved, but the groan of metal told her she was hung up on the curb.

She might be trapped, but maybe she could outwit Alfred. All she needed was a local tow truck to come for her car, preferably with her inside it. Pressing charges barely crossed her mind. She didn't need the hassle of the accident showing up on the evening news with the inevitable rumors she'd been drinking—or worse. Even if it was ten o'clock in the morning, viewers might believe the rumor mill, and her agent, manager, and publicist would be on her case.

Intent on calling AAA, Merline plucked her phone from her handbag. When her call wouldn't go through, she refrained from banging her fist on the air bag. Instead, she released a sigh of frustration and called Lilly, her personal assistant.

"Merline Sullivan's office." Lilly's upbeat voice came over the line from LA to Maryland as clear as the photographer's view of Merline through the front windshield.

Merline swore and she imagined Lilly's frown into the phone. "Merline? Is that you?"

"God makes artists. The devil makes paparazzi," Merline complained, realizing that her very plush, very slick red Corvette was heating up in the morning sun. A decade of practice avoiding the flash of cameras, of hiding behind big Gucci sunglasses and bigger Ferragamo hats grew tiresome on a good day. And today was far from good.

Lilly's voice sounded vibrant, annoyed. "If it weren't for your photographs in the rags, I wouldn't even know you're still alive. We never talk anymore."

"I'm calling now, aren't I? Besides, I'm on vacation." Merline had no idea how long she could maintain the front that everything was fine, that she was merely taking a career break. She'd canceled her world tour, claiming her broken wrist prevented her from playing guitar, but rumors had started. And when the paparazzi had caught her sneaking out the back door of a world-renowned voice specialist who'd diagnosed her partially paralyzed vocal cords as a reaction to the anesthesia during her wrist surgery, the rumors had escalated. It wouldn't be long before the entire world knew for sure that pop-sensation megastar Merline could no longer sing a note.

Avoiding the tinted side windows, flashbulbs popped through the front windshield, the bright lights warning of the blinding attention she'd receive if she reopened the door. The damned paparazzi seemed to travel in packs and at least five cameras now pointed her way. Sometimes the price of fame was more than she wanted to pay.

So far, Merline had kept her career-ending disaster from her friends, coworkers and recording company. Not even Lilly knew the truth. No one did—except her doctors. Luckily the business world mostly ignored celebrity rumors. Her recording studio hadn't called her to make a statement. Yet. But word would break soon. Someone would hack into a computer. Or overhear a nurse talking about her doctor's famous client. Word would get out that Merline was washed up. Ruined.

"You don't answer my calls."

"I've been busy."

Merline had no idea how long she could keep hiding. From the paparazzi. From her life. From the truth. From her fans. While the medical experts had given her little reason to hope, Merline hadn't given up. In her short twenty-eight years, she'd been stepped on often, suffered numerous setbacks, and had learned to fight to keep up a brave front.

"You're supposed to be resting after surgery."

"I am. Or I would be if my car didn't have a flat." She refrained from giving more details that would require more explanations. After all she was supposed to be resting her throat. From the nifty GPS on her dashboard, she ascertained her address and passed on her current location to Lilly. "Send AAA?"

"Sure."

Locals and tourists had exited the shops and gathered on the sidewalks. Likely the sound of her blowout had initially attracted their attention and then the paparazzi had increased everyone's curiosity. People milled, all waiting to see who would exit the Corvette.

Let them wait. Merline had no intention of budging until her tow truck showed. As perspiration beaded her upper lip, she reconsidered starting the car and running the AC, but even if her gas tank hadn't been low, she had no idea what kind of damage she'd sustained, and the possibility of starting a fire terrified her.

From a local shop with a sign that read "Second Chance," a woman gestured to her with an open palm, clearly inviting Merline to come inside. Slim, with shoulder-length blond hair and a tattoo on her ankle, she possessed intelligent blue eyes and a kind face.

Merline's phone rang. Caller ID told her it was Lilly. "What's up?"

"AAA can't tow you for another two hours. The truck's already out making a call."

"Give us a head shot, Merline," one of the paparazzi shouted. "Open up. Come on." He pounded on her window.

"What's going on?" Lilly sounded worried. "Should I call the police?"

"I'll be okay, Lilly. Thanks."

Merline changed her mind about exiting the vehicle. After grabbing her guitar case from the backseat, she pulled her hat low over her sunglasses, opened the door, and exited, using the case as a shield. Although the crowd surrounded her, experience told her if she walked quickly, people would move aside. Ten steps later and she was inside the shop.

Second Chance appeared to be a combination antique store and art gallery. The woman sold paintings, furniture, and vintage clothing. And her store smelled of fresh coffee and pastries. Even better the cool air-conditioning helped dry the sweat on Merline's palms. Towering urns filled with ferns and tiger lilies the color of lemons and ripe bing cherries soothed her. Deep green vines crawled over a brick walled fireplace that looked so old she wondered if the store had been built around it. As if waiting for customers, nooks and alcoves were filled with paintings and overflowing with big leafy plants; bronze statues and delicate miniatures flanked wall sconces. A silver tea set and a collection of ivory-handled canes rested on an antique sideboard.

When the woman locked the door behind them, Merline knew she'd found a friend. "Thanks."

"You're welcome. I'm Sara." She smiled warmly. "You can stay as long as you like."

The paparazzi knocked on the door. Sara lowered the blinds over the store's plate-glass windows, and after her kindness, Merline decided to buy a painting—even if she didn't like any of them. But as she spied a Linda Lekinff and then an original oil-on-canvas Tarkay, she relaxed further, and slung her guitar strap over her shoulder.

"You have beautiful artwork here."

"Feel free to look around. Would you care for a soda or coffee?"

"Something cold, please." Merline appreciated how the owner didn't ask personal questions, not even about the frantic paparazzi still knocking on the front door. "What about other customers? Aren't you worried you'll lose business?"

Sara grinned. "I own this place and profit isn't everything."

"Still—"

"Besides, after you leave, the town newspaper will

publish a story about you hiding out in my store and tourists will flock in. I'll make a tidy profit . . . so you needn't feel obligated to make a purchase." Sara held out an icy cola.

Merline accepted, figuring either Sara was uncommonly perceptive or she'd read her mind. "Thanks. Are you always so kind to strangers?"

"Only to superstars." Sara's blue eyes twinkled, letting Merline know not only that Sara recognized her, but that she was teasing.

"So you get a lot of us superstars here, do you?" Merline sipped the icy drink between parched lips and it tasted like heaven.

"You'd be surprised. I enjoy guessing which art will appeal to which customers. Now, you haven't even glanced at the Peter Max but Lekinff calls to you."

"I own several of her paintings," Merline admitted. "I like the mood she sets—peaceful, yet independent, and she's a good investment."

"Liking a piece is the only good reason to buy. There's an artist whose work I hung in the back that I believe you might enjoy viewing," Sara suggested. "The painting is called 'Midnight Magic.'"

Merline hated pushy salespeople, but Sara honestly seemed more interested in her opinion than in making a sale. As Merline wandered toward the rear of the store, careful not to let her guitar case knock into any of the paintings, Sara picked up a feather duster and lovingly ran it over one picture frame after another.

The paparazzi finally stopped banging and Merline actually felt safe. The piranhas might be waiting outside, but for the moment she was free. Taking her time, she roamed through the gallery, admiring old masters and up-and-coming artists, as well as the work of several talented locals.

But when she reached the back room, her breath caught in her throat and she held tight to her guitar. Something about 'Midnight Magic' drew her. While she wasn't an art expert, she recognized the technique. The painting was abstract, pointillism. Colorful. Filled with tiny dots of thick oil paint in primary colors, the technique caused the eye to blend the images until Merline saw secondary colors that were brighter than the original paint. The slashes of color were stunning.

Sara joined her. "The painting is very old, and legend says a brokenhearted magician painted it with magical paint."

Merline couldn't stop staring. It was almost as if she'd been meant to blow out her tire, stop in front of this store, and find this painting. "How much do you want for it?"

"Sorry. It's not for sale."

Disappointment washed through her. She would have enjoyed hanging the painting in her studio and marveled that the more she stared, the more her eyes blended the dots. "I understand why you want to keep it. Are there any other works by the magician?"

"Just this one. The legend claims that the painting has magical qualities that cause some viewers to travel to the right place at the right time to cure what ails them. When the painter finished, he traveled into the world he'd created on canvas and never returned."

"Now, that's a fanciful . . . idea." Merline gazed at the pinpoints of clouds swirling into the dark sky. She stared harder. Was that a star, a planet, or a satellite?

Weird.

She felt light. As if she was being pulled into the painting. The effect startled her. Merline liked art. She owned a bunch of paintings. But never had she felt this connected. How had Sara known? And why did she feel as though the painting was calling to her? Beckoning her?

Almost as if caught in a magnetic force, one moment Merline was standing in the antique shop, talking and breathing normal air, the next . . . she floated right into the painting . . . and she was . . . in a vortex of spinning light, swirling sound.

Oh God. Was that her screaming? Had her mind finally snapped?

Merline had left the gallery and Sara's antiques far behind. Sucked like a cork into a powerful whirlpool of purple slashes and pink ribbons of light, she tumbled and fought for balance. But she had no leverage. There was no gravity. No floor beneath her feet. No up. No down. Only Merline and her guitar wildly spinning.

Gyrating wildly, she suddenly popped through the fantastical tunnel. And her eyes widened in shock.

Frantic to find something familiar, she looked around some kind of busy domed building with large windows that let in . . . starlight. She blinked, trying to erase the images of beings—some of whom sported blue skin. Others had tails and wore feathers. Some floated, one snaked, and another crawled across shimmering gray metal that looked like no substance she'd ever seen. She felt as though she'd been transported onto the set of *The Outer Limits* or *Star Wars*.

Had Sara put a hallucinogen into her cola that she still held in one hand? So why was the liquid rising from her glass, bubbling away into the . . . atmosphere?

When she noted her own feet were no longer

attached to the deck, she screamed again. Surely not even LSD could make her float above the gray metal like an astronaut in space? What the hell was going on? Why couldn't she breathe? Was she hallucinating from lack of air? Or having a panic attack?

Her stomach roiled and she swallowed hard to keep down breakfast. This couldn't be happening. The stress of the past few weeks must have caused a complete nervous breakdown. She'd gone insane. She'd heard of pulsing blue lights causing mental instability, could the points of paint have caused an imbalance in her brain?

Alien humanoids couldn't be staring and pointing at her. They weren't there. She closed her eyes, attempted to draw deep breaths, but still couldn't pull air into her lungs.

Don't panic. It's all in your head.

But when she again tried to refill her lungs, there still was no air. Her eyes flew open. The alien world was still there. And she'd floated dizzily higher.

Oh God.

She needed oxygen. Her lungs burned. She released her glass and it traveled upward, end over end. Her vision narrowed, tunneled on a large man who'd floated into the air and who grabbed her shoulders.

She clutched his shirt. "I can't breathe."

He answered in a deep and melodic voice, speaking a foreign language she couldn't understand or identify. While his big brown eyes set in a suntanned face and framed by long dark hair looked concerned, she read puzzlement in his gaze. Obviously she didn't belong here, wherever the hell *here* was.

Her vision narrowed to a pinpoint of light. And then the light went out.

*   *   *

Merline dreamed. She had to be dreaming because she could hear the sweetest, purest male voice, singing a song she didn't recognize. Each note speared her with the need to touch and be touched. To love and be loved.

A natural singer, one who sang from the heart with both technical perfection and emotive qualities, was rare. He sang and evoked images of seductive whispers, hot kisses, and sensual moves. By the clear resonance of his voice, she could tell that he opened his throat without straining or tension. His singing was like a gift from the gods, natural and genuine. Words in the love song matched the tempo to perfection and suddenly she was no longer in darkness but a mist-filled twilight.

And though the singer kept serenading her, he was kissing her at the same time—an impossible feat, but she didn't care how he did it as long as his wondrous lips kept caressing and coaxing. As long as his seductive voice kept arousing.

Never had lips tasted so delicious. Or tones caused her blood to pump with need. Arching her spine, she flung her arms around his neck, pressed her breasts into his warm chest, and caught fire.

Burning with need, she demanded more. And he gave with his mouth and his hands. Her fervor escalated. Her breasts swelled and her nipples pebbled against his warmth as heat seeped between her thighs.

He placed one clever finger between her parted legs and she moaned into his mouth, her hips pumping. Faster. Harder. More. And when she exploded, not once, but twice, the electric sensation bolted through her like heat lightning. Delicious spasms ebbed slowly, leaving her glowing and satiated and happy in her amorous fog.

Like the sun rising at dawn to shred the mist, the light display brightened. She squeezed her eyes tightly shut.

Oh, so gently, the singer once again prodded her. "Come on. It's time to wake up."

Merline opened her eyes to find her fully dressed rescuer on the far side of a hospital room, his big brown eyes staring into hers with compassion. She pulled a sheet up tight against her chest and accepted that the lovemaking hadn't been real, but instead had been a dream-induced fantasy. And no wonder she'd dreamed of him—his had been the last face she'd seen before . . . oh, God. She was still here.

She'd traveled through a magical painting into a world full of alien beings. She'd almost suffocated. Blacked out. Had an erotic dream. It was insane. Crazy.

Closing her eyes, she took a deep breath, willing calm, telling herself this was a delusion and would be gone when she reopened her eyes. She breathed in. Out. Opened her eyes.

He was still there.

Although she'd sensed this man had been trying to help her, and she suspected that he might even be the reason she hadn't suffocated, she couldn't stem her rising panic. The magical painting, the aliens, all of it should have disappeared upon her awakening. But she was still . . . here. Wherever here was.

"Are you better?" he asked, his tone just as melodic

as she remembered, though now she could understand his language.

"What happened? Where am I?" She tried to sit up but couldn't move. Yet she could breathe. And she didn't care how scrumptious he looked with his aristocratic cheekbones, full lips, and squared jaw, or how compassionate his expression; she wouldn't accept confinement. "Release me, at once."

"You're immobile for your own safety." A tiny hologram image of a woman spoke to her and Merline blinked in wonder. She could see through the small three-dimensional image, but the woman appeared completely lifelike, down to her buffed nails and efficient bedside manner. "Let my program finish healing you and then I will release you."

She must be in some state-of-the-art medical facility. Although Merline wasn't up on the latest computer breakthroughs, she supposed if Disney World could create talking holograms, so could any decently equipped hospital. "I'm not sick. Let me go." She thrashed her head back and forth but couldn't free the invisible bonds that kept her immobile. Air seemed to freeze in her tightening throat. Panic, shock, and confusion warred with the aftermath of pleasure from her erotic dream.

Turning her head convinced her she was no longer in the busy terminal, but in a room that looked like no hospital she'd ever seen. Gadgets she couldn't identify hung suspended from the ceiling and the walls seemed to grow out of the floor.

In fact, the only thing human in sight was the strange man hovering over her. And to keep whatever fragments remained of her sanity, rather than deal with the alien equipment, she focused on him. His broad

shoulders and powerful chest led to a thick neck corded
with muscles. He wore simple clothes of a fine material, cut, and design she didn't recognize.

"Please. Be calm," he instructed. "Let the machine
heal you." The brown-eyed man with the puppy-dog
look slipped his hand into hers. As his warmth heated
her, she clung tight and tried to tamp down the fear
that she'd lost her mind.

"Where am I?"

He replied with an honest mien, without hesitation.
"Space Station Alpha-Gamma Five."

"Huh?"

He ignored her groan and soothingly rubbed his
thumb in tiny circles on the back of her hand. "Let me
introduce myself. I am Tomm Jabal from Siraz."

His direct gaze held hers, shooting an electric arc of
intensity at her, making her very aware of him as a
man. Hot enough to star in her dream-induced fantasy
or in a feature film, he emitted a rough confidence she
couldn't help but admire. Not to mention that he'd
saved her from asphyxiation and then had stayed to
make sure she was OK, an act of kindness that was
rare.

The tiny hologram floated above her and piped in, "I
am healer Gajar. Are you in pain?"

She shook her head. She had no physical pain. However, the mental agony of knowing she was having a
mental breakdown brought tears to her eyes.

"Please respond by voice. Different gestures mean
different things to different beings."

"I have no pain."

"Good. The suit translators seem to be working
properly."

"Suit? Translators?" Merline frowned, recalling that

when Tomm had first spoken to her, his words had been alien. But now he seemed to be speaking English, although she was having difficulty understanding his meaning. She'd never heard of Space Station Alpha-Gamma Five.

Gajar spoke like a teacher giving a lecture, her tone matter of fact. "Every Federation citizen is given a suit. I have placed your suit's control in the automatic mode until you learn how to operate it. The suit will adjust air quality to match your physiology and gravity to whatever you are accustomed to, as well as translate language, clothe you, clean you, and take care of waste. When you develop your mind, you'll learn how to operate other features such as null-grav, shielding, and breathing filters."

"*Okay . . .* " Merline had always been creative with her songwriting, but her mind had certainly imprisoned her in a very interesting world. Until now, she hadn't known her imagination was quite so bizarre.

Tomm pointed to her clothes that were neatly folded by her side. Yet when she looked down, she appeared to be still wearing them. "Your suit can duplicate any outfit. We thought you'd be more comfortable in something familiar."

"Thanks."

His tone was kind, his gaze curious, but she sensed an intensity about him she had no trouble identifying— attraction. Merline's voice might have won her a Grammy, but she'd have never made it to the top without her looks. She'd been blessed with features men found attractive and that women yearned to emulate. Plastic surgeons reported that women came in for surgery asking for J. Lo's butt and Merline's breasts, nose, and lips.

So Tomm might have been summoned straight from her inspiration, but he was reacting like most men—except he was making an effort to keep his eyes on her face and she gave him credit for that.

For a big man, he spoke gently. "Could you tell us where you're from and how you got here?"

"I'm from LA."

"LA?"

"Los Angeles." When he still looked puzzled, she added, "California."

"You just popped right onto the space station. One second the spot was empty and the next, you were right there in front of me. How did you do that?"

"I have no idea." She shrugged, wondering if all crazy people's delusions appeared so real. Still, she played along, wondering if she worked her way through to the end of her vision if she'd suddenly pop back into the real world.

The hologram, Gajar, seemed to have direct computer access. "My database places California on the North American continent of Earth, a planet in the third quadrant of the Milky Way galaxy—but no one has referred to California as a state for more than three hundred years."

Oh great. Her mind had totally flipped out. She wasn't on Earth. Wasn't in her own time, but had traveled three hundred years into the future. She recalled the owner of Second Chance and her words—that the painting could send people to any place or time to cure what ailed them.

And her sick mind had taken the story and created a fantasy world. She'd envisioned a gorgeous, considerate man who seemed to care for her—not her fame, not her fortune, not her damaged voice. She couldn't have thought of anyone more comforting or more attractive to appear . . . and so she must have summoned him up during her nervous breakdown. But no matter his appeal, she couldn't stay in a dream world. She had to go back to reality.

With a sigh she closed her eyes. *Focus. You are in St. Michaels, Maryland, in a shop called Second Chance. Your car will soon be fixed. The paparazzi will soon be gone.*

She would buy a painting from Sara. She would make a new life for herself without her voice. When she opened her eyes again, she'd be back . . . in front of the painting, in the real world.

Her eyes flew open. He was still there. The hologram was still there. Oh, God. She truly was insane and her hand trembled in his.

Perhaps she needed merely to work her way further through the craziness to return to reality. "Have you ever heard of a painting called 'Midnight Magic'?"

"There's nothing about it in my data banks," the hologram said.

Tomm shook his head, a dark lock of hair falling rakishly over his forehead. "Why?"

"Because the last thing I remember is standing in front of a painting. The owner said it was painted with magical paint and a magician disappeared inside it and never returned. I thought it was . . . a legend . . . or a fairy tale."

"It's possible the painting was a time portal," the hologram told her, then finally released her bonds. "How you ended up almost in the middle of the galaxy is a mystery and not my field of expertise. You had some neurological damage that caused paralysis in your vocal cords, but I've healed them. And your broken wrist is now whole."

Merline raised her hand. Her wrist. With everything that had happened, she'd forgotten the injury. Her cast was gone. She flexed the wrist and it functioned as if she'd never broken it. And her damaged vocal cords? Merline hummed, clearing her throat. Could her voice really be back? Would she really sing again? As her hopes rose, she softly hummed a few chords and reached for her guitar.

She might be crazy, but at least she'd created a world in her head where she could sing. And she'd rather be able to sing in this world than go back to her old one. She strummed her guitar and sang softly, testing her vocal cords, warming them up with an easy scale that sounded . . . perfect.

At the sound of her voice. Tomm's face lit up with appreciation. "You can sing?"

Apparently she could. She opened her mouth and belted out one of her favorite songs. And her sultry voice was back to sounding as if she'd never stopped singing.

She was healed.

She could sing, and tears of joy misted her eyes. Tomm signaled her a thumbs up.

Wow. She was really good to go. In the crazy world she'd created, she was healed. She had her health, her voice, and the sexiest man she'd seen in a long time who seemed very concerned about her welfare.

Nothing made sense. And she didn't care. She could sing. She didn't want to go back to the real world— even if she was insane.

The hologram doctor released Merline from the facility and she was free to go. But where? Unless she was living in an illusion, everyone she'd ever known had been dead for more than two centuries. Since she didn't believe she had an imagination vivid enough to create aliens and hologram doctors, she had to assume she wasn't hallucinating and that this place was real. She was not crazy.

Somehow the magical painting had brought her here. Oh, she didn't believe in magic—there had to be a scientific explanation—but perhaps the painting was a genuine portal to other times and places like the computer had suggested. Right then and there, she vowed to stop doubting her sanity and deal with her new circumstances.

Which meant she had to build a new life from scratch. However, she'd like to return to Earth . . . somehow.

After wedging her clothes into the guitar case, she slung the strap over her shoulder and headed out of the room, and Tomm accompanied her. The hallway appeared to lead back to the busy space station, but at the moment, they had the corridor to themselves.

She glanced sideways at him, wondering about his intentions. Merline hated being so suspicious, but while saving her and obtaining medical help had been a good deed, he'd stayed by her side, And now Tomm seemed reluctant to leave her to her own devices.

No matter his reasons, she owed him. "I never thanked you for saving my life."

"You're welcome." Tomm shrugged powerful shoulders, almost as if embarrassed, then shortened his long-legged stride to match hers, reached into his back pocket, and offered her a golden oval disk no bigger than a peanut. "What will you do now?"

She'd do what she always had done. Work. "Return to Earth."

"Space travel is expensive. You are far from home."

"I'll find a job singing. That's what I do." She peered at the disk and saw it was stamped with a logo or icon and thought it would be a shame if this was his idea of a snack. At the notion of food, her stomach rumbled, reminding her that it had been too long since she'd last eaten. And she absolutely refused to think about the fact for more than a mind-boggling second that she might not have eaten in more than three hundred years. She let the disk roll in her palm. "What's this for?"

"You don't have any credit here. That should buy you food and a sleeping cubicle for a few rotations."

"A few rotations?"

"We use Federation Time on the space station. I

know it seems strange, but you'll adjust." His tone implied differently, almost as if he feared that she might start screaming again any moment.

However, while she was trying to accept that she'd really traveled through a magical painting to a space station in the galaxy's center, she still remained confused. About her new world. About her reactions and that she was no longer so terrified but adjusting. About him and his motivations. In her experience, usually when people were as helpful as he was being to her, they wanted something in return.

Merline stopped in the hallway, tilted back her head, and frowned into his startled eyes. "Why are you being so nice to me?"

He chuckled, his laugh rolling through her like warm wine. "Because I have an ulterior motive."

At Tomm's easy admission, she shoved a lock of hair from her eyes without bothering to hide her surprise. Just because he'd so charmingly saved her life didn't mean she'd do whatever he asked. And after the heat he'd thrown her way, she could think of only one reason why he would offer her charity. But as yummy as he looked, as much as she wondered if he could be as good as her dream, she wasn't putting anything but her voice on the market. She might have just lost her home, her recording studio, and millions of dollars, but she had the most important thing in the world—her voice. She would survive because that's what she had to do.

"I would like to hire you to sing." His eyes twinkled.

Twinkled? He was most definitely flirting and she couldn't prevent her jolt of awareness that although he was the only person she knew in this galaxy, she would have found him attractive in an audience full of fervent fans. Merline recalled the hot dream and blushed. She'd assumed the cure was medical—perhaps it was more.

"I only perform private performances for my closest friends."

Damn. Now she was flirting right back. But she had to cut herself some slack. Still it was difficult to believe a painting would place her exactly in the path of a man who required her services as a singer. Unless the painting had done exactly what Sara predicted. And if the painting were the key, she needed to find it. If the painting had sent her here, maybe it could send her back home.

The idea set her heart racing. "Can you bring me to where I first appeared on the space station?"

At the sudden change in subject, Tomm shot her an odd look. "Sure."

Several minutes later, he'd taken her back to the exact spot she'd popped into the future. She saw the same shimmering metal walls. The large overhead dome. Lots of aliens. But no painting.

She checked nearby shops. She asked anyone who would stop and talk to her about the painting. And as she came up with nothing, disappointment washed over her.

Obviously, there was no easy way back. Get a grip. Life had never been easy. She had her voice and could earn a living. She would find a few gig and work her way back to Earth. It couldn't be more difficult than working the club circuit, waiting for her first big break.

With renewed determination, she turned to Tomm, ignoring the aliens passing by on the space station. "This job of singing you offered me. Would I work here on the space station?"

Tomm didn't hesitate, "It's on Siraz, my home world, where I could offer you an audience of hundreds of thousands."

She fisted her hands on her hips, suspicious as hell. "Would going with you to Siraz bring me closer to Earth?"

He shook his head. "It's the opposite direction, but you'd be well paid."

"I'd earn enough to buy a ticket back to Earth?"

"Ticket?"

"Pay my fare back to Earth." She used different words, realizing the translators didn't work perfectly.

"Perhaps you'll like Siraz—"

"No one likes Siraz." A man flanked by what could only be two bodyguards strode down the hallway. Merline had been around enough self-important people to recognize the power the stranger wore like a golden cloak. "Siraz is worse than the Seven Hells of Darica."

"That's not true," Tomm disagreed, his voice pleasant, but steel darkening his eyes. He bristled and placed his arm through Merline's. So tense the cords in his neck tightened, he was almost acting . . . *possessive,* although she'd only just met him.

The stranger ignored Tomm, as if he was of no consequence, and spoke directly to her. Dapper, dressed in black trousers and a matching jacket with gold braid, the newcomer peered at her with blue-eyed interest as he waved his manicured fingers exuberantly. "Besides, I can make you a much better offer than he can."

"Excuse me?" Merline felt like Alice who had just stepped into the rabbit hole.

"Let me introduce myself." With a quick smile and an offer to shake hands, he smoothly stepped forward.

"I am Dubane Fik of Marsadan Five. I have viewed ancient holovids of your performances and—"

"Holovids?" She was having difficulty with the translator again.

Dubane patted her shoulder. "Recordings of your concerts were saved on ancient computers and reformatted in three-dimensional vidstreams."

Okay. She didn't get all the technology, but she understood that her work had survived and that Dubane was familiar with her music. Still, it seemed odd that with an entire Federation of planets and so many years having passed that he could know about her past. "How did you hear about me?"

He preened, obviously quite proud of himself. "I collect music, among other things."

"I meant, how did you know I was on the space station?"

"Through my finders."

"Finders?" Tomm growled.

"I pay a variety of people commissions to find me interesting things. Today one of them spotted your precipitous arrival, and the strange case you carry. Once I obtained a holovid of your startling appearance and ran the unusual shape of the object you carried through my software and learned you played a musical instrument, I just had to have you."

Merline blinked. Surely the translator must have mistaken his meaning. "Me?"

"I'll pay you to perform tonight at my lounge. If you prove as popular as I suspect, we'll talk about an extension."

She'd needed work. He was offering. But she had been in the business too long not to negotiate. "What's the split?"

"Twenty for you, eighty percent for me."

"Fifty-fifty or I find another lounge."

"All right."

"You're accepting?" Tomm's eyes widened in aston-ishment and he released her arm. "You don't know Dubane."

"I don't know you, either. And I need work. Besides, I don't want to travel even farther from Earth."

"I offered you—"

"Work on Siraz."

"A terribly primitive place," Dubane spoke dismis-sively.

Merline didn't like the man's manners, but she preferred to be in the more populous part of the galaxy where she stood a better chance of finding an appreciative listening audience than on one faraway world where she might become trapped by lack of opportunity. "And your lounge is here on the space station, correct?"

"Very correct."

"So I'll sing here tonight," she told both men. "And after we all see the audience reaction, I'll consider a long-term contract."

"Excellent." Dubane pressed buttons on a PDA-like device attached to his wrist. When a disk ejected, he handed it to her along with a heavy sack. "Here's your contract for tonight's performance with all the perti-nent details, including advance payment."

She opened the sack and golden ovals spilled into her hand. Beside her, Tomm hissed out a breath and she suspected she'd been paid well. Accepting the disk of data, she nonchalantly replaced the credits in the sack, acting as if accustomed to doing business without her agent and manager. "Thanks for the opportunity."

"I expect you to make the most it," Dubane spoke over his shoulder as he departed.

"Count on it."

Merline couldn't read the menu in Federation Standard, but at brush of her finger over the words, the menu read itself to her. But she had no idea what *Dangor* meat with *Limop* sauce was, never mind any of the other selections. She snapped shut the menu in frustration.

"Need some help?" Tomm looked at her over his menu, breaking the brooding silence that had existed between them since she'd accepted Dubane's offer.

She wasn't certain why the big guy had stayed, but she appreciated his help . . . and his company. When they'd entered the establishment, a dimly lit bar with exotic music, strange aromas and a crowd dressed in everything from capes to feathers, a few of the male clientele had raked her with glances that had left her uneasy and feeling a bit vulnerable. She knew so little about this time and place, she supposed it was normal to be disoriented.

She'd had to adapt to the fact that the impossible had happened. Inexplicably, she'd traveled through the magical painting to the space station. And now she had to adjust to her new future that included miniature hologram doctors, suits that breathed, talking menus, and intelligent aliens in all shapes and sizes.

While the man beside her, Tomm, was not the kind of person she usually sought for a friend, she took comfort in his presence. Merline's good friends were busy people, type-A personalities and more forthright with their opinions. Tomm seemed to be laid-back, weighing his words, considering exactly how to handle her.

"Why don't you order for us?" she suggested.

He placed a thumbprint next to the dishes he selected, then dropped the menu into a slot at the table. She assumed someone in the kitchen read the order and would cook the meal. So when a slot in the table immediately opened and covered dishes of savory food rose up before her, she sniffed with appreciation.

"Wow. That was fast." Always rushing and on the go, she could easily become accustomed to such convenience.

He lifted covers from the plates, revealing a variety of foods in different colors and textures. "Please, serve."

Relieved that nothing wriggled or looked the least bit unappetizing, she inhaled a tangy sweet aroma and her mouth watered. "I'm not sure where to begin."

"Wait. I'm engaging privacy mode on our suits."

"Privacy mode?"

"Our suits have the ability to change the sound waves so only we can hear our words. Now we needn't fear being overheard." He waited a moment, as if timing his next words to make certain she was paying attention. "You could dump Dubane."

"I've already accepted an advance." She used a spoon with tines on the end to transfer food from the platters to her own plate, then offered him the serving piece.

Tomm hesitated for a moment as if he'd expected her to serve him, then helped himself, taking giant portions of some dishes and much tinier portions of others, but leaving plenty for seconds. "Dubane goes after exactly what he wants."

"So do I." She placed a tidbit of succulent white meat between her lips and grinned as the buttery and lemony flavor melted over her taste buds.

"Good?"

"Very." She tried a crunchy blue vegetable and winced at the bitter flavor.

"It's an acquired taste."

"One I won't be acquiring anytime soon." Gingerly she moved on to the potato-like food that teased her nostrils with the scent of garlic. Shocked to find the dish actually tasted like garlic mashed potatoes, she dug in with gusto.

"I'm not being clear. Dubane is wealthy. When he sets his eyes on something or someone he wants, he goes after it . . . and he doesn't care if he breaks the laws to attain his goals."

"So?" She noted that the utensils clung to the table with a light magnetic force. Drinks came in containers with straws and some kind of sipping valve to prevent leakage. The new sights, sounds, and tastes kept distracting her from the conversation.

"So right now, he wants you."

"And he has me—on his stage." Merline knew how to manage wealthy patrons. She licked the tines on her spoon before food particles drifted away. While huge ceiling fans suctioned air to keep the eating facility tidy, she noted most customers took care not to let their food escape their plates. "I agreed only to—"

"Do you think a man like Dubane cares if you agree?"

Although Tomm kept his expression neutral, as a trained vocalist she could pick up nuances in sound. And Tomm's previously mellow voice now cut with an edge, drawing her attention.

She sipped water that came out of the packet cold and considered his words. "You make Dubane sound dangerous."

"He is."

"Surely you have laws here?" she prodded, wondering if Tomm's depiction of Dubane was accurate. Was Dubane dangerous because Tomm considered him a rival, or because he was a cut-throat criminal—or some variation between?

"Dubane's wealth allows him to skirt the laws on the space station."

"And how long have you known Dubane?" she asked. Tomm's knowledge might be influenced by rumors, then again he might have personal dealings with Dubane.

"I don't know him at all." Despite the privacy mode apparatus in their suits, Tomm leaned forward and lowered his voice to a cutting whisper. "Dubane has a ruthless business reputation."

"He's already paid me for the evening. Are you saying if I negotiate a long-term contract, he won't abide by the terms?"

Tomm stared at her. "Don't you ever think about more than business?" Before she could respond, he clasped her wrist. "You're a beautiful woman. Dubane may want more than a business contract."

"Most men want more than a business contract." She sucked a bit of mashed potato from her finger and wasn't surprised to see Tomm's gaze drift to her lips. She might be playing dense, but she was listening very closely. More important, she watched his muscles tense, his eyes harden, his lips tighten and knew he believed every word he'd spoken. Yet if she agreed that his assessment of Dubane was correct, Tomm might be reluctant to say more. And she needed all the information she could get. So she shrugged her shoulders and tossed her hair over her shoulder as if she could take care of herself.

"Dubane isn't most men. He possesses things, businesses, and people. Rumor says that once he owns something, he doesn't let go. Ever." Tomm's hand closed over her wrist, not painfully, but as a punctuation mark to his words. "Don't toy with him. Take my advice. Sing for him tonight and leave the space station while you still can."

"You want me to base my decision on rumors when one night's work will hardly pay my fare back to Earth?" At her words, Tomm scowled and she reconsidered. "But I suppose I don't need to earn the entire fare at once and could work my way home. See the galaxy. I've always loved to travel."

"You could come with me to Siraz," his voice lifted with relief and a tad of hope. "It's an interesting world. I could show you around."

"But your world isn't on my way home."

He shrugged. "Unfortunately it's light-years in the opposite direction, about a three-day hyper-drive journey from here, but if you stayed one full season, you could earn enough to pay for a deluxe trip back to Earth, stopping at the major tourist planets."

Tomm sounded earnest and convincing. However, even if he were a music expert—and from the calluses on his hands, she suspected he might be—he still couldn't be certain the people on his world would like her music.

Her business sense might be saying, "No, no no," but as she eyed Tomm across the table, she wondered why she didn't just throw caution away. She had no one special waiting for her back on Earth, and although that saddened her, after three hundred years, she had no guarantee her music would be appreciated there any more than on Siraz.

Growing up an orphan, she'd planned every minute of her life to become a star, but success had cost her her social life. Between her busy schedule and the constant traveling from one show to the next, she'd hadn't had time for much more than a short fling with a backup guitarist, and a slightly longer affair with an ex-manager. The steady regard in Tomm's gaze suggested he might offer more than the initial superficial attraction that made her fingers itch to smooth the hair off his forehead, snuggle against his powerful chest, and find out if he tasted as good as he looked.

Instead, she leaned back, her stomach contentedly full. She could have been in a lounge on Earth, having dinner with a sexy man—if she could ignore the snuggling pink-tailed couple in the next booth, or the totally ugly creature at the bar. "Tell me about Siraz."

He hesitated, then chose his words with care and pride. "We don't live on the planet itself but a low orbit asteroid belt."

"You live in space?" She wondered if that's why Dubane had dismissed Siraz. For all she knew there was some kind of status system in place where the wealthy lived on planets and the poor were relegated to asteroids. Or perhaps the planet was uninhabitable.

Her ignorance had begun to bother her on many levels. She couldn't depend on her judgment when she had so little knowledge of her environment, including the culture and customs, history, and social standards of this society.

Tomm rubbed his chin. "We like living above our world. It's comfortable, interesting, and makes interplanetary travel less expensive when our star-ships don't have to fight the deep gravity well of a planet."

"Does this space station have a library?" Merline was beginning to realize that her lack of knowledge could cost her dearly. Suppose she sang a song tonight about love and it violated the local religions? Or suppose she inadvertently insulted her host by praising the simple life?

"You wish to go to a place full of written material?" He shook his head. "No such thing exists. We store our data in computer systems."

Merline supposed that made sense. "Where can I access—"

"Right here." He tapped a console and a panel opened. He reached into his pocket for a credit and dropped it into a slot. Apparently there was a charge for computer time. She preferred to pay her own way. Men who paid for things often expected more personal payment in return. But it seemed unkind to be so suspicious when he'd done nothing but help her.

Still she placed her satchel in a handy spot so she could pay for the next round, "What do I do?"

"Ask whatever questions you like." He smiled but didn't talk down to her. She liked that he didn't equate ignorance with stupidity.

Although there was much she needed to learn, what she needed for tonight's performance took on primary importance. "I'd like to hear the most recent and popu-lar song on the space station."

"Compliance." A computer voice spoke politely, even prompting her, "Would you like to see the perfor-mance as well?"

"Yes. Please."

"Two additional credits, please."

She pushed her satchel of credits toward Tomm. "I'd prefer to pay—"

"You must come from a world where the women are very independent." Tomm spoke with amusement, seemingly taking no offense, and that relieved her.

"Don't women have careers on Siraz?" she asked. But before he could answer, the computer started a miniature, three-dimensional hologram show of an exotic golden-skinned and green-eyed woman whose movements reminded Merline of a belly dancer. Nimble, sensual, her fluid movements undulated with a sexy rhythm that captivated her audience before she'd opened her mouth in song. Merline waited impatiently to hear her voice, and finally the singer slowly began to hum.

The holo audience seemed to hold its collective breath. The humming increased in tempo. Musical instruments Merline couldn't identify joined in, providing background, but never grew loud enough to drown out the steady humming.

Humming was not singing. Yet, the vibrations seemed to hold the audience enthralled in a trance . . . but it was . . . so . . . boring. When the woman finished, the audience broke into wild applause.

Perhaps Merline hadn't phrased her request correctly. "Computer, I'd like to view another popular selection, one where the singer uses words."

"Singing on the space station isn't done with words," Tomm told her, eyeing her oddly.

"Oh." Her stomach plummeted. "Why not?"

"Did you notice that the audience consisted of many kinds of beings?"

"Yes."

"I doubt you could sing words that some being

wouldn't find objectionable. On Abadore, working is considered a crime. On Dena, sex is forbidden except with a relative. Osarians have no eyes. Zenonites don't have bodies. Do you begin to see the difficulty?"

"Yes." Her head was spinning. If she hadn't consulted the computer before her performance, she might have started a riot or ended up in the space station's equivalent of a jail. If seemed a cruel twist of irony that she'd gotten her voice back and now couldn't use it.

Tomm must have sensed her shock. "On Earth you sing only with words?"

She nodded, wondering why Dubane had hired her if he'd listened to her old music and knew singing with words was unacceptable. Although she'd worked with strange agents and peculiar record producers, Dubane seemed odder than most.

"So what will you do?" Tomm asked.

She wasn't about to give up. "I still have my guitar. I'll play and let the music speak for me." Her words sounded so simple, but she wondered how many other ways she might err. "Computer, I need to see popular hairstyles, makeup, costumes. Show me every choice I must make as a performer to ready myself for an acceptable presentation."

Tomm eyed her with appreciation. "You are willing to adapt."

"Do I have a choice?"

"Many would complain." His eyes warmed. "You are taking so much in stride and I find your attitude admirable."

"Is that why you've stuck around? Because of my attitude?"

He laughed, totally at ease. "I'm a simple business-man between starflights with nothing better to do than share a meal with a beautiful woman. I have just enough time before boarding to watch your performance."

He seemed at ease. Mellow.

So why did she have the strongest feeling that he was keeping secrets from her? Important secrets. Dangerous secrets.

Even as the computer showed her costumes, makeup, and hair arrangements, she couldn't shake her impression that Tomm wasn't all he seemed.

Merline took a deep, cleansing breath and opened her eyes. The computer had adjusted her suit until her makeup and her outfit suited the current standards. Normally she didn't wear quite so much eyeliner, and the bright sequins that sparkled from the corners of her eyes up into her hair were a bit much, but when in Rome. . . . She could become accustomed to the convenience of her suit, and the amount of money she'd saved on shoes alone, never mind her dress, was extraordinary. To think that every Federation citizen was given a suit was a splendid introduction to this culture, her new future.

Still, no matter how many times she'd performed, she was always on edge in her backstage dressing room before she went on stage. Tonight was worse than usual. While her entire future didn't hinge on tonight's performance, she hadn't worried about pleasing an audience enough to make a living for a long time.

And playing only guitar, instead of merely using the instrument to accompany her voice, increased the knots in her gut. While she was a solid guitar player, she was a much better singer.

Even worse, when she'd asked for a sound check, she'd been told that her request was archaic. The acoustics and mikes would automatically adjust to maximize her voice. The lounge had been locked up and she hadn't been allowed in earlier.

The computer chimed. "Five Federation minutes until you're due on stage."

Merline sipped water from a packet, slung her guitar over her shoulder, and headed down a hallway, following a path of computer-generated blinking lights so she wouldn't take a wrong turn. When she arrived, the sight of the spectacular auditorium stole her breath. The entertainment lounge area of the space station reminded her of a giant geodesic dome. The audience sat in semicircular balconies that surrounded a stage, and once she stepped into place, the stage elevated her to the widest part of the dome. Lights played over her face and an announcer mentioned that she was recently from Earth.

Standing quietly, she was pleased to spy Tomm sitting front and center. He shot her a smile of encouragement. Since he needed to catch his flight immediately afterward, she might not have an opportunity to say good-bye and now wished she'd asked how to get in touch later. Perhaps the computer would know.

The sellout audience shifted, settled. The announcer finished his spiel and all attention focused on her. Her nerves increased and only years of stage presence kept her from biting her lower lip. She began to play softly, an upbeat song with pleasant chords to warm up her

fingers. Meanwhile, she watched the audience for reactions. Merline picked out a humanoid couple in a
nearby booth. The man seemed much more preoccupied with looking down his companion's blouse than
in Merline's music. Beside the couple sat two men,
their antennae curiously turned to her. A third party of
women were busy checking out the food in front of
them, seemingly the least interested in her.

"Good evening." Merline strummed her song and
after her greeting, she watched what she interpreted as
a ripple of surprise go through the audience. "My name
is Merline Sullivan. I'd like to thank you for coming tonight." She chose her words carefully. Certainly no one
could take offense at such a benign statement.

The audience listened and fidgeted uneasily. She
played a little bit more and could see eyes drifting
from her to the neighboring boxes. She was losing her
audience. She had to do something to reach them. Fast.

"On my world, we use words to sing, but as a
stranger here, I have no wish to cause offense and don't
know enough about this audience to know which customs and words might be insulting."

The crowd's attention refocused on her and they
seemed to be holding its collective breath. She dared
not sing even the simplest song, but her guitar playing
simply wasn't going to cut it.

She stopped strumming, let her gaze rest on Tomm's
for encouragement and tried to speak with confidence.
"So tonight, I'm going to improvise. The words I sing
will be meaningless to me. Please ignore your translators or if possible turn them off during my songs.
Please know that I will sing sounds that are not words
in my language, and I hope they don't translate into
words in yours."

She had them again. Electric silence sizzled with rising expectations. She strummed once, and performed a song that had gone multiplatinum. But she didn't use real words for fear they'd still be translated. Instead she substituted nonsensical scat rhythms she'd learned in New Orleans.

Ever so slowly, she saw her audience's jaded skepticism turn to interest and then to approval. The men never took their antennae from her. The man who'd been looking down the female's blouse actually took his partner's hand and tapped his foot, and the woman seemed to forget him as she stared at Merline. And the three women stopped eating, sat back, sipped drinks, and relaxed. Best of all, Tomm beamed her a bright, "I knew you could wow them," smile that never dimmed.

Merline had performed many concerts, but she'd never realized how much emotion she could convey with her voice when she didn't use words. Sometimes she carried a throaty longing, other times her voice was bright and clear, and once, during a sad song, she depicted sorrow. And the audience stayed with her, captivated. She didn't need the wild hissing that was the equivalent of Terran applause at the end of her performance to know she had entertained them.

But what was even more important was the bittersweetness of being back in the limelight—singing, performing. If she hadn't come through the painting, she might never have sung again. As she stood in the lights and took her final bows, she felt at home in this faraway place.

But it wasn't until she spied Tomm's empty seat that she realized how much she'd wanted to share the experience with him. But he was gone. He'd had a starship to catch.

Before she had time for disappointment to sink in, the peaceful hissing and adulation altered. The adoring audience exited their balconies, floated toward her, trying to rush the stage in a frenzy of exuberance. As Dubane's bodyguards surrounded her to protect her from the swelling crowd and quickly hustled her away, she felt very alone.

She'd probably never see Tomm again and was surprised at the sharp sadness welling in her chest. She wouldn't soon forget him because he'd saved her life, because he'd fueled an erotic dream, and because although they'd only known each other for a short time, the connection between them had been amazingly strong.

Merline expected security to escort her back to her dressing room, but instead, once they left the performance area, they took a sideways elevator. When it kept going for a while, she realized they were traveling to the far side of the space station—the residential side.

She frowned at her guard. "Where exactly are you taking me?"

"Dubane has invited you to a celebration."

She didn't like his guards whisking her away, even if it was for her own safety. And she didn't appreciate his assumption that he could appropriate her time whenever he wished. "But I didn't accept any—"

"You are the guest of honor. Dubane also mentioned he wanted to talk to you about a contract extension."

She was about to refuse, but the elevator stopped and the doors opened into a room so sumptuous she was shocked into silence. Opulent tapestries threaded with silver and golden threads framed portals that revealed a spectacular view of the space station against a backdrop of twinkling stars. Starships flew into a giant spaceport and out of bright landing bays.

Inside the room, three-dimensional images of Merline replicated her performance. Her voice emanated from hidden speakers and the partygoers helped themselves to fizzy drinks passed out by servants wearing little but what looked like body paint. None of the sophisticated guests seemed the least bit disturbed that the servants kept their heads bowed, their eyes downcast. One slight woman serving canapés tripped and almost dropped her tray. She trembled terribly as if she feared she might be punished. The absolutely gorgeous men and women servants with downcast eyes made Merline uneasy as she recalled Tomm's warnings about Dubane.

"There you are," Dubane separated from the crowd and greeted her with a refined smile. "My dear, you were splendid, dazzling!"

"Thank you. You've been very kind." Complaining about a party in her honor seemed rude, but she didn't want to talk to these people. She wanted to find the equivalent of the Beverly Hills Hotel and sleep undisturbed for at least twelve hours. "Although, I appreciate the party, I hope you'll understand that performances tend to exhaust me."

"But on Earth, I thought it was customary for an opening night party." Dubane lifted two drinks from the tray of the servant to his right and handed Merline a glass.

She sipped cautiously, then grinned with pleasure. "How did you know a martini, extra dry, is my favorite?"

"Research is my business. There's little about you I don't know."

She arched a brow. "Really?"

He took her arm and drew her toward a private alcove that overlooked the spaceport. "I'm very impressed. Your voice is superb and I believe we have much to offer one another."

"Such as?"

"You will sign an exclusive contract with me and I will make you a star."

She didn't like the way he'd phrased his offer, as if she had no choice, as if he were giving orders. Perhaps the translators had failed to capture the nuances, but she also didn't like the manner in which he crowded her—just a little. Not enough to touch, but enough to force her to take a step back from a conversation more intimate than she'd have liked.

"If you know me as well as you claim, then you understand I'm already a star."

"Not here."

"No matter whom I choose to do business with, it won't take me long to build my fan base."

Dubane's polite demeanor suddenly hardened and his eyes lit with banked irritation. "Working for me—"

"I don't work *for* anyone." Needing to be perfectly clear and feeling safe in the room filled with guests, she set down her martini and faced him. At the fiery temper she read in his eyes, she barely refrained from shuddering, but she refused to place her career even partially into anyone's hands without fully checking their credentials. "Before we do business, I need a lawyer, an agent, and a manager to look out for *my* interests."

"You don't understand. I will be your lawyer, agent, and manager and take an eighty, twenty cut. The twenty part is yours."

His offer was outrageous. Offensive. "I'm so sorry. I must have heard incorrectly. I thought you said—"

"I did. And our dealings aren't up for negotiation, my dear." Above her head, he caught the eye of one of his security people. She thought Dubane might have him escort her out of the party, but instead Dubane lowered his voice. "You need a tour of my collection. I think you'll be impressed."

She shrugged away. "I don't think so. I'm sorry. I'm really tired and it's time for me to depart for—"

The floor beneath their feet suddenly dropped Dubane, his guard, and Merline into the floor below the one they'd just stood on. She hadn't realized why he'd separated her from the crowd until it was too late to react. The ceiling panel above closed and they were suddenly very alone.

"Come. My interesting collections will keep you awake. I'm sure of that."

Knowing she had no choice, Merline followed, but her stomach churned with trepidation. The air down here seemed dirty. The scent reminded her of stale sweat and fear. And the glimmering flicker of red lighting made her think she'd dropped into hell. "What do you collect?"

"I appreciate talent of all kinds."

"I don't understand."

"I adore artists. Singers. Dancers. Painters."

Merline didn't like being isolated, didn't like how he'd maneuvered her. Her gut tightened with apprehension. She was alone here on this space station and if she disappeared, no one would search for her, no one would care. Except Tomm, but he'd left for Siraz.

"Where shall we go first?" he asked.

"Back upstairs to the party." Recalling the trembling servants above, she decided to extricate herself immediately. "I'd like another drink."

"Ah, to appreciate my collections, you should be

sober." Dubane placed his arm through hers and sensing she had no choice, she pasted a curious look on her face, but her instincts were signaling that she was in trouble. "Come, I know just the place to stimulate your senses."

He led her into a room that reminded her of a photographic studio. "Please, have a seat."

She was glad to sit before her wobbly knees gave out. Her mouth was dry. She had no idea what to expect, but from the soft sobs coming from behind a dark curtain, she braced herself for something unpleasant.

"Fanda is the foremost dancer in the galaxy. Like you, she was reluctant to sign with me at first, but she soon understood the benefits of working exclusively for me." Dubane nodded and the curtain disappeared.

Merline gasped at the sight of the woman on her knees. Her body was lean, graceful. Her beauty alone would have made her a top fashion model on Earth. She possessed gorgeous eyes, high cheekbones, and a proud and graceful neck. Her breasts heaved as tears streamed down her cheeks.

Merline's mouth went dry. "Why is she crying? Is that part of the dance?"

Dubane didn't answer. Fanda began to dance, her movements slow, subtle, beautiful. And every line of her body depicted sorrow and a broken spirit that caused Merline's heart to ache.

When Fanda completed the dance, she ended once again on her knees. And her entire body trembled. Tears still rained down her cheeks.

Dubane shook his head and spoke softly, like a deadly viper. "Next time, you will dance happily. This constant sorrow doesn't please me."

The dancer bowed her head and her entire body shook so hard that Merline had no doubt the poor woman had been badly mistreated. A woman of her talent could perform for the masses. "Fanda dances only for you?"

"She's part of my collection." Dubane stood and the woman cowered.

Merline's lower jaw dropped in shock. Oh . . . my . . . God. Dubane *collected* talented people.

"Fanda lives here?"

Dubane gestured down a long hallway with many rooms. "I like to view my collection whenever the mood arises."

On the way out, Merline noted the security arrangement. The room was a cell, with a force field that held Fanda a prisoner. And room after room down the hallway was filled with more "talent."

Dubane was insane. A monster.

Sickened, she pressed the back of her wrist to her mouth. Merline had to find a way to escape. As if sensing her horror, Dubane gripped her arm tightly and drew her into the next cell.

A man stood naked in chains. Before him stood an easel, a palette of paint. His eyes glowed with the rage of a caged wild beast. The moment he spied Dubane, he spat. The spittle bounced off a force field, never reaching the intended target.

Dubane seemed not to notice. "This is Lenatob. He paints images so beautiful that even the Emissary of Medane begs for a portrait. So far, the great Lenatob has refused to paint me, but he will come around—all my talent eventually does."

Merline didn't speak. She was too terrified to talk as the full measure of her predicament struck. Dubane was showing off his collection because he didn't fear her. She had no doubts he intended to keep her—just like the dancer and the painter. And no one would stop him. She had no friends here. Dubane could do whatever he wanted with her and she doubted she'd be any more successful at escape than Fanda or Lenatob.

"Paint." Dubane ordered.

In response, Lenatob tossed the palette at the force field. Dubane snapped his fingers and his guard pressed a button. Electric lights suddenly arced over the poor man's skin. His face contracted in agony and he flopped to his belly, writhing, the sounds emitting from his mouth inhuman.

"Stop." Merline squeezed Dubane's arm. "Please stop. You're killing him."

"I would never kill such talent. Once he learns to cooperate, the pain will stop."

Merline realized Dubane was showing her what he would do if she didn't cooperate. In shock, she didn't resist when Dubane escorted her to the next empty room. No way could she fight him and the guard—even if she knew how.

Dubane led her toward a cage. She dug in her heels, but her effort to resist was useless. She punched and kicked, but she might as well have fought a rock for all the effect she had. Oh God. He was going to lock her up. Was her fate to spend the rest of her life in a cell, facing torture if she refused to sing for a madman?

Suddenly being back on Earth and unable to sing seemed a much better place than where she found herself. Alone. In a cell. At the disposal of a madman. And when the lock clicked in place, she couldn't hold back a terrified sob.

One day later, Merline had learned that waiting for Dubane to show up was almost as torturous as the

boredom of having nothing to do in her cell. She'd
been given nothing to drink or eat—no doubt to wear
down any resistance to obeying his orders whenever he
finally returned. Her austere quarters consisted of four
bare walls, a ceiling, and a floor. While she had her
guitar and could have played, she'd refused to do so
knowing that her music was her only bargaining chip.

She should have listened to Tomm and heartily
wished she'd left with him when she'd had the
chance—even if the journey had taken her in the opposite direction from Earth, she wouldn't have been
locked in a cell. Damn. She'd made such a mess of her
life. Back home, she'd let her career rule every decision. Had she repeated the same mistake here?

No matter how many opportunities she had, she
wondered if she'd always screw up. Her choices had
always been made with logic; perhaps she should have
trusted her heart.

Exhausted and emotionally drained, Merline dozed
and once again dreamed of a man singing. Only this
time when she opened her eyes and found herself still
confined in her bleak cell, she still heard the unique
song. Suddenly it cut off.

And she held her breath.

When Merline heard a footstep outside her cell, she
shoved to her feet, expecting Dubane. She tensed,
clenched and unclenched her fists, and tried to will the
nausea at bay. At the moment she was too scared and
angry to think what she should do. However she didn't
think she could resist whatever he asked if he subjected
her to the same kind of pain she'd already witnessed.

Already she trembled and wondered how long it
would take for her to cow from Dubane, just like his
servants she'd seen upstairs. Still, she had some

pride left and lifted her chin, unwilling to show her fear.

The force field crackled and a door burst open. Despite her intention to appear courageous, she gasped and jumped back.

And stared at . . . Tomm. With a hefty gun in hand, a cocky smile, and a familiar intensity in his eyes that made the blood rush to her head, he gestured for her to come with him.

He looked so solid, so real, she couldn't be hallucinating and yet . . . she was so shocked, she spoke the first dumb words that came out. "Was that you I heard singing?"

"I used a song to calm the guards."

His words made no sense, but they didn't have time for detailed explanations. Still, she had to know. "What are you doing here?"

"I knew you were up to your graceful neck in trouble so I came back to rescue you."

"How did you know?"

"Dubane's passion for talent is well known in some circles. I should have warned you more forcefully to stay away."

"You did. I didn't listen. I don't know how to—"

"You can thank me later. Let's get out of here before Dubane realizes I short-circuited his entire security system. The man's practically hardwired into his computer system."

She slung her guitar over her back. Tomm grabbed her hand, tugging her into the hall where people of all shapes, sizes, and colors poured into the hallway.

Apparently he'd freed every single one of Dubane's talent. She hoped they would all escape. They merged into the crowd of excited beings and she marveled at Tomm's ingenuity. He'd come in alone and found her.

She wasn't about to stop and ask questions—like where he was taking her and how he intended to get them off the space station.

So when Tomm steered her out of the crowd of talent fleeing through the complex and through a wall panel, she didn't hesitate to go with him. They ended up in a narrow area of wires, pipes, and gadgetry she didn't recognize. Tomm had to crouch to walk, but she merely had to bend her head and hold her guitar behind her so it wouldn't bang on the narrow walls.

The area was dark, spooky. But she was so relieved to escape Dubane she didn't care. And Tomm—she marveled over his willingness to risk his life to save her. No one had ever done so much for her. Despite her weakness due to lack of food and water, his effort to save her energized her.

Shots behind them zinged off walls and screams of pain and terror echoed. Obviously not everyone had escaped.

"Hurry." Tomm urged, his voice normal so she assumed he'd engaged the privacy mode.

He helped her under a mass of heavy cables. Her guitar case caught and when he didn't tell her to leave it behind, but instead reached behind her to help free it, she hit one of those turning points in life where everything seemed clear.

Throwing her immediate future into Tomm's capable hands seemed a no-brainer, especially with Dubane's insane pursuit. They'd be lucky to get off the space station alive.

But if they escaped, she planned to be open-minded and grateful, no matter where she ended up. After experiencing Dubane's cage for just one day, she'd rather go anywhere, even if she couldn't sing, than go back to his "collection." Hell, she'd rather be dead than sit in a cell forever.

Heart pounding, nerves ragged, she forced once foot in front of the other through the narrow passageway, on the one hand hoping the tunnel would end soon, on the other, dreading when she'd have to exit and expose herself to recapture.

She whispered, despite the suit's privacy mode. "How much farther?"

"I'm not sure."

She hugged a massive pipe and squeezed around it, then placed the guitar on the floor to drag it through. "Does that mean we're lost?"

"I know where we're going. I'm just not sure where we are."

"Huh?"

"On the building plans, this passageway leads a direct path to the landing dock."

"Won't Dubane and his men have the area covered?"

"This dock isn't in his plans. Computer systems mark the area as a water treatment plant—enough to discourage the curious."

"And once we reach there? Then what?"

"We stow away aboard a freighter."

"Sounds dangerous."

"Staying here is dangerous."

"You have a point." She bumped into his broad back. He'd either stopped to take his bearings, to let her rest, or to figure out how to get around a blockage in the passage. She took a moment to draw in deep breaths and to relax her tensed shoulders. When he remained silent, she asked, "What's wrong?"

"Someone else is here in the passage. They're up ahead."

A horrific scream sliced the air behind them and then cut off suddenly. Merline shuddered. The passageway that had seemed dark and protective had turned into a trap. She pressed against pipes on one side, slick metal on the other. While they might need a cutting torch to get out, Tomm had brought a weapon with him and maybe he could shoot their way through.

She attempted to tune out the shouts, her pulse pounding and her mouth dry. "Going back isn't an option, but what would happen if we broke through a panel?"

"The walls are bendar, one of the strongest manufactured materials in the galaxy."

"So what do you suggest?"

"We keep going."

He stepped forward and she followed. Putting down each foot as soundlessly as possible, she strained to hear a rustle of clothing, a footfall, a breath that might warn of imminent attack. When her guitar banged on a pipe and echoed through the tunnel, she winced. And her stomach knotted at the knowledge that she might as well have announced their presence.

"Mudsucker." To his credit, Tomm didn't say more than the one low-pitched curse word.

"Sorry."

"I wasn't swearing over the noise. That doesn't matter. They already know we're here."

She swallowed hard. "They?" No wonder he was cursing. It was bad enough to think of one enemy awaiting them, but several? Even if Tomm shot their way through the passage, they'd have to climb over bodies. God . . .

"I hear two distinct sets of footsteps."

His hearing had to be much keener than hers. Either that or she just couldn't discern the faint sounds over the thudding of her heart and the blood rushing in her ears. Every step forward, she expected to hear shots fired. To feel shooting pain. To be exposed by the light of a flare.

But the narrow passageway remained dark. And as difficult as it was for her to squeeze through, it must have been harder for a man Tomm's size. Yet he maintained a fairly steady pace.

"Make that three sets of footsteps," he corrected his earlier statement. "And one sounds much lighter and smaller than the others. So stay alert."

"What for? Do you expect me to swat a flying beast out of the air with my guitar?"

He chuckled, stopped, and pressed a weapon into her hand. "Try not to shoot me. Although the setting is only on stun, the jolts' sting goes right through the suit."

She recalled the screams behind them and trembled.

Back in Los Angeles, after an overzealous fan had turned into a stalker, she'd learned to fire a handgun on a shooting range. But this sleek weapon was so light in her hand that it felt like a toy.

"What do I need to know besides pull the trigger?"

"Aim first."

"Very funny. I can't see squat in the dark."

"Watch for stun bursts. When these weapons fire, they emit a signature barrage that begins with a round that's bright and distinctive. Once you mark the stun burst and aim at the fire ball, you've a good chance of hitting your target."

She wouldn't be shooting a target, but living beings. The idea of hurting someone made her a little sick. She hoped she was up to the task. Intellectually, she had no problem with the idea of shooting to avoid being shot. But when it came down to the moment, she hoped she had the right stuff. And she didn't want to think about whether the weapons about to be fired at them were set on stun—or on a more lethal setting.

In contrast to her ragged nerves, Tomm seemed so skilled at this search and rescue business, so proficient with weapons, never mind at ease—as if he encountered life and death situations on a daily basis. And his demeanor remained calm, even upon discovering they might be trapped.

"You never said what kind of business you're in," she said, her way of finding out more about her rescuer before she found herself in even more trouble.

"I export *Frelle*."

"*Frelle*?" The name didn't translate and had an exotic pronunciation—exotic and extraterrestrial.

"*Frelle*'s a spice. Very rare. Extremely difficult to produce. And it's only produced on Siraz."

"Why is that?"

The conversation helped distract her from the trouble ahead. But she never forgot the enemy was there, standing between them and a chance at freedom. She had no reason to be optimistic. Dubane seemed to have all the advantages. Nevertheless, she clutched the gun in one hand and her guitar case in the other and forged ahead.

Tomm's tone changed to a thread as hard as the bendar walls around them. "They're coming close now. We'll stop and make them come to us."

Her heart raced. "Okay."

"Drop low so you can fire between my ankles."

"Give me a second." It took a moment to bend into a prone position, locate his feet in the darkness, and place her stun gun between his ankles to avoid hitting him by accident. Not only was his big body shielding hers, he'd asked her to lie flat and she'd watched enough cop shows to know he was protecting her while he took all the risks.

She still couldn't hear them. She most definitely couldn't see them. She couldn't even see her own hands in front of her face. "How close are they?"

"Fifty paces."

Merline's hands shook so hard she had to brace her elbows on the floor to steady herself. "Ready."

Every second ticked by like a minute. The minutes passed like hours. She didn't want to wait. Didn't want to wonder if she was going to live or die. She wanted the confrontation to be over. She wanted to shout, "Come on. Come on. Come on."

Sweat beaded on her brow and upper lip, under her arms, but the suit quickly absorbed it. Squinting in the darkness, determined to do her part, Merline tensed, her finger on the trigger.

The bright light from the first signature blast might have blinded her if she hadn't already been squinting. But luck was with her. She got a clear look at her target, aimed, and pulled the trigger. Tomm fired a split second before she did.

The enemy went down with a muffled yelp. Merline didn't know if she'd hit him or Tomm had, and slightly queasy, she preferred not knowing. At least she hadn't frozen as she'd feared.

However, the shooter's weapon had damaged a nearby pipe and water now sprayed over them. Her suit kept her dry, but her guitar case wasn't waterproof. And the wet walls were slick and the floor slippery, which made holding still to take the another shot more difficult.

The next fire pinged off the ceiling, a wild shot that lit up their targets. Tomm quickly stunned another man, and the third, a birdlike creature, took off the other way with a squawk of outrage.

She edged back and shoved to her feet, grabbing the guitar as she rose. "You okay?"

Tomm didn't answer but remained on his feet and wedged between the walls. Oh, no. Had one of the blasts struck him and she hadn't even known?

She reached out and shook his shoulder, panic setting in. He couldn't have died trying to rescue her. Not big, strong Tomm. *Please, God . . . no.*

Shaking, sick at heart, she clenched his suit, reached for his neck in search of a pulse. "Tomm? Tomm. Wake up."

He moaned softly, his breath fanning her ear. At least he was still alive. Breathing.

But they had to get out. That squawking thing might have been a pet, but she suspected the bird was intelligent and had gone for help. They had to exit the tunnel before the bird returned with Dubane's men, but she had no idea how much time they had.

Tomm groaned. Louder this time.

"Tomm. Talk to me. Are you hurt? Can you move? What can I do to help?

"Hush. Head hurts."

"Sorry," she whispered. "What can I do to help?" she repeated.

"Wait."

She wished she could do as he asked, but likely he wasn't fully aware that time was running out. And while she'd have liked nothing better than to hold his hand and give him all the recovery time he needed, she couldn't.

"That third creature escaped and no doubt will soon return with Dubane's men. We have to make our way to the end of the tunnel. Can you go on?"

"Soon." He lifted his head, grunted and took an unsteady step.

She had no idea how badly injured he was, or how much pain he was in, but he dragged himself forward and she followed, wishing she could do more to help. She tried not to think about climbing over the bodies. If Tomm could do it injured, she could do it, too. When they finally exited the passage into an empty service corridor, she expected shots. She looked right and saw empty corridor. She looked left, saw more empty corridor. There was no one.

But she finally got a good look at Tomm. His eyes were glazed with pain, his lips tight. But she saw no bleeding, no bruising, no external injuries. And the steady determination in his eyes never wavered.

Even in his pain, he must have sensed her concern.

"I'll be all right. Tomorrow. Luckily, the blast only nicked me."

He took a step, using the wall for support. With each step he regained his balance. But they should probably be running.

She kept glancing back over her shoulder. "How far to the shuttle bay?"

"Not too much farther." He stumbled through a door that she hadn't known was a door, then decided it was a hatch as it sealed behind them, leaving them in what looked like a gigantic flight hangar.

She expected security to spot them immediately, but for a secret place, there was an amazing amount of activity going on. The port reminded her of a seaport on Earth. Except instead of cargo ships, she saw spaceships in sleek designs as well as big clunkers. Instead of people, there were beings in so many shapes and sizes and colors lined up to board a passenger vessel that she had to remind herself not to stare.

Tomm took her hand. "Welcome to the creditless economy."

"Huh?"

"These people operate outside normal channels. Barter is often the means of trade, not credits."

"Are they criminals?"

"Some." He led her past robots loading pallets into a ship's cargo bay. "Many worlds have so many rules and regs they strangle legitimate business. So people leave, hoping to make better lives for themselves in places where laws are less of a factor. Space ventures sound glamorous to many dirtsiders, but it's dangerous out here. Planets have enough trouble patrolling themselves and space is vast."

No one paid them any attention, but Merline didn't

relax. With this many beings in on the secret hangar's location, surely Dubane knew about the place and would be sending his security—if they weren't already here.

They strolled by a particularly dilapidated vessel. The hull bore pits and scars. The plating had obviously been patched many times. The *Raven*, its named carved into the hull, was one of the last ships she would have picked to board, but when Tomm pulled her into an open hatch, she didn't hesitate to follow.

"The *Raven*'s heading to Siraz and the captain has the rep of a harsh but fair woman. If she catches us stowing aboard, she may not push us out an air lock."

"Now that makes me feel so much better," Merline muttered. She climbed in and hauled herself up, and noted that Tomm seemed to know exactly where he was heading. "Have you been on board before?"

He shook his head. "I studied her plans last night. She's due to depart in less than an hour. When I checked, I altered the computer manifest so this cabin won't be booked and we can stay here unnoticed."

"What about alarms?"

"Paid a mechanic to turn them off."

"Why not purchase our fares?"

He shot her a sheepish grin. "I'm a little short of funds right now. I didn't plan for . . ."

"Me. Sorry about that. I'll pay you back when I can." She slung her guitar aside, wondering how long they'd be stuck in quarters half the size of her closet, but not about to protest. Even a coffin-sized cubicle was better than going back to Dubane. "You purchased the seat front and center for my performance. Wasn't that expensive?"

"I splurged." He closed the hatch behind them. "At

the time, I didn't know I'd need to fund an escape—"

"Hey. You did great. You're great. I'm not complaining. It's just that—"

He raised an eyebrow. "You're accustomed to luxury?"

She shook her head. "It's just that I feel as if I went to I-am-an-idiot university. This entire world is so new that I haven't adjusted yet. I keep saying and doing the wrong things and I suspect it's going to keep happening."

"You're doing marvelously well . . . considering."

"Not so well." She sighed. "If not for you, I'd be stuck in a cage at the mercy of an insane man. I don't even know why you came back for me."

"I told you I have an ulterior motive." He opened a cabinet and tossed her a water packet.

She opened it and sipped greedily, wishing she had some food to go with it. As if reading her mind, Tomm handed her a packet of warm food. "Space rations. They're tasteless but fill the belly. We'll be sick of them by the end of the trip."

"How long until we reach Siraz?" The room had no beds, no chairs, no furniture and she leaned against the wall and slid until she sat on the floor before digging into her rations.

"A day. Maybe two."

He was right. The food was tasteless but filling. "You make it sound as if your world's far away."

"It is." He sat beside her, his thigh against hers, and attacked his own food. "This ship will spend more time in real space, putting a safe distance between us and the space station than it will take to complete the entire hyperspace journey."

"What's hyperspace?"

He shrugged. "The theory is that space folds like a blanket and we travel through where the folds touch. Without the folds the distance is much greater but the folds shorten the distance."

"So you why don't know exactly how long it takes to get to your world?"

"The folds aren't stable. Neither are the planets or the stars. The entire galaxy is always in a state of flux."

"The idea is making my head hurt."

He chuckled. "I take it you never studied theoretical astrophysics?"

"I wasn't much of a student," she admitted, "except when it came to music." Oh, so casually, she shifted until their legs no longer touched and then oddly, she missed the intimacy. "And I'm still waiting to hear about your ulterior motives."

An alarm sounded. A purple light flashed a warning.

She jumped to her feet. "What's going on?"

"We'll be leaving soon." Tomm also stood, gathered the leftover food and drink receptacles and stashed them in a bin. Then he placed his palm on a hidden panel and a padded couch opened out of the wall.

She stood and frowned, looking from him to the bed and back, relieved the alarm had stopped making so much noise. "Are you saying your ulterior motives are sexual?"

He laughed, his mouth curving to show a dimple in his chin. "I'm not that hard up."

"You better not be up at all," she quipped, but her tone was defensive—and she wondered if he liked her the same way she liked him or if she'd been reading his heated glances wrong. The electricity sparking between them was hard to miss, but she wanted to believe there was a mental connection as well as a physical one.

He speared her with a speculative look and she suspected the translator had twisted her little jest into something bizarre—either that or she'd violated some decency code or insulted some cultural belief.

"We need to lie down and web in."

Web in? First he told her he had ulterior motives, then he pulled a bed out of the wall, asked her to lie down, and now he wanted her to *web in*? She'd have to be naive to think that "webbing in" wasn't some kind of metaphor for sex.

"Excuse me?" She fisted her hands on her hips. "If you think I'm going to let you tie me down so you can have sex, you're mistaken. I thanked you for saving my life, but I didn't ask you to do it. I don't owe you more than the credits—"

"Everyone must web in for the hyperspace jump." His eyes glinted with amusement.

Sheesh. She raised her hand and clamped it over her mouth, then slowly lowered it. "Oops. I did it again, didn't I? I thought webbing in was—"

"When I start making love, you'll know it," he teased, a promising heat in his eyes. "And I damn well won't be asking."

She swallowed hard. "You won't?"

"I might spend most of my time on Siraz, but I do know when a woman is willing."

The implication that he only made love to willing women should have reassured her. However his comment that he wouldn't be asking steamed her. How could he be so damn sure she'd be willing when she was so confused?

With a sigh, she gestured to the couch that looked too small to hold them both. "What do I do?"

"Lie down so I can place the webbing around you."

"Fine." She agreed, still feeling foolish and a little wary. Gingerly, she took a spot on the couch. And then he pulled a net from the wall, floated it over her, locking her in tight.

"This will protect you during the jump into hyperspace. That's why the alarms sounded."

"You could have told me that before," she muttered, hoping he wouldn't understand that the heat rising to her face was a sign of embarrassment.

"And miss the lovely blush on your cheeks?" he teased and webbed himself in.

"You're enjoying my mistakes way too much."

"I take enjoyment where I can."

She eyed him from her position on her back. He was lying next to her, his large body between her and the door. She suspected the cabin was meant for one, either that or two smaller beings. Although she'd scooted all the way against the wall, they were shoulder to shoulder, hip to hip, thigh to thigh.

"Is your life difficult on Siraz?"

"Depends how you define difficult. Producing Frelle is labor intensive, but only during the harvest."

The purple flashing lights disappeared. Engine vibrations rocked her and she clenched her fists. She was about to fly into space. To an unknown world. With a man she'd known for only a short time.

But she wondered if the painting had the ability to draw her back through time, back to her own world, and if she had the choice, would she want to go? No one special was waiting for her on Earth in her own time. And right now, the idea of traveling with Tomm, seeing his home and his world excited her. She was looking forward to her future in a different way from how she had in years.

And she very much wanted to get to know Tomm better. She couldn't help liking his humor, his bravery, his quiet strength. And she wanted time to explore their developing attraction. She couldn't help noting how aware she was of his warmth, his size, his protective nature. And instead of feeling like a singer who was also a woman, with him she felt like a woman who could sing.

Merline tensed, waiting for liftoff.

When the cabin door slammed open, she gasped. With difficulty, she lifted her head. A woman with two men backing her up burst through the door, weapons aimed.

They'd caught them. And they hadn't even taken off yet.

Beside her, Tomm tensed, released the webbing, and sat up in a blurry speed of movement.

But the intruder was faster, the woman pressing the blaster directly between his legs. "Don't move."

Tomm kept his hands up and his voice nonthreatening. "Captain, I'm sorry we had to stow aboard, but if you kick us off your ship, Dubane will kill us."

"And if you don't leave, *I* will kill you."

Merline fumbled with the webbing and finally un-snapped it and sat up. "If this is a passenger ship, I'd be happy to provide entertainment in exchange for our transportation."

"What kind of entertainment?" A short humanoid male with a stocky frame, a large forehead, and a barrel-like chest leered at her.

Without removing her stunner from Tomm, the tall and lithe female captain jammed a hard elbow into her subordinate's chest. "Petroy, one more comment like that and I'll ditch you along with them."

Petroy paled but kept leering at Merline.

"I sing." She gestured to her guitar case.

"Shit." The captain glared at her. "You're the Terran singer who caused the riot and then released Dubane's collection?"

"Yes."

Petroy licked his full lips. "Captain, he'll kill them for sure if you kick them off."

"Not my problem." Nevertheless, the woman eased up on the weapon between Tomm's legs, but she didn't holster it, either. "What's your story?"

"I'm a simple *Frelle* farmer from Siraz trying to go home."

The captain rolled her eyes at the ceiling. "For certain you're a liar, because there's nothing simple about disabling the *Raven*'s sensors." She turned her sharp green stare on Merline. "Merline Sullivan from Terra?"

Merline squared her shoulders and raised her chin a notch. "How do you know so much about me?"

"It's my business to know. Besides, you caused so much trouble your name is being toasted in every bar from here to Devron IV." She scowled at Merline and then focused again on Tomm. "I've heard life on Siraz is hard. Does she understand the hardships?"

"I was a little too busy saving her life to explain."

The captain snorted, holstered her weapon, and offered her hand to Merline. "I'm Angel." She glared at Tomm. "Captain Angel to you."

"Captain." A dwarf-sized creature came up behind Angel and tapped her shoulder. "Dubane's men are asking permission to board and search the *Raven*."

"I don't converse with pervs."

Petroy seemed to regain his composure. "Captain, Dubane has a fleet of starships at his disposal. Perhaps—"

"Prepare to blast off as soon as I hit the bridge." She turned back to Merline and Tomm. "I expect a full report on how you disabled my alarm."

"Of course. May I ask how you found us?"

"Heat sensors. Web in and stay out of my way."

Tom nodded. "Thank you."

Angel spun on her heel and spoke over her shoulder. "Don't thank me. Thank Merline. We Terrans have to stick together."

Angel was Terran? Was that why she'd allowed them to stay? Or did she have a soft heart under her harsh attitude?

The cabin seemed strangely empty after the captain's departure. They webbed in and Tomm pressed a button. The hull turned transparent allowing them a giant window into the shuttle bay. As the *Raven*'s engines roared, security guards backed away, but she couldn't forget Dubane's fleet might be in swift pursuit.

As interesting as she found the view, Merline turned a troubled gaze to Tomm. "I think it's time you tell me exactly what you want from me."

"Your singing voice. Your tone, your rhythm, your unique pitch is perfect for making *Frelle*."

She blinked. "Excuse me?"

"On Siraz, I have a large spread of grazing *Siltarees*."

"*Siltarees?*"

"Eight-legged animals who appreciate fine music."

"What?"

"When we sing to the Siltarees, they enter a blissful state that elevates their *Frelle* levels. The better the singer, the higher the state of bliss and the more *Frelle* the *Siltarees* secrete into their fur. We shear the fur to process the *Frelle*."

"Why don't you use recordings?"

"The *Siltarees* know the difference. We aren't sure why. They are very sensitive to technology. That's why we live above the clouds, in order to avoid disturbing them. It's also why we cannot wear our suits when we're down on the planet."

"I see." And she didn't like the idea of giving up her suit. The technology boggled the mind, but she already had come to rely on it. She imagined that after an entire lifetime in a suit, it would be even more difficult to go without one.

"As you can imagine, not many people want to sing to animals, give up their suits, and spend time without technology, but the financial rewards can be extraordinary when the *Frelle* is sweet enough."

He spoke with pride and eagerness. His tone and the light in his eyes told her he loved his work and his world. "My parents used to sing to the *Siltarees* together and we produced the sweetest and most expensive Frelle in the galaxy. After their deaths, the farm became mine."

She recalled the sound of his smooth voice. The first time she'd heard him sing, she'd thought she'd been dreaming. "After I first arrived, while I was unconscious, did you sing to me?"

"My voice sometimes calms people." She also recalled him singing to the guards before they'd escaped. Obviously, his singing possessed unique qualities, too.

"So you sing to the *Siltarees*?"

He nodded. "But my voice alone is not enough. I hoped you and I could work together." Tomm clasped his hands behind his head and stared at the ceiling as if he was waiting for her rejection.

Although she'd vowed to remain open-minded, she was having difficulty. "You want me to sing to animals?"

"Yes."

"How often?"

"Once a day."

"For how many days?"

"An entire season would make the *Frelle* sweet,

smooth, and valuable. I can offer you one-quarter of the profits. It should be enough for you to go back to Earth, but if our arrangement works, perhaps you'd consider staying."

On a backward planet where she sang to animals? She didn't think so. Although the idea of seeing his home and spending more time getting to know Tomm appealed to her, she liked her creature comforts and her singing career too much to stay out of the public eye for long.

"How long is a season?" she asked, pleased that her tone sounded level as she reminded herself she didn't yet have a career in this part of the galaxy. And now she would be pursued by Dubane.

"Thirty days."

She owed him that much. And agreeing would give her time to decide what she wanted to do next.

"All right."

"You'll do it?" He turned his head and his eyes burned hotly into hers. "You'll sing with me?"

"Yes, but I want you to understand that I'm a city girl. I like performing for people, so I won't be staying past the season."

"I understand. But you also must understand that I'll try to get you to change your mind."

She arched a brow. "And how will you do that?"

He grinned, his eyes shining with amusement. "Now that wouldn't be fair, telling you my secrets."

She would have teased him back, except the *Raven* soared out of the shuttle bay and the starscape stole Merline's breath. Stars twinkled across the heavens and below, the giant space station shrank with amazing speed until it disappeared. With the naked eye, she could see faraway galaxies, nebulae, and the occasional passing starship.

"Prepare for hyperspace jump." A computer system blared a warning.

Merline watched the stars outside turn to ribbons of multicolored light. Her stomach lurched and her vision sharpened. The vibrations seemed to rattle every nerve and she could have sworn she heard her own escalating heart beat. And with Tomm's shoulder against hers, his hip to her hip, the touching suddenly injected her with a new awareness of him.

Puzzled, she stared at him. "What's going on?"

"Senses are heightened during hyperspace travel."

"Oh." Was that why she had the sudden urge to pounce on him, press her mouth to his, and find out if kissing him was as good as she imagined it might be? Or was her reaction simply the afterburn from the adrenaline rush of the last few days?

"Is something wrong?" He unfastened the webbing and neatly placed it back into the compartment.

"Everything's just peachy." What could be wrong? Her hands still shook and the cold of space seemed to have invaded her bones. She'd been drawn through a magical painting into the future. Her one singing engagement had gotten her locked up in a people collection, and she'd escaped to go to a world she'd never heard of to sing to animals. She took one look at the heat in Tomm's eyes and her banked frustration overflowed into a raging river of need.

After removing the webbing and closing the distance between them, he gathered her into his arms, tucked her head under his chin and held her close. His heat banished the cold and as she breathed in his very male scent, she tipped back her head. She wasn't going to settle for comfort when he might have so much more to offer.

She slid her hands up his hard chest, over muscular shoulders, past his corded neck until she threaded her fingers into his thick hair. Locking gazes, she slowly tugged his head down until their mouths were an inch apart.

A smile played over her mouth. "Kiss me."

"Are you certain you—"

"Kiss me."

His eyes narrowed. "You are reacting to hyperspace sensitivity."

"I'm reacting . . . to you. Now, shut up and kiss me."

She tugged harder and when the corner of his mouth turned up and his eyes lit, her heart skipped in anticipation. For once, she was doing exactly what she wanted. Hyperspace had nothing to do with her urge to kiss him.

"But—"

"If you don't stop talking, I'll tell you what I really think."

"Now there's a scary thought." His eyes twinkled and his lips grazed hers in the wispy light caress of starlight, shooting sparks directly into her system.

Merline thought she'd been prepared, but Tomm's kiss was delightful sorcery that cloaked her in a cape of magical sensuality. He nibbled. He nipped. And his big hands stroked up and down her back, and all the while her nerve endings went on overload.

The big man could kiss. In absolutely no hurry, he seemed intent on both savoring and ravishing her mouth until her pulse elevated and her lungs strained and her heart beat a sexy rhythm against her ribs.

Perhaps his spectacular kiss was solely due to the effects of hyperspace. But that would only account for her physical reaction and not her happiness of being with this special man. Because even as she savored his embrace, even as she appreciated her swept-away excitement, she liked the way he made her feel about herself.

As he gently broke their kiss and boldly searched her gaze, she knew one kiss would not be enough. She already craved another. And yet, she found staring back into his gaze, twin stars of bright light just as compelling as his kiss.

She licked her bottom lip. "So on a scale of one to ten, one being terrible and ten being awesome, would you say that kiss was off the charts?"

He drew his brows together. "I'm not certain I can agree."

"Why not?" She let the answer rip before realizing he was teasing.

"One kiss simply isn't enough to develop a rating system. I need more of them—for a comparison test."

She laughed and leaned in to kiss him again. "Greedy man."

"I will consider those words a compliment."

And then their talking ended. Words ceased to matter. She assumed their kisses would progress to lovemaking. But she assumed wrong.

The computer interrupted. "The captain wants you both on the bridge."

"Later."

"Now," the computer insisted. "The *Raven*'s under attack."

Merline and Tomm followed the computer's blinking light display to the bridge to find focused chaos. Angel stood on the crowded bridge, her hands on her slender hips, her green eyes defiant while her crew busily checked monitors, put up shields, fired weapons, and tracked the closing enemy ships.

"I didn't want you two to miss the excitement," she muttered for a welcome.

"How can we help?" Tomm offered.

Angel crooked her finger at Merline. "I want to broadcast you singing."

"I don't understand."

"Look, we don't stand a prayer in the universe of getting away from Dubane. His ships are faster, his weapons better. But if you sing, they may decide not to aim so well."

"My songs don't stop weapons," Merline countered.

"Put a pretty women in front of men and they've been known to do foolish things. Like disobey orders."

"That's what you're counting on?" Merline strode forward. "Surely you have another—"

"Course I do." Angel winked at Merline. "But I need you to buy me the time I need to charge up my handy-dandy secret blaster gun."

"You're kidding, right?"

Angel rolled her eyes as a blast hit the ship and they all hung on or risked tumbling. "Do you see anyone laughing?"

"Fine. What do you want me to sing?"

"Something distracting—the sexier the better."

Merline wished she'd thought to bring her guitar. But even she could see the rapidly closing ships and she didn't need to be a military specialist to understand the closer they got the bigger a target they became. "What do I—"

"Petroy, hook her into the com," Angel ordered. "Engineering do you have my damn power?"

"Ten minutes, Captain," came a harried female reply.

"Make it five," Angel ordered.

Tomm escorted her to the main communications console and Petroy placed her in front of a monitor. Leaning over he pressed several buttons. "Ready?"

"Sure." She nodded and broke into a sexual ditty she'd once heard in a bar. Angel signaled her with a thumbs up. Petroy turned beet red, and Tomm sang harmony in a deep voice that hit every note, every beat, and seemed to blend perfectly with hers.

Shocked at how good a singer he was, her gaze flew to his face and watched his mouth twitch in amusement. He'd told her he sang to the animals, but he was so good he could have a sensational singing career if he'd desired it. And damn that man—he knew he was that good and now he was laughing at her astonishment.

She picked a technically difficult song with a catchy tune and he stayed right with her. She sang it fast and he kept right on tempo. And the sound they made was amazing. The bridge noise faded into the background. Time seemed to have no meaning.

She didn't understand how he seemed to pluck the notes out of the air of songs he'd never heard. But together they were magical.

"Ready to fire, Captain," a voice from engineering blared.

"Let her rip."

The *Raven* might have appeared dilapidated, but Angel had obviously outfitted her ship with superior weaponry. When they fired, a bubble of force shot through hyperspace. As the force traveled, the bubble widened. And Angel's shot caught their pursuers in the force, buffeting Dubane's state-of-the-art starships as if they were toy ships in a hurricane, effectively scattering the fleet.

"Captain." Merline spoke to Angel. "I don't know how we'll ever repay you."

Angel grinned at her. "That ammunition was dated. If we didn't use it, we'd have had to deep space it."

"Still, you've risked your ship for strangers. Thank you."

Angel hugged her. "Not strangers. We're both from Earth."

That night they celebrated. Merline would have guessed that the narrow escape from death would be blamed on them and that the crew would have been glad to be rid of their stowaways, but she was totally wrong. The narrow escape and the successful battle seemed to make the crew fond of them.

After partying through the night, the group had bonded. Tomm had promised to have a case of *Frelle* waiting for them as payment for passage when the *Raven* returned. And the next morning when Angel dropped them off at Siraz, the captain hugged Merline good-bye and promised to check on her if she made it back to this part of the galaxy. Strangely, in just the short time Merline had been aboard, she felt as though she'd made a new friend for life.

Perhaps the bond was because she and Angel both came from Earth, but Merline believed the connection went deeper. Angel had revealed pieces about her life and she had just as rough a childhood living on the streets as Merline had had in foster homes.

As the *Raven* docked, Tomm practically vibrated with eagerness to leave and show her his home. He'd invited the entire *Raven* crew, but their schedule dictated an immediate departure to scavenge a ship a space miner had spotted floating in an asteroid belt three systems away.

The Siraz spaceport looked similar to the one on the space station, but here, the dominating life-form was humanoid. Other races still passed through, but the ratio of human to nonhuman was much higher. Tomm guided her into an empty sideways elevator and she felt a shift in their relationship. This was his home, his turf, his world.

She'd left everything behind to come with him and she was beginning to have second thoughts. Angel would have let her stay on the *Raven* and eventually would have taken her home to Earth. But by the time Merline had known that, she'd already agreed to accompany Tomm.

And after that spectacular kiss, she wondered how good the lovemaking would have been if Dubane's ships hadn't interrupted. She couldn't imagine spending a season here without finding out. But after partying all night, she needed sleep. As curious as she was about Tomm's home, she figured she could wait to explore until she didn't have to fight to keep her eyes open.

But those thoughts scattered when the elevator stopped and the doors opened. And Merline gasped at the unbelievable view. "Oh . . . my . . . stars."

The elevator had opened into a giant room with twenty-foot-high ceilings and floor-to-ceiling windows that overlooked the planet below. Furnished in a rich decor, the room served to frame the green and aqua world below. With shimmering polar ice caps, the vast majority of the world consisted of green forests, lush pasturelands, and rolling hills.

"That's Siraz." Tomm slung an arm over her shoulder and guided her forward into the living area. "Welcome to my home."

"It's lovely." She didn't have to fake enthusiasm. After Dubane's sneers, she'd been expecting primitive conditions, but Tomm's home above the clouds and in low orbit sported lovely tapestries, beautifully woven carpets, and lots of green plants. And she loved the quiet privacy. There were no noisy neighbors or vehicles whizzing by, no paparazzi, just the soft trickle of the waterfall.

"Tomorrow we'll go down to Siraz, but today we'll rest." He led her to a cozy room decorated in soft whites with plush furnishings and shimmery white walls. "Will you be comfortable here?"

"Yes, thanks." She slung her guitar from her shoulder and placed it in a corner. "And where will you be?"

"Across the hall." His eyes issued an invitation, but she was so tired she wanted sleep. "There's food in the kitchen. Make yourself at home and don't be alarmed if you see any medium-sized animals prowling the house. All are friendly."

"OK." She shut the door after him, grateful that the suit kept her clean. Bathing wasn't necessary. After pulling back the covers, she climbed into the first actual bed she'd seen since she'd arrived in this time. Apparently, most people simply employed the null-grav in their suits and slept while floating in the air. Since she had yet to master her suit, floating wasn't an option for her. But apparently on Siraz, after going from orbit to planet side where one didn't wear a suit, one became accustomed to furniture.

As she snuggled into the bed, she didn't care about the reasons. The sheets were ultra soft, the pillows comfy. She closed her eyes and stretched. Her toes bumped into something soft. Something furry. Something . . . alive.

She sat up with a gasp, flung the covers aside and stood on shaking legs and peered into the eyes of a very large feline, about the same size as a collie. The black catlike creature raised a haughty head and sent her a dark green how-dare-you-disturb-me glance, then proceeded to lick its front paws, ignoring her.

"Shoo." Merline thumped the bed. The cat didn't deign to even look at her. She recalled Tomm telling her that none of his pets would harm her and decided to try sharing the bed with the creature. Gingerly, Merline climbed in and took care to avoid crowding the cat.

The cat didn't move. And slowly Merline relaxed. The cat inched closer and cuddled into the curve of her stomach. Sleepily, she dropped a hand to its head and scratched behind its ears. At the animal's loud purr, she fell right to sleep.

Merline slept through an entire day and night. She awakened the following morning to the scent of crisp fried bacon, scrambled eggs, and coffee. Surely she couldn't be back at home. Panicked, she opened her gaze and was reassured by the big lazy black cat, the white bedroom, and the sound of Tomm happily humming as dishes and silverware clinked.

She petted the cat, rose from bed, and stretched, feeling totally renewed. She padded into the kitchen. "Did you make me bacon and eggs? And coffee? Oh . . . God . . ." She reached for a cup and sniffed, then savored the first sip while Tomm kissed her cheek.

"Did you sleep well?"

"Oh, yeah. How did you . . ." She gestured to the food.

He grinned. "Angel thought you might enjoy some familiar food."

"That was very thoughtful of her. You know, for a woman who tries so hard to appear fierce, she has a soft heart."

"She liked you. If she hadn't, she might have turned us over to Dubane for profit."

Merline didn't argue. She'd heard a few stories about Angel during their night of partying. And she was glad the woman wasn't her enemy.

After the wonderful breakfast, she removed her suit with a special electromagnetic device, changed into her clothes from Earth, and grabbed her guitar. Along with the big black cat, named Wisdom, they took Tomm's private shuttle down to Siraz. It seemed strange to wear her clothing again. The fabric rustled against her skin and the scent reminded her of home.

"We can't wear suits because the technology harms the Siltarees, correct?"

"Yes. It's inconvenient, but technology upsets their systems and when they are nervous, they won't produce Frelle."

"I thought the suits translated for us. How is it that I can understand you?"

"I learned your language."

"When?"

"Last night. The computer force-fed me a program. It can't be done often, but—"

"You learned a whole language so you could talk to me?"

"If you can sing to my *Siltarees* I figure I should learn to sing in your words."

Impressed, she watched Tomm pop the hatch. Wisdom bounded out without a backward glance. The scent of wild grasses and crisp air struck her. And then the gorgeous blue sky with billowing white clouds made her homesick for a moment. But Earth hadn't been this clean, at least not the parts she'd seen, for hundreds, maybe thousands of years.

Untouched by civilization, Siraz possessed a beauty Merline had only seen in wildlife parks. Immediately in front of the shuttle was a stone terrace with a tiki hut and two lounge chairs that overlooked a grassy meadow. Craggy mountains rose precipitously on three sides of the green meadow and behind them meandered a wide glacial blue river that sparkled under the blazing sun.

After Dubane's description, likening the planet to hell, she'd been wary. "It's beautiful."

"I think so." Tomm stepped beside her with a crossbow held casually at his side. "You have to understand that Federation citizens are accustomed to the comforts and protection of their suits. To most, sweating is uncomfortable and it's very warm here. Soon we'll perspire and begin to smell."

On Earth, in her time, perspiring had been an everyday occurrence and once again, she wondered about the painting. It seemed as if not only had the painting placed her in Tomm's path, but she in his. Adapting to the time she hadn't worn a suit was not a problem for her.

She shrugged. "We can swim in the river."

He shook his head. "It's not safe. The planet is wild. Although we'll be safe on the platforms, there are predators in the forests and grasslands along the river."

Uneasy, she searched the valley, but aside from a few circling birds, she saw no sign of animal life. "Are we in danger?"

He held up the bow. "Stay with me on the platforms and you'll be safe enough." He led her up a few steps to the shade of the hut. "My father built this to keep the sun from darkening my mother's fair skin. The roof's shape attracts a breeze and we can sing from here."

She frowned at the empty meadow. "Sing to whom?"

"If we sing, the *Siltarees* will come." He sounded so certain. Already his bronzed skin glistened, emphasizing the angles of his cheekbones, his reassuring blue eyes, and the set of his powerful shoulders.

She sat on the lounge chair, removed her guitar from the case. She strummed a few chords, adjusted a string to tune it, and then cocked her head at him. "What shall we sing?"

"Whatever you like. The *Siltarees* key in on sound. Words don't matter, but the emotion does."

"All right." Feeling a bit apprehensive, Merline started to sing, and was shocked to find that the acoustics of the natural valley were as fine as most amphitheaters. And when Tomm joined in, singing with her, the notes blended and harmonized before floating out over the grassland and into the forests at the base of the mountains.

At first, nothing happened, but as they sang, Tomm's sexy voice merged with hers and the grass far below them started to sway. Watching in fascination, she saw the tiny brown dots grow into sleek eight-legged *Siltarees* that looked like a cross between tan sheep and sleek seals.

For some reason she expected the giant herd to remain silent, but they noisily, honked, hooted, and brayed as if joining into the song. The animals chased one another, frolicked, nipped, and if she hadn't known better, she would have thought they danced.

She didn't pause for breath between one song and the next. She didn't want to break the spell they were casting over the appreciative animals. And she couldn't doubt their enjoyment. They skipped, jumped, and gamboled. All of them. Full-grown *Siltarees*, their children and babies, even older gray-haired ones came to listen to the music.

Merline marveled at the sight of thousands of animals and wondered if she'd ever sung to such an appreciative audience. And oddly, a golden mist seemed to form over the herd, rising higher and higher in a golden cloud. Her gaze flew to Tomm's and his eyes widened, almost in surprise, but then he smiled into the golden mist. She breathed the mist into her lungs, and despite so many wild animals so close by, a wonderful aroma seeped through her nostrils and deep inside—a scent that was tangy and rich, provocative and lusty.

She twisted around again to find Tomm watching her with an unmistakable burning heat in his eyes that made her gasp and actually miss a beat. As he sang, his words caressed, stroked, and teased. Nothing could have been sexier than singing with this special man in a cocoon of golden mist. Only years of practice kept her fingers strumming and the vocals in sync when every cell in her body ached to stop singing, toss aside the guitar, tear off his clothes, and make love to him under the open sky of Siraz.

It was if their singing together had wrapped them in a private bubble of need, intimate and cozy. She'd been attracted to Tomm from the first moment she'd opened her eyes and seen him leaning over her with concern, and the feeling they should be together had grown steadily. But what she felt right now was spinning her out of control. Her pulse was up, her breathing ragged. Her breasts ached and dampness pooled between her thighs.

The milling animals below, the scent in the air, plus Tomm's penetrating heat were all escalating her needs. She didn't know how much longer she could ignore the sensations crashing over her, drowning her in a storm of emotions. Somehow, she belted out another song. Then another. But his melody wrapped around her, carrying into a state of excitement she didn't understand.

She'd never felt so . . . on edge. As if a thousand

tiny prickles of sensation danced and cavorted across her flesh. She was wearing way too many clothes. And as the pressure kept building, growing, and intensifying, a wild longing to throw herself at Tomm, to ravage his mouth and take everything he could give sent her into a frenzy of song.

She'd never reached such notes. She'd never carried such depths of emotions. She'd never sung so well. And his voice was right there with her, carrying her higher, farther, deeper than she'd ever reached before.

Sitting was no longer possible. She had to stand and dance, and Tomm joined her on his feet. Below them thousands of *Siltarees* cavorted as if the songs had a direct pipeline into their brains. The *Siltarees* emitted a wondrous aroma that she breathed in, and the scent increased her energy, fed her rhythm, and kept the notes pure.

She had no idea for how long they sang, but Tomm's fervor for the music appeared as strong as hers. And when she could sing no more and set aside her guitar, she would have collapsed if he hadn't gathered her into his arms.

"You were wonderful," he murmured into her ear, his voice tender and husky, his eyes hot.

Worn out, sweaty, and filled with lusty need, she wrapped her arms around his neck, pulled his mouth down for a kiss. He tasted of coffee and sweet juice, and his kiss fed her hungry soul.

Kissing him seemed so right, so natural. Being here with him, singing with him to the *Siltarees* in the golden mist was a special experience she'd remember for a lifetime. And she suspected that only making love to him could top the otherworldly experience.

Merline had kissed Tomm before, but not like this. As if desperation had replaced her blood, as if desire had replaced every thought, she could think of nothing more than his mouth on hers. The man kissed better than a dream, better than a fantasy. And made her want so much more.

But even through her growing passion, at this moment, she knew she was finally in the right place at the right time with the right man. All doubts disappeared into the mist.

He carried her to a rock bathing pool of crystal-clear water surrounding by ferns and fed by a waterfall. With the mountains and sky as a backdrop, the private setting encouraged her to let go. Merline disrobed before him and took pleasure in slowly unbuttoning her shirt and watching his eyes go molten. And when she revealed her lacy bra and panties, he swallowed hard and stared.

His deep voice was a silky whisper of appreciation. "Do all Terrans wear such provocative undergarments?"

She spun around slowly. "See anything you like?"

He shot her an approving grin. "You are so magnificent."

She toyed with him as she played with a bra strap. "You aren't so bad yourself. At least what I can see of you. But unlike your singing when you kept perfect pace, you're falling behind."

"Hmm?"

"You're wearing way too many clothes."

He folded his arms across his chest and his forearm muscles glistened in the sun. "I'm not missing one moment of your disrobing."

"And suppose I stop taking off my clothes until you catch up?"

"Then I would be sorely disappointed." His tone filled with regret, but his eyes glinted with amusement. He was teasing her and she liked this side of him.

And she knew just how to tease back. She slipped off her bra straps, letting them fall loose over her shoulders, then reached behind her to unfasten the clip. Her damp skin kept the bra from falling until she replaced the lace with her hands. Slowly, seductively, she cupped her breasts, offering her flesh to him.

He had no difficulty translating. His eyes darkened, and he bent his head, taking her nipple into his mouth. His lips tickled, his teeth nipped, and his tongue seduced, causing an immediate swooping sensation in her stomach.

She'd thought he was going to kiss . . . her mouth again.

But you love surprises.

But this was even better.

Agreed.

She heard his thought in her head.

The golden mist is allowing us to hear one another's thoughts.

What? Startled by the rush of his thoughts, his meaning, his emotions, she couldn't quite grasp his words. She felt as though his mind were a deep ocean, his thought a surging tide where she caught flashes, a series of images, a slice of emotion, slashes of sensation. Nothing whole, nothing distinct, but streaming segments—all Tomm, portions of his very essence.

And strongest of all was her sensing how much he wanted her with a force that made her knees go weak. He wanted her enough to tremble with the need. She actually felt his hardness, his craving, almost overwhelming desire to delve inside her. And yet he held back.

She heard him talking to himself. *Wait.*

Wait.

Wait.

Merline needs pleasure. Must give her more.

His emotions wrapped around her. Under her. Over her. Sliced through her.

And all the while, he kept his mouth on her breast. His tug laved her hardened nipple. He sucked and the tug seemed to draw deeply from her core. She raised her hands to his head, combed her fingers through his hair and held on tight.

Yes. He was incredible. He was applying exactly the right amount of pressure and heat, a delicious tongue lashing that left her knees weak and about to buckle. No one could be that intuitive.

She hadn't believed him before, hadn't understood the implications. *He was reading her mind.*

And what an interesting mind. He chuckled, right inside her head. *When were you going to tell me?*

"Tell you what?" She was squirming. Inside and out. What he was doing with his mouth should have been illegal. And as her nipple pebbled, her other ached for attention.

That you want . . . me to love you like this. His tongue dipped into the erotic circles of her fantasy.

Oh . . . my . . . god. He was delving into her deepest thoughts, into places she didn't go—at least not often. But he was giving her exactly what she'd always imagined. She didn't know if she could take the pleasure.

Yes, You can.

At his determination, she shivered, uncertain. She'd always wanted to know that a man loved her, not her singing, not her body, but her essence. And his mind was open and she was catching pieces of his thoughts that fed her need and had her so excited and already damp with desire. He knew what she wanted. He read her mind. And he understood that she liked a man who would give her exactly what she asked for.

She liked the emotion to be all about Merline the woman, not the singer, the star. And he was thinking about what she wanted. She could feel his approval like a storm of need breaking inside her.

He wanted to fulfill her every desire.

And she wanted to take everything he offered.

And yet . . . this sharing of thoughts was so intimate, so daring that she hadn't realized he'd removed her panties. Not until he nudged her legs apart.

Open for me.

She wasn't . . . ready to share her thoughts while she made love. And yet . . . she was too aroused to even think about stopping. He wanted her. He wanted Merline, her singing was a bonus, her body was extra. He craved her. Liked her. Wanted her and it was like coming home.

As if she belonged. Staying and making love to him was so right. Being with Tomm was where she was meant to be. Her spirit had found completion. Now her body needed to get there, too.

She wanted to experience everything with Tomm. Her body burning, her blood simmering, her thoughts in flames—she wanted it all and she opened her mind to him, allowing him to feel what he was giving her, what she still needed.

And in return she took in images of him kissing her breast, her neck, her bottom, and his impatience to plunge between her legs. His desire ripped through her. And she poured toward the temptation he offered. Her heart churning as her own needs pounded her and his hammered her, too.

With a shimmy of her hips, she pressed into him.

And he scooped her into his arms and carried her into the bathing pool. Warm water lapped her skin. But the fire in her mind burned scarlet.

Tomm removed his clothes and tossed them aside with his bow. And then he placed his hands on her waist, lifted her onto a molded lounger in the pool and then he parted her thighs so her legs bent at the knees, allowing him access to her core.

Yum. She heard his approval. Saw a picture of her lush lips in his mind. And as he breathed in her female scent, he shuddered with male satisfaction.

Tensing with anticipation, she clenched her hands, wondering what he would do. She couldn't see all the pieces of the picture in his mind. She only got flashes. Excitement. Pink. Warmth and rock-hard determination. Eagerness.

Stay with me, he urged. *Stay. Stay. Stay.*

"I'm right here. I'm not going anywhere."

He grabbed her wrists. Placed his mouth over her center and she arched into him with a gasp. And then exactly following the very clear picture in her mind, he made every tiny lick last for long, lingering, lush seconds.

Her hands reached to clench him. His wrists held her fast. *Got you right where you want me and where I want you.* His satisfaction seared her.

Want more.

Good.

More.

Yes, he agreed.

And he gave her more, more time, more tenderness, more heat, more love. And he was thoroughly enjoying himself, completely caught up in tasting her flesh, of keeping her open, on edge. And she was just as determined to keep her lust at bay until he was inside her.

You're enjoying having me . . .

Exactly as you want me to enjoy having you.

The mind communication allowed her to let him know precisely what she liked. Merline had never been shy about expressing her needs, but no one had ever understood her so perfectly. All she had to do was think, *a little more. Yes. There.* And he complied instantly, brilliantly and then he took her satisfaction for his own.

Shared sensations increased the intimacy. He was inside her mind. Inside her body. His tongue on her flesh fired her every nerve impulse into tapping a happy dance.

As her excitement increased, she sent it to him, and he fed on her emotions and they came back to her so strong she was awash in need.

Now, her mind shouted.

And he was there the moment she wanted him there, lowering his body, entering her, inch by delicious inch and filling her with an incredible ease. She arched into him, drew him closer for another kiss.

His tongue dipped into her mouth and greedily, she held on. Mouth to mouth, chest to chest, hips to hips, she adored being so close, reveled in the heat of his skin, savored his hard muscles, cherished every lingering caress as his tempo escalated.

To him she was warmth, softness, and tightness. His need for friction battled with his need to hold back, a battle he was losing as she urged him with her mouth and hands and hips.

She was so ready, her mind enveloped his. Her arms wrapped around his neck. She locked her legs around his hips. Timing her movements to his was so perfect because she could feel what he felt. She knew as soon as he did what he would do and when he would do it.

And just as she was in his head, he was in hers, drawing out each movement, giving her exactly the sensation she craved at the exact second she asked. Erotic pleasure sizzled across her flesh and through her mind with one stroke. Delicious need matched otherworldly lust.

Radiating in pleasure both hers and his, they exploded together, taking one another along. And she gasped at the force of his eruption even as he marveled at how she spasmed again and again.

And when his ragged breathing eased, when his heart stopped hammering her chest, he placed his cheek against hers and whispered into her ear. "You are amazing."

"So are you, but," she frowned, "you aren't in my head anymore."

"Nope."

He looked way too innocent. And now that lust no longer clouded her mind, she was thinking about her experience differently, trying to figure out just what had occurred between them. "That golden mist was some kind of aphrodisiac, wasn't it?"

"Yes."

She had to give him credit. He didn't avoid her gaze or attempt to lie, but his admission turned her world upside down. Her gut clenched. She could think no better of him than a man who'd secretly placed a drug in his unsuspecting date's drink. And it took every bit of self control not to slam her fist into his too-handsome jaw.

CHAPTER 8

"Damn you," Merline swore.

After all his tenderness, she couldn't have felt more betrayed. She hadn't required an aphrodisiac to make love. She'd been willing. But he hadn't told her what she was volunteering for. Instead, he'd brought her here, let her breathe in the mist without warning her of the consequences, and she felt . . . used. Bitter. She shoved him away, pushed to her feet, and dressed, needing the barrier of clothing.

But like a shield raised too late against a slicing sword, she rocked back on heels and fought the agonizing tightness in her chest. She'd started to let herself care about him—okay more than care. She'd been falling for him.

He'd slipped on a pair of pants and joined her as she stared at the valley, trying to blink back tears. He'd betrayed her trust, and now all she wanted to do was leave on the next shuttle. She shouldn't have come here. She should have stayed with Angel. Eventually she would have made it back to Earth.

The cat, Wisdom, padded up to her, stood on his hind legs, placed his paws on her shoulder, and gently licked away a stray tear. She buried her face in the big cat's neck but refused to cry.

She was too tough to cry, at least on the outside. Inside, she was sobbing as regret flayed her with pain. She should have known a man couldn't be trusted, especially one with a self-proclaimed ulterior motive. And now she couldn't get away fast enough.

"Are you in pain?" Tomm's kind tone caused a lump to well in her throat.

She shook her head.

"Did I do something . . . unacceptable?"

She sniffed back a tear. "You should have told me."

"Told you what?"

He sounded genuinely puzzled, but she wasn't good at reading the intentions of men from Earth, never mind a man from another world. And with a voice as skilled as his, he could inject any emotion into his tone whether he was feeling it or not.

She couldn't bear to look into his eyes. Not now when she ached with what he'd done. "Go away."

Wisdom went down to all fours. She scratched behind his ear and the big cat purred.

Tomm shook his head. "I'm not leaving you here. It can be dangerous."

"No kidding." He hadn't warned her about alien men who could rip out an unsuspecting girl's heart.

"I'm very serious. The *Siltarees* have natural enemies. They leave people alone unless we wander onto the grasslands but—"

"Can we leave now?"

"I'm sorry. Not just yet. The *Siltarees* require a few hours to make the *Frelle*. If a departing shuttle disturbs them, our efforts will have been for nothing."

"Fine." She sat on the edge of the patio, pulled her knees to her chest, and stared over the valley. The *Siltarees* were rolling on their backs, leaving behind huge tufts of fur. The process would have been fascinating if she could have focused on them.

As if sensing her pain, Wisdom curled up beside her. He nudged her until he could settle his head on her thigh.

"I have offended you in some way, haven't I?"

"Yes."

"I am sorry."

"It's too late for an apology." She turned her head and scowled.

He spread his hands wide. "I'd hoped to please you enough so you'd want to stay."

"That was your plan?" She practically spat the words at him and watched him flinch.

"I just said so."

"You failed."

His voice resounded with frustration. "Why?"

"Because you tricked me."

"I did not." His tone was indignant and every muscle in his body tensed from the cords in his neck to his muscular chest to his fists. Yet he didn't move, simply waited for her to explain.

"You should have told me the mist was an aphrodisiac."

"If we'd stopped singing in order to talk, the mist would have disappeared. The *Siltarees* wouldn't have made *Frelle*." He sounded as if he was being reasonable. "The process is delicate and cannot be interrupted."

She ground her teeth. "Why didn't you tell me beforehand? Like when we were still on the spaceship and I still had a ride home?"

He shrugged. "It never occurred to me."

"It never occurred to you that I would want to know that I was about to breathe in an aphrodisiac? That we would link minds? That we would make love? You didn't think I'd want to know?" She glared at him. "What kind of man are you?"

He ran a hand through his ragged hair. "When I saw the golden mist, I thought I was dreaming. Legends tell of such a thing—if the music is sweet enough, it is said the golden mist will rise from the *Siltarees* and sweeten the air. But I had never seen it or known anyone who had. So I didn't expect . . ."

"Are you telling me the golden mist doesn't happen every time you sing?"

"Of course not. Creating the golden mist is a feat of legends, as are the aphrodisiacal properties. I never imagined that you and I would create such music. And once I breathed it, I could think of nothing but you. Of kissing you. Of holding you."

A stick snapped. She jerked her head toward the sound, searching for danger.

Dubane came around the side of the waterfall and pointed a blaster at Tomm. "Merline's way too smart to fall for your slime crap."

Dubane had found them.

In horror, Merline stared at the man who'd seemed to come right out of the rock face. Wisdom wisely bounded away and she wished they could have done the same.

"What are you doing here?" Stunned that Dubane had followed her all the way to Siraz, she instinctively backed away. "How did you get here?"

"I never release anyone from my collection." Dubane spoke as if he was being the most reasonable man ever born, but rage glittered in his eyes. And as he spoke and the translator worked perfectly, she realized he was still wearing his suit. "At least," he said with a sinister gleam in his eyes, "I don't release them while they're still alive. As for how I got here, I took a shuttle. Yesterday. Since I couldn't be certain which site Tomm would chose, I positioned myself between the three most likely targets. And thanks to your song, my efforts will be most lucrative."

Dubane gestured to a skimmer that was already gathering the Siltaree fur.

"You came to steal the *Frelle*?" she asked, trying to keep Dubane's attention on her as Tomm edged toward the crossbow he'd left by the pool.

Dubane shook his head. "After you escaped and caused me so much trouble, I decided you owed me. So I came up with a plan. Selling the spice will help me replenish my collection. You two shall be my first—"

Tomm dived toward his bow. Dubane fired and the bow burst into flames. Below, the skimmer neared the animals and the *Siltarees* milled, then stampeded. The valley thundered with the echoes of their hooves pounding the flatland.

"Halt or I'll fry her." Dubane issued his threat in the calmest of tones.

Tomm stopped and shot her a look of apology, an anguished grimace, as if he expected her to blame him for failing to protect her. And in that moment she feared he would do something that might get them both killed.

Dubane had surprised them. At the moment, they had no option but to obey his orders and she shook her head slightly, hoping Tomm would pick up her mes-

sage not to risk any dangerous maneuvers that would
further put their lives in jeopardy.

Tomm replied with a brief nod.

Dubane reached into his suit and pulled out a tiny
machine no bigger than a deck of cards and tossed it to
her. She caught it. The sides were smooth and metallic,
the faceplate plastic.

"Press your thumbprint into the faceplate," Dubane
ordered.

"Why?"

"It's your recording contract."

Surely no one would expect her to honor a contract
made under duress? That wouldn't be legal on Earth—
yet here, Dubane seemed a law unto himself. "I don't
understand."

"I'm your agent, manager, and business partner.
First you will continue to sing for the *Siltarees* herds
and create *Frelle*. Then after I have gathered it, I will
destroy Siraz."

"You are insane." She stared at him, unable to conceal her horror. Wouldn't the Federation track down a
man who destroyed an entire world? Or could Dubane
pay off that many officials? She didn't know and
looked to Tomm. When her gaze met his, she saw
banked fury in his eyes, determination to stop Dubane
in every tense muscle.

But Dubane held the weapon steady. "My idea is
pure genius. Once Siraz is gone, I'll have the best and
only supply of *Frelle* in the galaxy. Prices will sky-
rocket, and after you thumbprint that contract all your
earnings will go directly to my account. You and
Tomm will perform concerts, both public and private."
Her skin crawled as Dubane ranted, but he always kept
complete control of his aim of the weapon. "You will

go from planet to planet and make me wealthier and more powerful than even I could dream."

She began to toss back the machine. "I'm not interested in singing for you."

"You'll sing or Tomm dies." Dubane's voice hissed with deadly threat.

She had no doubt he'd kill Tomm as he had most of his collection. Bowing her head in defeat, she placed her thumbprint on the machine.

Dubane dropped them at the next herd and departed. He'd assured them his guards would inform him if they refused to sing to the herd. Tomm had told him that the *Siltaree* would not make *Frelle* if the guards wore suits and Dubane had been forced to concede the point. Tomm and Merline's only advantage was that the guards couldn't understand their words, so they could speak freely.

The beauty of Siraz failed to capture her attention. Under the hot sun, the memory of their lovemaking in the pool seemed like days ago instead of hours. The mountains here protruded from the ground in a dark and forboding manner, and the lack of cover over the vast plain made escape appear impossible.

"Can we disappear into the forest with the *Siltarees*?" she asked.

Tomm shook his head. "Even if we could find a way to escape the guards without injury, we'd never survive in the forest without weapons. The wild *katars* would eat us before nightfall."

"Will Wisdom be all right?" She recalled the big cat licking away her tear as if trying to give comfort, and then his running off after Dubane's arrival.

"He'll be fine—until Dubane destroys the planet." Tomm's voice hardened and the guards shifted nervously.

"Surely that was an idle threat?"

Tomm shook his head.

"You have those kinds of weapons?"

"I don't. Dubane might." Tomm placed her guitar into her hands. "We have to find a way to escape and stop him. I won't allow him to ruin this world, our way of life. I won't let him destroy you." She'd learned not to underestimate Tomm's quiet determination and yet, what could one unarmed man do against Dubane, his guards, and his superior weaponry?

"Dubane's had years of practice at controlling his collection. The only reason we escaped before was that I came in from the outside . . . from a direction he didn't expect." Tomm spoke with care, as if deep in thought.

"I'm sorry. This is all my fault. If I'd listened to you, I would never have sung for Dubane at the space station. He would never have added me to his collection and you wouldn't have had to save me. Now your entire world is—"

"I came after you of my own accord. It was my decision and not your fault. But even if it was, we have no time for regrets. We need to find a way to escape." Again he dropped into what appeared to be deep thought.

"And?" she prodded.

"Perhaps when Dubane takes us to his ship, we will find the means to—"

One of the guards issued a sharp word she didn't recognize, but he gestured to her guitar and his order was clear. They needed to sing.

She wasn't in the mood. Singing was a joyful experience, but to do it on command sickened her. But until they figured out a way to stop Dubane, they had little choice. Idly, she wondered if the golden mist would rise from the *Siltarees* again. And what would happen if the guards breathed in the mist?

While one guard had blue-tinged skin, they both were human. Despite the heat, icy fear shot down her spine at the idea of how they'd respond.

She turned her guitar and strummed a bit, settling into position on another wooden stage set high above a clearing on a rocky crag. "Perhaps we shouldn't sing quite so well. If the guards breathe in the mist, there's no predicting their reactions to the aphrodisiac."

She didn't have to point out she was the only woman here. Tomm's eyes hardened. "I won't let them—"

"They are holding all the weapons. Perhaps we should sing off-key?"

Tomm shrugged. "If the *Siltarees* don't make the *Frelle*, Dubane will not be pleased. I won't take the chance of his harming you."

His guards stayed too far away for Tomm to surprise them. And they remained close enough to watch their every move. They really had no choice, exactly as Dubane had planned. "So we sing our best?"

"Only until we find a way to free ourselves."

"Agreed."

And so they sang and their voices carried on the wind, across the plain and into the forests. Drawn to the song, the *Siltaree* herd streamed toward them much like the first time, the wild creatures enthused by the music. And despite the soulful sadness in her tone, the *Siltaree* listened and cavorted and gathered ever closer.

Once again her voice twined with Tomm's and together, the sounds were more pleasing than either

alone. Once again the *Siltarees*' scent filled the air, and
once more the golden mist filled a Siraz valley and
again she and Tomm breathed in the mist.

So did the guards.

And it wasn't long before she became uneasy at the
lust glimmering darkly in their eyes. Yet, if one attacked her, perhaps Tomm could defeat the other. She
was about to suggest the notion to Tomm when he cut
off the song in mid-note and changed to one she'd
never heard.

He'd never done that before. In the past he'd always
allowed her to choose the music. Perhaps he'd also
seen the guards' interested looks in her and thought a
change would help. But she could only guess. She
couldn't yet read Tomm's mind.

The tempo was upbeat yet repetitious. Almost
hypnotic. Below them the *Siltarees* still scampered and
played, but the pace had changed from frenetic to mes-
merizing. When she caught Tomm's eye, he nudged
his chin in the guards' direction.

Expressions glazed, they swayed in time to the music.
They no longer held the blasters aimed at them. One
guard appeared to blink repeatedly, as if forcing himself
to stay awake. She didn't understand what was happening. How could the mist be making them sleepy?

Or was it the song? And if the music made them tired,
how could she and Tomm use it to their advantage?

Before Merline and Tomm could sing the guards to sleep, Dubane had returned to collect them and had sent his skimmers to gather the *Frelle*. He'd transported them by shuttle and locked them inside a dimly lit spaceship cabin. With no supplies and nothing to do, she tried to shrug off the effects of the aphrodisiac.

But it wasn't easy. Dubane had given them suits, a necessity to survival in space, and Tomm's black jumpsuit molded to every muscle. A lock of dark hair had fallen over his forehead and he raked his hand through it, with no realization of how good he looked. As he paced from one side of the tiny room to the other, he moved with the grace of a caged cat. Powerful legs ate the distance and when he reached the far wall in three paces, he spun with complete balance, barely breaking stride as he headed in the opposite direction.

Very deliberately she moved in front of him, forcing him to halt.

"What?" he blinked, as if he had no idea what she was talking about.

"Stop trying to fight the effects of the mist."

He stiffened. "I do not take what isn't freely offered."

"I'm offering." She placed her hands around his neck. He didn't move one muscle, but his nostrils flared.

His eyes narrowed. "And after we make love will you then hold my actions against me?"

"Of course not. Last time, I thought you knew in advance what the mist would do and had failed to tell me. I was wrong to believe you would commit such a dishonorable act. Can you forgive me?"

He spoke stiffly, through a clenched jaw. "I . . . don't . . . know."

"I understand." She should have dropped her hands from around his neck, but she couldn't find the strength. Instead, she tried to make him understand. "In my past, I was famous. Men courted me for their own reasons, for my music, my wealth, my connections. No one ever wanted me just for me. And when I learned you also wanted me because I could sing . . . I assumed that you were like the others. So when the mist appeared," she shrugged, "I jumped to the wrong conclusions."

"You don't trust me."

"We haven't known one another that long. You saved my life, but you also had much to gain from my singing."

"You think I would risk my life for *Frelle* and credits?" he practically spat the words at her. His eyes hardened to granite.

"I've come to expect the worst."

"Our minds were linked. What did you see?" Gaze

ominous, he stepped back and crossed his arms over his chest.

"Bits and pieces of thoughts. Flashes. Pictures. It wasn't enough to convince me of anything except how much you enjoyed making love." She worked up the courage to lean into him. "Perhaps we need to link again so that I can know you even better."

Despite his anger with her, a corner of his mouth quirked in amusement and his eyes twinkled with both passion and humor. "Nothing would please me more."

Sensing that he might not have given in so easily if not for the lingering effects of the mist, she kissed his chin, his neck and as he leaned closer, his ear. "I plan to please you . . . a lot."

Merline cared about Tomm's feelings, yet she knew how difficult it was to recover from a breach in trust. But she sensed he had enough self confidence to get past her mistake. And so she showed him with her lips and her fingertips exactly how precious he'd become.

She had no idea what the future held. Dubane might execute them tomorrow. But they had right now and she didn't want to waste another moment. If they died, she wanted Tomm to know how much he meant to her.

And as her mouth found his, their suits went transparent. She didn't question him. Instead, as they mindlinked, she hoped he could read her better than she'd read him and she opened her mind and her heart. For her the trust was a new beginning.

As he sent back approval through the link, her boldness grew. With a mental thought, he shot her a vision of null-grav, the suits' ability to float them in midair. And so she wasn't surprised, but pleased, when he activated the mechanism. Suddenly they floated on a cushion of empty space.

Wow.

You like?

Oh, yeah. I like our privacy. And I like who I'm shar-ing the privacy with.

She snuggled right against him, unaware and un-caring of which wall was up or down of sideways. Her focus was concentrated on Tomm. She scooted up his big body, appreciating the way he anticipated her move.

His hands clasped her waist, she parted her legs. But she didn't take him inside her. Not yet. First she wanted another kiss and he chuckled, clearly surprised that she was teasing him. But he obliged with another hot kiss. And then another. Each kiss was different. Sometimes he teased, sometimes he demanded, and sometimes he let her take charge, but she always set the pace and she was in no hurry at all.

And he slid his hands down her back, over her bot-tom, using heat and friction to pull her close. She nipped his neck, tweaked his nipples, and watched his eyes glaze with passion. She threaded her hands into his hair and locked gazes.

"Tell me what you want," she demanded.

"You."

His message was simple and stabbed her to the core. And through the mindlink she felt the truth. Sure, the man might have initially gone after her for her singing, but he wasn't thinking about singing at the moment. He was thinking about her heat, her arms and fingers and lips. And he was thinking how right she felt.

With one pelvic tilt, she took him inside to the hilt. He hissed in pleasure. And then he took her breasts in his hands and caressed as she began to move over him. Slowly. Erotically.

And all the while she stared into his eyes, read his mind, and saw what she looked like to him. Perfect. Beautiful. Special and sensual. He wrapped her in approval, appreciation, and a sensual harmony that caused her heartbeat to escalate, her breath to come in rasps.

And then he showed her a vision of desire. But she didn't want to release him.

Let me adjust the suit to please you.

She drew the thought from his mind and as she felt the hot lick between her legs, she understood he was directing the suit, and gasped in wonder.

Oh my.

Is that an 'oh my' yes?

Yes. She increased the pace of her hips. Pleasure from his hands, the suit, and his hardness radiated through her. He was touching her everywhere, her flesh, inside and out, her mind, in the deepest recesses. And he poured his own excitement into her.

Her breathing came in greedy gulps. She couldn't hold out much longer. Nothing had ever felt so good, so right, so undeniably exquisite. And suddenly he ripped right over the edge, taking her with him and setting off her own fiery explosions.

"Ready to sing?" Dubane had ordered Merline and Tom to the bridge to watch him wipe out Siraz. The sick bastard had ordered them to sing as he set the charges to bust apart the planet. Worry and excitement gnawed at her nerves. Nevertheless, she followed the plan she and Tomm had come up with after making love, and she tried to look beaten and defeated.

Tomm squeezed her hand and released it. This was

the moment they'd been waiting for. Would all their practice work? Heart dancing up her throat, Merline looked at Tomm and began a count. "One and two and three and—"

He jumped in right on the beat. Over the last few weeks of captivity, they'd sung to the *Siltarees*. Dubane had collected all the *Frelle* and had stored it aboard his ship. While guards had watched their every move as they'd sung on Siraz, they'd had time to perfect their singing. She hoped they had it down to an exact science.

Tomm had come up with the brilliant idea to use their voices to place their captors in an altered hypnotic state. Producing the desired effect took a special blending of tune and notes and timing, but their experiments with the guards on the planet had seemed to work. Certain repetitious notes combined with a syncopated tempo had induced a trancelike state. And when the guards had awakened from their stupor, they seemed to have no notion of passing time or that anything had been wrong.

Merline still didn't know if they could affect Dubane or the bridge crew. All were humanoid, but every alien race had a different susceptibility. But this was their first chance at Dubane, and while he'd brought them onto the bridge to gloat about destroying Siraz, he'd unwittingly given them their opportunity.

"Place charges in orbit," Dubane ordered. One of his crew worked busily over a console.

Merline concentrated on her singing and stared out the vidscreen. The launch of the weapons shooting into orbit distracted her, but Tomm nudged her knee with his and helped her recover. Through the entire ordeal he'd been her rock.

And as the weapons tracked into position, she sang

and kept the complex tempo required. Already one of the crew seemed to be catatonic. Another stared at the floor. Others moved sluggishly.

But Dubane seemed too keyed up for their singing to slow him. Tense, she tried to relax her throat and redoubled her efforts. After another full minute, the guards and the crew seemed to go under.

"Set timers." Dubane still paced, issuing his orders without any regard for his crew's condition.

But he must have been less alert than he appeared, because he didn't seem to notice that no one was responding to his order. However, with impatience he reached over the console and jabbed the settings, displaying extraordinary will.

Merline kept singing. Tomm tensed beside her. They were running out of time. In moments the timers would blow and blast apart Siraz and the *Siltarees*, along with Wisdom, who remained on the world.

Tomm kept singing, but he stood and walked toward Dubane. Clearly, the man wasn't himself. He didn't question Tomm, but he wasn't out like the rest of the crew, either. His glazed eyes told Merline that in another few minutes they would have him where they wanted him, but they didn't have minutes.

While she tried to keep the beat, Tomm, still singing, leaned past Dubane, his finger ready to press the stop button. But Dubane jerked, coming out of his partial trance to knock Tomm's hand away.

Tomm countered with a punch to Dubane's jaw that knocked back his head. The men began to fight, moving at speeds so blurry she couldn't follow. She suspected the suit sped their movements somehow, but she wasn't about to let that stop her from advancing to the command console.

The crewman standing before the console moaned. Before he came out of the trance, she confiscated his blaster from his hip and placed it to his temple. "Turn off the timers."

"But—"

"Do it. Now." She dug the blaster into his head. And his fingers fumbled over the vidscreen.

Meanwhile, Tomm took a vicious blow to his head, bounced off a wall, and used his null-grav to flip in midair. And he caught Dubane with a kick in the gut. Dubane roared his outrage, waking a few crew out of their dazes. Before they could go for their weapons, Merline fired her blaster into the floor.

"Put your hands behind your heads or I'll shoot your first officer."

"Do as she says," the first officer ordered.

Dubane shouted at his crew. "Kill her."

But they didn't listen to Dubane. Instead they placed their hands behind their heads. Merline took the opportunity to lean over the console to check the weapons' status.

But while her suit translated language, Merline couldn't read the words or diagrams. "Computer, what's the orbital weapons status?" she asked.

"On hold."

"Disarm and recall them," Merline ordered.

"You do not have authorization to order—"

She jabbed the crewman again. "Give the order or I'll see if this blaster is set to stun or to kill."

He didn't hesitate to comply. "Stand down. Recall the planet busters."

Tomm's elbow jammed into Dubane's face. Dubane cursed and blood spurted over the bridge of his broken nose. His suit couldn't stop the blood from trickling into his eyes.

Legs shaking, hands trembling, Merline aimed the weapon at Dubane. "Freeze or I'll shoot."

With a blur of speed, Dubane kicked off the wall, changing his angle of attack from Tomm to her. Without hesitation, she pulled the trigger.

The blast caught Dubane full in the chest. Surprise and horror widened his eyes. And then he collapsed to the floor.

Merline swallowed, nausea rising in her throat. The man deserved to die, but she would prefer if it wasn't by her hand. "Is he dead?"

Tomm felt for a pulse and straightened. "Yes."

Merline thought she was going to be sick and swallowed hard. Tomm lifted a blaster from another crewman, but clearly they had no intention of fighting. With Dubane gone, they wouldn't risk their lives to carry on.

Tomm hurried to her side, concern darkening his eyes. "Are you all right?"

"I will be."

But even an hour later, after Tomm had spoken to the authorities, recovered his stolen *Frelle*, turned the crew over to the Siraz police, and reunited with Wisdom, she still shook. The hot drink Tomm pressed into her hands and Wisdom's purring couldn't calm her nerves.

Tomm placed an arm over her shoulder. "You had to shoot Dubane. It was self defense. If you hadn't he would have wiped out an entire planet."

"I'm not shaking because I regret what I did." She clenched her fingers. "If I had it to do over, I'd shoot him again. I'm glad he's dead." She looked up at Tomm. "I'm glad . . . and that's not right, is it?"

"What's wrong with being glad that Dubane will never hurt anyone again?"

"You're right. I've just never thought I'd be so glad to be alive and be with you." Merline didn't feel as if she was the same person anymore. Ever since she'd stepped through the painting, she'd sought to put her singing career back on track. Now, with Dubane gone, with no one to stop her, she couldn't work up any enthusiasm for the idea.

"What are you thinking?" Tomm sat beside her and placed an arm over her shoulder.

"That I've been trying to restart my career since I got here and I'm no longer certain that I want one."

Tomm's concern turned to mock horror. "You aren't giving up singing?"

She cuddled against him and enjoyed Wisdom's deep purr as the cat placed his head on her lap. Merline scratched behind Wisdom's ears and titled back her head to look straight at Tomm. "How long until next season?"

"Time enough for me to take you home like I promised."

"I already am home." The words felt right and she knew she'd made the correct decision.

His gaze bored into hers. His eyes twinkled. "And here I thought I was going to have to build you your own recording studio to convince you to stay."

"That would be nice. But all I really want . . . is you."

TEMPTATION

BY

JEANIE LONDON

1713, St. Michaels, Maryland

Blessed or cursed?

Nina de Lacy considered the question as the priest blessed their small household congregation and bowed low before the altar. She'd been accused of both during her life, and given her rather unique abilities, she supposed either judgment had merit. It depended upon one's point of view.

So, blessed or cursed?

When she thought about the looming hours ahead spent sitting for a portrait, Nina leaned toward the latter.

"I'm not languishing, Gray," she informed her guardian as they made their way from the chapel. "Honestly."

"Of course not, my dear. Today is for celebrating."

She would have celebrated a reprieve from this portrait sitting, but Gray Talbot, Earl of Westbury, would not be gainsaid. Nina had appealed to his reason already.

He was unreasonable. He wanted to celebrate the arrival of her eight and tenth year in a grand fashion, since they were forced to celebrate the event far from their London home.

"You look as if I've proposed a trip to the gallows," he said. "Not a birthday gift."

"Do not attempt to deceive me. You want to fill that bare spot on the gallery wall."

Gray laughed, and the rich sound rolled through the hall with such life that she noticed a faint echo, as if these well-appointed walls weren't used to holding such a lively sound.

"Of course I do. I am setting my home to rights, but I would never fill the spot with any but the worthiest treasure. You, my dear, qualify."

Wrinkling her nose at him, she earned another chuckle, and even more than his praise, his laughter raised Nina's spirits with a sense of triumph that felt far worthier than any portrait ever would. Gray didn't laugh often anymore, hadn't since he'd lost his wife in childbed scarcely more than a year past.

He wore the weight of his loss heavily. Not in careworn lines or wrinkled creases, but in an expression so stern her guardian could seem almost intimidating.

Except when he gazed upon her.

"In the civilized world," she said, "any face painter worth his fee would have come to the manor."

"But, my dear Nina, we are dealing with Master Verbrugges, and in this part of the world, he is considered the authority. We must accommodate."

"Is that your way of saying we're no longer in the civilized world?"

"'Tis my way of saying we must look to each day as an adventure." Gray extended his hand to her.

Nina glanced down at the strong fingers silently beckoning. Raising her hand, she grew breathless with the anticipation of slipping her fingers inside his . . .

Warm skin met warm skin. Muscles flexed as he caught her in his grip, a touch gloriously familiar and strangely foreign.

Nina felt the faint pulse of life in his fingertips, a strength that was firm without being possessive, the touch of a man who would not pull her along, but walk beside her.

Tipping her head up, she met Gray's gaze, saw the melting softness in his deep eyes. As always, he recognized the ceremony of clasped hands, understood how utterly she craved touch that was no more than it should be—a simple touch.

Touching Nina was never simple.

Except for Gray. She didn't know why, only that with him flesh was only flesh, clasped hands only clasped hands, which made his touch the most important in her world.

She savored the sensation while walking across the hall, where a liveried footman swung the door wide before retreating discreetly. Gray led her into the mist-soaked morning to the coach awaiting them in the lane. Clinging to him, she memorized the warmth where their hands met, a tingly sensation that glazed her skin soft as a whisper.

He helped her inside the conveyance then sat opposite, and Nina released him. The moment was broken, their connection vanishing as a mist blown away on a breeze.

Trying to shake off the sense of loss, she stared

through the coach window at the river, at least what she could make out through the fog. Trees were towering shadows on the far bank. The swift water glowed beneath the rising mist.

So much about this place reminded her of her childhood home on England's Welsh border, land lush and untamed, the villages so rich with life and memories, hopelessly rural compared to cosmopolitan London, where she'd spent her latter years.

" 'Tis lovely," she said.

Gray nodded. "Are you sorry we moved into town?"

This wasn't the first time he'd asked the question. Nina knew it wouldn't be the last. Not until they settled in according to Gray's standard. "I had no desire to grow tobacco. Neither did you."

"It would have been quieter on a farm."

"Wasn't that why you wanted to move into town?"

His knowing gaze pierced the distance, making Nina feel exposed. "I only want you to be happy."

"I know."

She wanted Gray to be happy. He needed to make a place for his loss and learn to move on. A man of great spiritual conviction and deep love, he deserved to be loved in return. The colonies offered him a chance to fashion a new life.

Queen Anne had granted him two hundred acres that had been much suited to tobacco farming, but Gray had chosen to settle in the small village of St. Michaels instead. He'd built a manor house befitting his station and opened a legal office.

Nina had been managing the office. His practice had been growing respectably as his circle of acquaintances grew and his sphere of influence increased; she had no doubt he would be made a judge then mayhap even a justice on the high court of appeal. Gray wouldn't stay away from politics for long.

Interest sparked his conversation whenever he discussed the doings in the legislative assembly or the latest bill to be introduced into the lower house. Councillors had been sending business his way, acquainting themselves with the character and ethics of this newly arrived nobleman.

As Gray's heart healed, he would become involved in shaping this country as well. So Nina hoped, for his sake. He could only spend so much time on his knees in prayer, as she was wont to tell him. There was no good reason why such a wonderful man should be confined to live in the shadows with her.

Master Verbrugges' home was a respectable brick house in a nearby town. Not nearly so grand in size or embellishment as Gray's manor, of course, which had been built closer to the village center for business considerations.

Yet the Dutch painter possessed a charming home, a sign he enjoyed success in a place so devoid of culture that itinerant artists often painted heads to place in stock pictures to satisfy demand.

"I believe we shall like the master," Gray said as he handed her from the coach. "From his correspondence, he seemed a likable sort, pleasant to pass time with . . . I hope."

Master Verbrugges turned out to be a lively fellow indeed, hurrying across the hall upon their announcement. He greeted Gray with a beaming smile, and Nina

thought him rather quail-like with his stout middle and
short thin legs. Grizzled hair stuck out on all ends of
his wigless head.

"Lady Kirkby, I am delighted, delighted." The master extended his hand to take hers in greeting, but Gray
neatly sidestepped the effort.

Nina retreated behind her stalwart guardian's broad
back in a dance familiar from their social outings and
smiled at the master in welcome. "Master Verbrugges,
'tis a pleasure."

While acquaintances could often be put off by
Nina's aloofness, the master's gaze grew wide, as if he
found her appearance more startling than her manner.

The expression passed so quickly she decided her
imagination must have run away. The master seemed
quite jovial as he escorted them into his studio, chatting excitedly about details of the portrait from his correspondence with Gray.

The studio proved to be a chamber with windows
that soaked the room with a warm light. A table covered with paint jars and brushes resided in the center,
appearing as if it was moved often, and easels positioned at various vantages bore up the observation. A
creatively chaotic place. Inviting.

"I shall paint you entirely, of course," Master Verbrugges assured her before hurrying toward a chair that
he dragged to the windows with the scrape of wood
over stone. "Milord and I discussed a dark background
to emphasize the beauty of your skin. The green gown
is a lovely choice on you, milady, just lovely."

Nina only nodded, unable to take credit for the
choice, for the gown, too, had been a gift from Gray.
He'd had the design fashioned with this sitting in mind,
and the decor of his gallery as well, no doubt.

A servant appeared with refreshment. Master Verbrugges had set up a comfortable chair for Gray's leisure, but dear, thoughtful Gray remained by her side through the lengthy process of posing her to best suit the light, ensuring that Master Verbrugges would have no need to touch her himself.

"I will sketch you today, milady," the master said when he and Gray had finally agreed upon a pose—one that strained her neck muscles unbearably.

She did not complain, though, as she'd been left with a view through the windows of the gardens as blessed distraction.

"I'll capture the details of your expression and your finery, so you and Lord Westbury may review the result and decide upon changes."

"Very good." Only then did Gray retreat to recite a rosary or review his legal cases, appearing utterly content.

Master Verbrugges' charcoal scuffed over parchment in bold strokes while Nina stared into the garden, noticing the burnt edges on fragile white azalea blooms, the wilted flower of a dogwood as it broke away from the stem and floated to the lawn. She wished to emulate Gray's serenity, to possess his knack for bringing his peace along with him wherever he went.

His strength came from prayer and a conviction that God guided him always, no matter how often he fell. Since losing Juliette, Gray had fallen often into despair, guilt, and anger.

Yet he rose each time, his faith to support him, and had Nina been looking through his eyes, she wouldn't see burnt blooms but the wonder that such loveliness grew to be nourished by the sun. She wouldn't see a

spent flower but the glory that had let the blossom
flourish before fading.

Birth. Life. Death.

'Twas the natural course, as she well knew.

Had she been looking through Gray's eyes, Nina
would see blessings rather than curses. Yet God hadn't
felt very close since their arrival in Maryland, despite
a private chapel in the manor and a priest who minis-
tered their spiritual needs daily.

She wasn't sure why, but each time she was forced
to pick up the tatters of her life, the threads grew ever
more slippery, more frayed and difficult to grasp.

"What say you, milady?" Master Verbrugges interrupted her reverie, and Nina resisted the impulse to turn
and spoil her pose. "Would you care to see the result?"

"Of course."

Setting aside his charcoal, he hurried toward her,
sketchbook outstretched. "I think you will be pleased
also, milord."

Gray only inclined his head, but Nina recognized
the hope alight in his expression, knew how much he
wanted this event to raise her spirits. And reaching for
the book, she vowed to adore whatever image greeted
her, to express pleasure and extol the master's talents.

But in his zeal, Master Verbrugges didn't quite bridge
the distance. The sketchbook bumped her hand, then fell
from her grasp, skating clumsily over the sweep of her
skirt toward the floor. Instinct brought Nina forward to
catch the book just as the master did . . .

Their fingers brushed, only a glancing stroke, but the
sensation crashed as a fist. No matter how she tried to
brace herself for what she knew forthcoming, Nina was
always surprised by the first blow of that iron fist, the

feeling that she reeled precariously whether or not she sat or stood, the slam in her chest that stole her breath.

Mattered not whether a touch was hard or soft.

Mattered not whether contact lasted a second or an hour.

With each touch the scene played out until the end.

Whoosh.

There was no other description for the rush of visions that hammered at her as gale winds might buffet her from all sides. Haunting images . . .

A beautiful, black-haired woman who sat inside a studio much like this one, her face turned toward the master as he had been in his youth, the woman smiling a smile meant to entice and the master giving way to the rise of desire.

"Follow your heart," Nina urged. " 'Tis always true . . ."

The master in his prime clinging to a young frail boy as he loosed his grip on life, the master's despair, so real his anguish brought tears.

"Grieve for your son, but don't give into despair . . ."

A painting, the canvas filled with thick dots of brightly hued paint, oddly changing the harder she tried to make out shapes that wouldn't come into focus, and the master older, staring into the painting, his longing for what was inside tangible. Heartrending.

"Wait, wait, bide each moment, resist the longing or lose the chance to atone . . ."

The visions were pivotal choices Master Verbrugges would make over the course of his life, choices that would lead to his salvation or condemnation at the moment of his death.

Nina saw that, too, a startling image.

He lay upon a bed, his talented hands withered upon a

faded coverlet. His face old, skin parched, gaze bright with fever, his chest rising and falling in broken rhythm beneath the coverlet.

For an instant she sensed his acceptance, a feeling of inevitability and peace that swept away all else. . . . Then death came, and with it the battle for his soul.

The clawing blackness, a blast furnace of evil.

The light as terrible in its own way. Ruthless, all-powerful, so brilliant it burned.

Shadows so raw the darkness ached as it warred with the blinding radiance to claim a soul that passed from this life.

Nina witnessed this passage to eternity from within the battle, shocked by the violence of other-worldly forces fighting for dominion. The visions of the master's life scalded her, revealing whether the choices he'd made through his lifetime would leave his soul strong or vulnerable in these first moments of death.

Nina could see the result . . . *always.*

Luminous light would surround the master's soul, fill it with a glorious serenity, or evil would sink malevolent claws deep enough to drag him into the black abyss.

Time fell away. Nina knew naught whether an instant or eternity passed as the dreaded knowledge of the battle beat at her from all sides until she was left gasping and aching, filled with the knowledge of choices that shouldn't be made, of paths that shouldn't be taken.

And with only the slightest effort, she urged the master toward the choices that would turn him away from the darkness and closer to the light.

Soul whispers.

She breathed encouraging words and precious guidance that would steer his soul toward salvation until his end, and while she could not change his past, she could remind him to atone in his present and help him stand firm in his future.

Her blessing. Her curse.

CHAPTER 2

White light. Peace.

Salvation, if the master would but stay his course.

Then a beloved voice whispered through the edges of her awareness, beckoning. "Nina. My dear, Nina."

Strong arms held her close, and the ambrosia of familiar male and spiced cologne seeped through her senses. Nina clung to Gray, feeling so utterly drained yet frantic with the need to speak, to reveal what she'd seen.

She had whispered to the master's soul, but 'twasn't enough. Not nearly enough. She must caution him, too, warn him where the pitfalls lay . . . a compulsion so strong that her mouth moved without consent, breathless gasps that slipped through no matter how hard she fought to stop them.

The battle had robbed her strength. Her fight was weak.

Because Nina knew, oh, how well she knew how fragile the promise of salvation could be.

Choices made over a lifetime swept a soul closer to salvation, then farther away again; an ebb and flow. Ceaseless. Unrelenting. Evil remained on perpetual guard for souls that slipped toward temptation.

The string of choices made over a lifetime was as delicate as pearls threaded on gossamer strands. Sometimes those choices would be monumental, requiring deliberation and heart searching. But all too often those choices would be subtle, naught but murmurs, quickly made with little thought, yet they could be cunning as they led a soul along the winding paths of morality.

Nina could urge the master toward the light, but only he possessed the ability to stay the course. Free will—another blessing and curse. But he stood a fair chance if she but warned him of the snares ahead . . .

Biting her lips, she buried herself in Gray's arms, the only arms that had ever held her without a backlash of revelation, an anchor as she resisted the wild urge to reveal all she'd seen.

Exposing herself, and Gray, to condemnation again.

Blessed slumber overtook Nina as was its wont after a touch, but soon she found her way back to consciousness again, forced her eyes to open, to focus, to remember.

Master Verbrugges' studio.

Her portrait.

The irony of Gray hoping to raise her spirits when he knew how truly beyond hope she was.

She stared into what appeared to be a guest chamber with shutters drawn to block the light. She sensed Gray's presence, wondered what he'd told the master about her episode.

Nina supposed she should feel grateful. The deaths she witnessed weren't always so peaceful. Often, they overwhelmed her with despair or shocked her by their brutality.

Yet how could she feel grateful? Watching the deaths of those she touched was a burden—not the knowing, for death came to all. But knowing that her nudges and revelations still didn't guarantee salvation to those who refused to listen, or believe.

Those people strong enough to take charge of their fates might think her blessed, but those who feared her message invariably believed her cursed.

And no one understood.

Least of all Nina. In eight and ten years, she had yet to divine the purpose of her ability. For the small measure of good she had wrought, she'd been condemned to a much greater degree, dragged into a maelstrom of self-doubt, and made an outcast.

Shoving aside the wave of self-pity that did her no credit, she sought out Gray and found him sitting across the room, watching her. "I don't imagine you wanted a painting of me on your gallery wall in full swoon."

He didn't smile, and she so desperately needed him to. She wanted to ease his mood and the worry that shaped his handsome features into such a solemn mask.

This man had borne too much heartache for one life, losing sweet Juliette and their newborn son, bearing the burden of her guardianship, a woman with no life or future. Instead of gratitude she heaped more grief upon his head.

Yet Gray wanted to save her, looked helpless that he'd failed again. And in that moment, despite Nina's avowals not to give in to despair, tears swelled inside.

"I am sorry."

Suddenly the mattress sank beneath his weight, and he was close, oh so close, *almost* touching when she so much wanted to feel his arms around her again. "My dear, you are the one who wants to conceal your gift. If there is blame 'tis mine, for forcing you to sit for a portrait."

Nina shook her head, the yearning to feel his touch a tangible ache, almost unbearable.

She was guilty, and of far greater sins than Gray knew. She wanted to feel his touch so much that she lay awake in her dark bed, yearning in a way that did him such dishonor.

"You take too much upon yourself." The truth shamed her. "'Twas a well-meaning gesture. You wanted to gift me with a reason for leaving the manor."

"I should know better than to force you."

His words were about much more than a portrait, Nina knew. "'Tis not your fault I had to leave London."

"I encouraged you to use your gifts. I did not heed warnings that your aunt and her Anglican friends were growing threatened. I subjected you to their judgment and cruelty."

"You only meant for me to bring good with my . . ." The word *curse* sprang to her lips, but she bit her tongue. Such bitterness would only fire a barb. "You are not to blame. Indeed, I am always grateful for how you worry about me. You are my guardian angel, a living one whom I can see and hear."

Her words were a fanciful truth she'd spoken before, but they had the desired effect. Gray relaxed.

"Do not take so much upon yourself," she said. "You've already given up your birthright and position to devote yourself to harboring me."

"I haven't given up anything you haven't."

"I appreciate the sentiment, but that's not true and you know it. I may have a title and rank, but my very existence isolates me from people. I had no life. You did."

His dark eyes smoldered. "Enough of guilt and blame. We agreed to start a new life for both of us. Let's look to the future and the peace we can find in this new place."

Unable to resist her need, Nina slid her hand into Gray's, felt his strong fingers close around hers.

His skin was warm, his pulse solid and steady. She finally knew gratitude for a physical connection that felt so solid in a world bereft of small touches, *her* world, such a barren one.

Lifting her gaze, she met dark eyes so filled with knowing. Gray knew how even his simplest touch was a kindness, yet he had the grace to be humbled by his power.

"What did you tell the master?" she asked.

He patted her hand reassuringly. "He seems a kind sort. I don't think he'll dispute a young lady in a swoon."

But Gray knew as well as Nina that she'd done more than swoon, and if the master carried the tale into the village then speculation would begin, the whispers.

"Do not worry yourself, my dear. We have weathered far worse."

Now there was a truth. Still, when Gray helped her rise from the bed then withdrew his hand, Nina had to resist the urge to hang on, to cling to him and the belief all would be well.

She whispered a silent prayer for strength as he led her from the chamber, but Master Verbrugges seemed genuine enough when he greeted them and asked after her health.

"I am well," she assured him, though she felt anything but.

"Lady Kirkby must rest," Gray added. "I'm unsure when we'll return. You will receive recompense for your time, of course."

"I have done nothing—"

"Your sketch."

The master waved a dismissive hand. " 'Twas a pleasure with such a lovely subject. I shall send the drawing to your home to make a birthday gift for the lady. But I beg you grant me one favor before you go."

She knew Gray would grant the master this favor rather than risk offense, especially after the man so generously gifted her with the sketch. She wondered if the master had counted on that reaction when he'd made the gift.

"What can we do for you?" Gray asked.

"I should like your opinion on a painting."

"Come, my dear." Gray took Nina's hand and said to the master, "Lead the way."

They were escorted into a gallery, a chamber rich with dark wooden beams where Nina was surprised to find paintings by many artists. Brilliant landscapes in vastly different lightings and textures. Portraits. Faces, busts, and even a full-length of the black-haired woman from Nina's vision. On the canvas, the woman didn't look enticing but triumphant, her expression reigning over the art in the chamber.

" 'Tis my private gallery," Master Verbrugges explained. "Paintings I admire and various techniques I study."

"Which painting did you want our opinion on?" Gray prompted, and Nina sensed his impatience to leave.

"Over here." He gestured to a turret in the south end " 'Midnight Magic'—'tis a very special painting."

"Special, how so?" Nina seized the opportunity to cast herself in a favorable light, to alleviate any lingering questions about her health.

" 'Tis a painting with a purpose, one that requires a certain amount of . . . care."

Gray's gaze narrowed. "What sort of purpose and care?"

"Nothing sinister, milord. Come, see for yourselves." He led them across the gallery.

The painting from her vision.

The canvas didn't depict a particular subject at first glance, but as Nina stared . . . the brilliant dots of thick oil paint blended and smeared until all Nina could see were bright slashes of color.

She gazed up at Gray, who seemed as taken by the painting as she, and even in profile, she could read the confusion on his face, sense him trying to understand the trick of the technique that made shapes out of random splotches.

"Look closely," Master Verbrugges urged.

As Nina turned back, those splotches came into focus, much as the visions in her mind formed whenever she touched a person. One minute she stared through a mist, then hazy edges faded and an image appeared . . .

A man.

High cheekbones. Full sensual lips. Chiseled jaw. Strikingly male. Deep auburn hair flowed behind his shoulders. His skin was fair. His deep-set eyes dark as a moonless night.

She had no hint who this man might be but recognized his expression, a look she saw often enough on Gray's face. Nina could never mistake *grim* while staring at it.

There were hard lines around the man's mouth that

contrasted dramatically with the silk sheen of his hair. Hairs prickled at the back of her neck at the sudden urge to smooth away those hard lines, to feel his lips curve in a smile.

Suddenly Nina's own pulse throbbed softly in her ears. "Who is he?"

"You see a man?" Master Verbrugges asked. "What do you see, milord?"

Such an odd question. What else would they see but the subject of the portrait?

"A man with red hair," Gray said.

"So you both see the same image? Interesting."

Gray scowled. "What trick is this?"

Master Verbrugges gave them a thoughtful smile and spread his arms in entreaty. "No trick, milord. I assure you. I told you that 'Midnight Magic' is different. There is no painting in the world like it. Legend claims the artist was discontented with his life, so he used magical paint to create a doorway to a place where he could be happy. 'Tis said when he finished the painting, he traveled into the universe he'd created on this canvas, and never returned to our world."

Gray's grip on her arm tightened, but Nina couldn't tear her gaze from the painting, sensing the intensity of the man's deep-set eyes, wondering what his voice would sound like. As hard-edged as his mouth? As silky as his hair?

"Is he real?"

"Indeed he is." Master Verbrugges looked thoughtful. "My former apprentice. A lad of a most rare talent. But he is not inside the painting, though he could be if he chose."

Nina could feel Gray stiffen beside her and knew full well he likely thought this painting a portal to the netherworld, or some other such Satan's lure. "What madness do you speak?"

"No madness, I assure you. 'Midnight Magic' offers second chances. Not for everyone, mind. Only those who can see the secret. I am the custodian. A very great responsibility."

Second chances? Is that what she'd seen the master doing in her vision? She needed to know. How was it possible to give away something so precious?

"Why are you showing us?" she asked. "Do you believe we have a need?"

Gray tightened his grip in warning, and for a startled moment, Nina thought he would drag her from the gallery.

The master shifted his gaze between them, as if taking their measure. Gray returned his gaze with a stony one.

"The man you see in the painting could also see inside 'Midnight Magic,' " the master explained. "I asked him to sketch what he saw. May I show you what he drew for me?"

"Please," Nina said, both demand and plea.

Master Verbrugges motioned back to the door. Gray didn't argue when she hastened across the gallery and back to the studio, where the master hurried to an oak armoire. Pulling open the doors, he revealed a haphazard array of gem-hued jars, glasses filled with paintbrushes and scraps of parchment and canvas of all shapes and sizes.

He searched through the shelves, brushing aside jars and pulling out rolled parchments only to shove them back impatiently when they proved not to be what he sought. Her own anticipation mounted apace. Gray's, too; she felt the muscles in his forearm tense with each agitated exclamation that emerged from the bowels of that armoire.

"Trust me. I touched this man," she whispered, knowing Gray would understand what that meant.

"Ah! Here we are." The master finally emerged, brandishing a half-rolled parchment as if waving a wand.

He was so clearly excited that Nina held her breath as he unrolled the parchment. His gaze caressed the sketch before he turned to them so they could see the bold charcoal lines that depicted two faces . . . a woman and a man.

The faces were drawn with strong, skilled strokes, the details unnaturally precise, smudged lines that conveyed such intense emotion.

The woman's face was the focus, and her whole expression yearned. Not the desire of one eager for a prize, but of one who knew she would never have what she wanted, as if the realization poised her precariously on the brink of despair.

The man's face loomed behind, his hand resting on her shoulder. His expression was that of a stalwart guardian, possessive, but there was something else, too . . . an unfulfilled desire that seemed to match the woman's.

There was an odd symmetry to the drawing, though, as if the space above her left shoulder remained curiously bare.

Gray appeared rooted to the spot, and when he didn't rally to comment, Nina struggled to find her voice. "Your apprentice looked into the painting, and saw *us*?"

"Remarkable that you should find your way here, don't you think?" Master Verbrugges asked. "I recognized you instantly. But forgive me. I thought we would have more time together for me to explain, to help you understand. But you see now why you needed to gaze upon 'Midnight Magic.'"

Nina could not seem to grab a hold of the feelings spiraling through her as she stared at the sketch, the shock and disbelief as she tried to comprehend the implications.

"Understand what?" she asked.

"Why you must meet Damian, of course."

That shook Gray from his daze. "That man is here? In Maryland?"

"Surely you have heard of Hart Hill. Damian is the youngest son in a family of shipwrights." The master fixed his gaze on the parchment. "Such an incredible talent. Alas, Damian did not get a fair chance to display his abilities. Despite his birth in Scotland, his colonial up-bringing was held against him. 'Tis an unfortunate bias that stains perception of more than our artists, I fear."

Remembering her earlier comments about civiliza-tion, Nina felt a flush warm her cheeks. She, more than most, should have understood the ill effects of bias.

"What does this man do now?" Gray asked.

"He works with his family building ships."

Damian Hart's face seemed etched in Nina's mind, his expression carved in stony lines. Building ships when he was clearly a talented artist. She understood disappointment and broken dreams.

"He saw us inside the painting," she said. "Does that mean he's a part of our second chance?"

Gray's fingers curled over hers, squeezed another warning. But Nina barely spared him a glance, curios-ity burning.

"'Twould seem. I beg you to meet Damian and find out."

"How can a painting give second chances," Gray de-manded sharply. "Are you suggesting we can somehow travel *inside* as you claim the artist of legend did? 'Tis madness you speak, man."

"I have seen many go through during my years as custodian, milord. Some go instantly. Others take time to decide. Yet always in the end the opportunity for a second chance wins out. 'Tis a wonderful gift."

Nina thought Gray would bolt then, polite behavior be damned. Master Verbrugges must have recognized it, as well, for he quickly said, "I cannot say why Damian sketched your faces, nor can I say why you see him inside 'Midnight Magic,' but clearly your fates are entwined. Pray meet the man. I'll not caution him of what you've seen. Decide for yourself."

"Enough," Gray barked. "'Tis naught but evil, and we will play no part."

Master Verbrugges stared at them, mouth drawn into a tight line. Then he said, "I know not what ails milady, but she fell into a swoon at the touch of my hand."

Nina winced, though the master entreated his words in a tone not meant to threaten, only beseech their co-operation with an almost regretted appeal.

"I beg you, visit Damian." He continued. 'Tis all I ask. Whatever comes of the meeting, you have my word I'll not mention 'Midnight Magic' or anything that took place here today."

'Twas hardly an offer Gray could refuse.

"Have you considered this painting could be God-given, Gray?" Nina asked him on their return home in the coach. "Think on it. You claim my ability is, yet there are many who condemn me for a witch. A second chance would be a generous gift."

"More likely Satan's temptation." He scoffed. "I've read naught of disappearing inside paintings in any Bible verse, but I have read much of healing the spirit. Our Lord forgives unreservedly. We have no need for second chances."

Nina wanted to argue the point. *She* needed a second chance to start life over again, a life where she might laugh and love, a life that was more than hiding.

Or yearning for the feel of a simple caress.

What would a life of touch be like? A life where she shared the interests of normal maids her age, of endless nights of parties, of dances and flirtations . . . of knowing what 'twould be to kiss a man, to *touch* one, to indulge those forbidden desires that awakened her in the darkness?

"I touched Master Verbrugges and felt no horns," she said. "I saw 'Midnight Magic' in my vision. What he accomplishes with that painting is on his path to salvation. I urged him in that direction. 'Twas right. You know I would never deceive you."

Gray scowled harder.

"How else can we explain Damian Hart's sketch?" she asked. "Those were our faces. How could he draw our likenesses when we have never met him? Before we ever came to Maryland."

How could she be so consumed by the mere sight of a man? 'Twasn't a question she would ask of Gray, who turned to stare out the coach window, clearly troubled.

But Nina wanted to know, *had* to know.

"We came to the colonies to start a new life." She tried to keep the urgency from her voice. "How can we possibly ignore what we've seen in that painting?"

Finally, Gray turned back around. "You are right. We have come here to start a new life, yet we seem to be at odds on how best to do that. You refuse to use your gift, which leaves you hiding yourself from people."

'Twas only with effort she held his gaze. "I pray to have your faith. I pray to see the meager good I accomplish through your eyes. But the simple fact is I do not. I can whisper to a soul and nudge it toward salvation, yet 'tis only a *nudge* against a lifetime of temptation. Every one of us must travel our own path. That leaves a soul far too much time to stray."

"Sometimes a nudge can make all the difference, my dear. Think of those who will hear your whispers through their lives when they are poised on the brink of faith or despair, or facing a choice between good and evil. If they hear your voice and you can help even one, shouldn't you try?"

His words shamed her, with her own selfishness and despair, with her own desire to place her needs against those of countless, nameless others.

Why could she not be as Gray, whose faith stood unwavering under the harshest of trials? He might fall, but he always managed to rise again. 'Twas during those times, he claimed, his faith carried him.

"Those few I help seem of little consequence against those I hurt in the process. You have no life because of me, and look at what your family has suffered. They have lost you."

"They have not lost me." He scoffed. "I receive correspondence on nearly every ship that sails into the harbor. Look at what they have gained. You brought my sister back to us when she had strayed. You helped ease Juliette's passing."

The admission clearly pained him, and she quickly leaned forward, took his hand.

"I am sorry. I did not mean to bring up such dark memories, yet I cannot ignore mine. What of my parents?"

"They died at the hand of zealots. You are not to blame."

"Those zealots believed I was Satan's spawn. My own aunt can't even stand to look upon me." Now Nina peered out the window, unable to meet his gaze as she admitted the worst truth of all. "Is it so wrong to want to live a normal life?"

She heard him move, suddenly felt his warm hand on her shoulder as he stared out the coach window.

"No, my dear. 'Tis not wrong to want."

Nina lifted her gaze, focused through her tears. "Then I want to meet him, Gray. I want to understand 'Midnight Magic' and how this stranger fits in."

She wanted a second chance.

An audience with the mysterious Damian Hart would have required more explanation than her guardian cared to give, so Gray insisted upon taking Nina to the Eastern Shore where Hart Shipwrights plied its trade. Under the pretense of inquiring about a vessel, they would make the man's acquaintance and see what came of a meeting with no mention of "Midnight Magic."

Nina agreed to his terms.

Upon their return yesterday, Gray had made inquiries into the Hart family then retired to the chapel, where he'd spent his night in prayer. She hadn't slept either. Visions of Damian Hart and imaginings of a painting that granted second chances warred with her own attempts at sleep, at prayer, at making any rational sense of her anticipation for what lay ahead.

The morning had dawned bright and clear, and Nina stared through the coach window into the sharp blue of the sky, noting how the clouds appeared crisp and sturdy, as if possessing substance enough to cradle her unspoken hope within their grasp.

She could smell the sea on the air as the coach clambered along the riverbank toward the shore, her tension mounting with each mile they traveled, the quiet heavier for the steady clip-clop of hooves over the dirt lane that marked their way.

Gray sat silent and sour of expression, and her own eagerness proved an unseemly contrast to his grim mood. Yet not even his disapproval could dull her eagerness when the shore came into view. The ocean backed up into the river valley and the result was a sweeping shoreline littered with docks and vessels in the haphazard display that made up Hart Shipwrights.

Hart Hill loomed in the distance, aptly named as the bay's shoreline was an otherwise even place, save for this hill where a stone house perched, a sentinel. The coach stopped and Nina disembarked, the wind snatching at her skirts, alive with that unique taste of fresh water mingled with salt sea.

Gray didn't get a chance to inquire about the whereabouts of the shipwright. The workers appeared well-versed in spotting potential business and directing such to the office of the man who reigned over this small kingdom.

Murray Hart.

The man himself looked as seafaring as the vessels he built. Tall and craggy, he walked with a sinewy strength that suggested he spent as much of his time testing the seaworthiness of those vessels as he did building them.

He sported a head full of waving gray hair streaked with a fading red, and if the color had not provided a hint to his ancestry then his brogue left no question. He greeted them with an introduction. "Milord, milady, what can I do for ye?"

"We understand you have a shipwright who creates custom designs." Gray provided the information he'd learned.

"Aye, me son Damian. What are ye looking for?"

They fell into talk of boats while Nina stared through the office's unshuttered facade, which allowed a clear view of the yard. She skimmed her gaze over shipwrights working on various stages of hulls and beams and riggings, over a lumber yard that hurled smoke into the clear morning and tinged her breaths with the scent of burning sap.

The bay ruffled with a strong sea wind, and in the distance, she could see a vessel with dual sails unfurled, skimming across the surface with a speed that matched her rushing thoughts. She couldn't help but wonder what 'twould feel like to chance the winds at breakneck speed, to outrun destiny.

If outrunning destiny were even possible. Before her trip into Master Verbrugges' gallery, she wouldn't have believed such a thing possible, but now . . .

"Damian's out with one of his customs now," Murray Hart said. "If ye'll set up a time—"

"'Tis unnecessary." Gray motioned to the door. "We'll just have a stroll along the shore and take a look at some of your work while we wait for him to return, if you don't mind."

The man motioned them toward the south end of the yard. "He'll bring her in there, if ye've a ken to stroll that way."

Gray led Nina from the office, and they walked along arm in arm, viewing the workings of this shipyard firsthand. They moved past the mill works to a place where long piers reached out into the water like spindled fingers. Some sat empty, while vessels of various sizes rode at anchor beside others. From this vantage, Nina got a better glimpse of the dual-sailed boat that cut swiftly across the swells.

This vessel was somewhere between the size of a bateau and a ship's boat, and there was no mistaking the man sailing her. Nina watched him prowl over the deck with limber grace, his motions sure and brisk as he trimmed sails, cut across the swells, and sliced over the waves, bow rising and falling sharply, water fuming in his wake.

Nina sensed defiance about the swath he cut through the morning, as if he rode those waves daring the wind to fail him. 'Twas only an impression—indeed, she could make out no true details of the man at this distance—or mayhap 'twas her own sense of confinement that etched itself upon him.

But watching him ride those waves, the sense of freedom, as if he did outrun destiny. . . .

She had no idea how much time had passed until Damian Hart finally steered his vessel toward the peer, but Gray edged closer, setting himself firmly in the wake of her whipping skirts, the gesture protective, familiar. Her last line of defense against any who might try to touch her.

Her pulse thudded in her ears, thick against the sounds of the wind as the vessel neared.

Damian Hart's face was now tanned by the sun. He wore his hair long, fashioned back in a queue that didn't contain the wild thickness, somehow as bold as the man himself. Lengthy strands whipped out behind him, shockingly bright tendrils in the glare of the sun.

He'd tossed off his waistcoat and shoes to sail, and while his dark breeches fell below his knee, without the benefit of a coat, the shape of his long legs was clearly evident.

Wind sliced down his unbuttoned collar, lifting the white shirt in the same manner as his sails. The parting fabric allowed Nina to make out the tanned lines of a muscled chest, the smattering of bright curls nestled within firm ridges.

"Unfit to meet with a lady," Gray muttered.

" 'Twas you who refused to request an audience," she reminded him, surprised at such criticism from a man who managed to find so much good in everyone. Even her.

Though she had to admit Gray made a point. Although she'd resided in his home for nigh on six years, she had never seen him in such dishabille. Gazing upon Damian Hart suddenly seemed as if they were intruding upon his privacy. A blush warmed her cheeks and she avoided looking at Gray, who was scowling.

Nina recognized the moment Damian Hart drew close enough to recognize his visitors. His body, so clean of line to be almost angular, went stock still. He might have seen them ashore, but he hadn't recognized their faces until that very instant.

He did not call out in greeting, nor did he wave, he only stared at them, as if he'd expected to see them one day and neither the time nor the place was of much import.

Nina felt speared on the edge of his dark gaze, a sensation as sensual as she imagined a hand might caress her bare skin. Her skin tingled with each brush of her skirts against her legs, of the wind caressing her cheeks. That wild trembling inside grew until she felt wound so tight she might burst.

She stood beside Gray as each moment stretched. Damian Hart moored his vessel and stepped onto the pier. His motions were whipcord strong and all contained energy, and only as he approached did Nina feel the full effects of his black eyes.

She stood rooted to the spot, amazed by the heightened awareness that made her heart race in her chest, each breath a strain, and when his striking gaze pored over them as if measuring their likeness against that in memory, or mayhap against the sketch he'd drawn, Nina's mouth went dust dry.

'Twas almost impossible to make his expression—his eyes were so black she could barely discern pupils.

Gray introduced himself and only after stating his purported business and clearly establishing that Damian Hart would be dealing directly with him did her protective guardian finally extend the courtesy to her. "This is my ward, Nina de Lacy, Lady of Kirkby."

She curtsied, though her limbs suddenly felt unsteady, and she was glad for Gray's solid presence as he stepped in to shield her from any attempt at polite contact.

"Lady Nina." The Highland lilt of Damian Hart's voice made her name fall from his lips as a caress. *Nee-nah.*

Neither she nor Gray could have foreseen this man's reaction to meeting his vision from "Midnight Magic". . . . He forcefully avoided Gray and grabbed Nina's hand.

Damian had no intention of being denied access to the woman from "Midnight Magic." Not even by this man. Not when Nina de Lacy stared up at him as though she'd waited forever to see him. Not when his own body responded in a way that reminded him he was a living, breathing man.

He might not yet understand who Lord Westbury and his ward were in the landscape of life, but Damian fully intended to find out. He'd always known they would cross paths, and while time's passage had forced that knowledge to retreat beneath the weight of more immediate concerns, he'd still known to expect them.

Nina was younger than he'd envisioned, much lovelier with surprise written all over her beautiful features than the longing she'd worn in "Midnight Magic." Her unusual amber eyes were round and wide as she stared up at him, full lips parted in a perfectly angelic *O*.

But when he touched her, she recoiled, swaying on her feet as though she might swoon.

"Milady?" he said, hanging on tighter lest he be forced to catch her.

Her hand stiffened inside his, though her skin felt as warm satin, even more tempting, and his own breath halted in his throat as the moment stilled to a crawl.

Damian could barely hear Westbury yell or feel the chill spray that suddenly moistened the air. He couldn't name what was happening except he knew something was.

Westbury lunged toward him in a move that made Damian brace to defend himself, and the lovely Nina held herself poised as if expecting the sky to crash down upon all their heads.

Then, the moment passed and everyone stood frozen, himself included, although he could not explain why. The seconds ticked by, marked only when Lady Nina's fingers finally relaxed within his. Their gazes held steady until both dared to breathe again.

Westbury, however, stood in stunned tableau, seized by some fit of incredulity that left Damian free to enjoy the feel of Nina's hand, to savor satiny fingertips against his own.

She peered up at him from beneath gold-flecked

lashes, and he read shock and wariness in her gaze, though he couldn't think of anything he'd done to warrant such a response.

Then a blush crawled into her cheeks, tinting her creamy skin in shades of sunrise.

Westbury, too, must have noticed her reaction, because he snapped out of his daze and growled, "Unhand the lady, Hart."

But Damian didn't let go. He held on when she tried to pull away, though the possession in Westbury's voice brooked no refusal. Damian could well understand.

Nina was an exquisite beauty.

Though dressed in the height of fashion for a proper miss, no unwieldy hoops could hide the fact that this maid was sleek of curve and long of leg. Just shy of tall and slender with lovely full breasts.

A few honey-hued curls had escaped the constraints of her mobcap to frame cheeks of lustrous hue, and Damian was struck by the urge to pull away the frilly cap and see her hair unbound, to arrange it around her face to frame her likeness.

He wanted to paint her. 'Twas a shocking claim, for the impulse to paint had not been his forever. His art had gone the way of his youth, his dreams, and the future he had once believed could be his.

Now he lived life as he'd sworn to live, free of the grand delusions that consumed him inside his studio, free of anything that resembled inspiration to infuse his soul with a fresh breath. He spent his creativity in hard labor in the shipyard that allowed him to fall into an exhausted and mercifully dreamless sleep each night.

He lived the life that contented his father and brothers and tried not to let the monotony of his days claim his sanity.

But Nina de Lacy. . . . Just gazing upon her loveliness breathed life into the dead places inside him. He wanted to capture her likeness, not as he'd done from the image in "Midnight Magic," but *this* woman. The woman who made his blood simmer in his veins. The woman who made him breach propriety for a simple touch of her hand.

He wanted to capture the nuances of her expression, the curiosity he saw glittering in her amber eyes, the hint of color riding high in her cheeks.

"Take your hand from my ward, Master Hart." Westbury shouldered him hard enough to unbalance Damian.

Nina pulled her hand from his grasp, and he turned to meet Westbury's gaze on equal ground because finally, *finally* Damian had a clue to the mystery of his second chance.

This exquisite young lady was his muse.

A missive from Hart Hill arrived the following day. The courier presented the letter while Nina worked in the office, filing correspondence. As Gray met with a client, she was forced to wait until he concluded his business before learning the contents of the sealed letter.

By the time he emerged, she found herself hard-pressed to keep from rushing to his side as he read:

Lord Westbury,
I have spoken with Master Verbrugges, who explained the arrangement regarding your ward's portrait. As he also informed me he would be unable to honor the arrangement, I am offering my services under the agreed-upon terms.
Damian Hart

"Hart wasted no time before running to his old master," Gray said. "I wonder if Verbrugges kept his word."

"Whatever your concerns about 'Midnight Magic,' I sensed no evil in the master. Nor am I surprised his former apprentice went to visit. Given his drawing of us . . ."

"'Twould seem Master Verbrugges was right that our fates are somehow entwined." Gray shook his head as though he still couldn't quite believe that fact. "Yet we know naught of this Damian Hart."

"We know of his family and his career. We know that he is a talented artist despite his ill fortune."

"We know naught of the man's character."

Nina watched Gray from across the reception desk, recognizing another sleepless night etched across his face, in the faint droop of his shoulders. Her stalwart guardian. What had he ever done to merit this thankless task of guarding her?

"What shall we do, Gray?"

She could not even bring herself to speak Damian Hart's name. Just this thought of him conjured the feel of his large, rough hand holding hers, a feeling that stirred her in places she dared not acknowledge.

Gray leaned heavily against the doorjamb, frowning. "I would shield you from this painting and the man depicted on the canvas, but we cannot ignore the facts. You can touch this man as you can no other, save me."

Nina waited, her own tension rising unbearably as she sensed his uncertainty. There were so many questions to answer.

Was Damian Hart her salvation or her damnation?

Would Gray deny her the chance to find out?

"I only wanted to see your beautiful face inside the gallery." He thrust a hand through his hair, looking fraught that this situation had grown so far beyond his control.

Nina, too, felt the weight of guilt for her changing opinion about a gift he'd so genuinely wanted to bestow upon her. A mere day before, she'd been ungrateful.

Today, she wanted his gift more than her next breath.

She should have released Gray from his promise, insisted they shouldn't pursue the situation. He didn't want to expose her to Damian Hart, no matter how fair he'd vowed to be.

But as she stared across the desk at this man who had come to mean everything to her, until a day ago the only man she had ever been able to touch, Nina could not bring herself to speak. She could only stare helplessly at him, her desire reflected in the resignation on his face.

And Gray, dear Gray, would oblige her as he did in all things.

"Then, my dear, I promised you a portrait for your birthday."

Damian heard the heavy footsteps climbing the stairs that led to his corner room studio and inhaled a heavy sigh at the confrontation on its way. He'd known from the moment he'd set the servants to cleaning the layers of dust from this chamber that word would reach his father's ears, and when it did . . .

"Damian, are ye up there, lad?" his father called out.

"I am."

Murray Hart appeared in the doorway, his whole body contained with the effort of appearing calm when he undoubtedly wanted to scream bloody hell to the rafters for being forced to climb three flights on bad knees to find his youngest son.

"What's this I hear about ye not heading to the yard this morn? Are ye ill?"

"Nay. I accepted a commission."

His father stared from beneath thick brows, disappointment in his eyes, but to his credit, he didn't explode. *Yet.* "What is this? I thought we had done with this foolishness."

In only a few words, what had once been Damian's very lifeblood was reduced to the whim of a squandered life, a path devoid of any value. A mistake.

" 'Tis only a portrait—"

"One will lead to two. Painting is an addiction with ye. Being up here all the day with yer head in the clouds . . . ye need to be outdoors, breathing the fresh air to clear yer mind."

"I am only taking the mornings to paint a lady's portrait. Master Verbrugges is unable to see to the task himself."

"We need ye in the yard. What about yer customs?"

"I'll fill my orders. You have my word. And Gordon and Blair have more than enough help to handle things if I'm gone for a few hours a day."

"Yer right there. Yer brothers have had years to handle the business without any help. We had an arrangement."

"I'm honoring it. I failed to establish myself in Europe as an artist, so I'm home to work for you. But think, Da, I've taken no free time since my return. 'Tis well over a year."

His father wanted to argue. Indeed, Damian could see a vein pulsing so violently he expected a rupture and flowing blood. But to his father's credit, he sucked in a hard breath and managed concern instead of a rebuke.

"I worry about ye, lad. Ye're restless. Ye drink too much. Ye whore in places ye shouldn't be whoring."

"Since when do you listen to alehouse gossip?"

"Alehouse gossip? Me own men have been spilling tales of yer carryings-on with the Leicesters. Both the lady *and* her husband."

"Did they also spill tales of the generous commission those carryings-on yielded your shipyard?"

"No son of mine need whore for my trade," his father roared. "How dare ye suggest it."

"I didn't. If 'twould make you rest any easier, then know I would have involved myself with the Leicesters with or without their commission. They're a nice couple."

His father stared at him as if he'd grown a second head. Damian didn't bother defending himself. He had no defense. How could he defend his need to venture forth into dark places, where only the perverse had any power to thrill him, to make him feel anything at all?

He'd grabbed at the feeling with both hands. Simple.

His father fisted his fingers, the show of greatest restraint. "Ye're nearly a score and ten. At yer age, both yer brothers had wives and wee ones to settle them down."

"So having me work in the shipyard isn't enough? Now you would tell me when to wed and bed a wife, too?"

"Do nae twist my words," Da snapped. "I only want ye to be happy. 'Tis what yer mother wanted above all else."

There it was—the truth. Another simple one. When his father had wanted Damian to follow along in his brothers' footsteps and work at the shipyard, he had honored his wife's request to allow their youngest son to pursue his art talent with costly tutors, even though Murray Hart didn't see the merit of learning anything that didn't serve a purpose.

To his way of thinking, painting served none.

His youngest son might have once created art with his hands, but seeing the beauty inside a painting couldn't compete with building a ship that could carry people across an ocean.

Damian didn't try to press his father to any other view. Once, he'd have argued the point until his own veins had threatened to burst. Now, he had no heart left for the fight. Where that heart had once been was only bitterness and resentment for a truth that made him a failure.

He had been cursed by the need to create. Would that he had been born normal as his older brothers, that he could work the shipyard and be content with the work his hands wrought.

Alas the routine was crushing his spirit no matter how hard he tried to make peace with his fate.

Until now . . . until Nina. She was a reprieve from the torture that ate away at his soul. His second chance.

For shelter from the storm that raged inside him?

Or for a chance at the future that should have been his?

"I haven't forgotten our arrangement, Da. I won't let my custom orders run late, but I will paint this portrait."

His father didn't seem to have much fight left, or any inclination to hide his disappointment and disapproval of his youngest son's choices. "Don't let this lust see ye to a bad end, lad. Make peace with yer life. 'Tis short enough as ye well know."

Suddenly, his mother might have been standing in

the room between them, her lilting laughter swelling in the silence, making father and son understand each other, making everything right with her smile.

Damian found no words to reassure. How could he explain his restlessness, his discontent? How could he admit the work his father and brothers esteemed above all else felt like naught but an endless waste of his time?

His father only shook his head and left. Damian watched him disappear down the stairs, suddenly seeing the age on his father and wishing he might have said the right thing. Just once.

Damian was still staring down those stairs when the housemaid called up his guests.

Shaking off his mood, he retreated to the far end of his studio as much to protect himself as to provide the best vantage of the door. He couldn't be sure of Westbury's reception as the lord's acceptance missive had been terse, implying that Nina had been the one to desire Damian's services while Westbury had chosen simply to accommodate her.

And when the lady appeared in the door, Damian thanked the fates for Westbury's indulgence.

Nina was a vision in her emerald finery.

When he had first seen her on the Eastern Shore, she'd been wind-tossed. The color had been high in her cheeks, her honeyed curls had escaped to softly frame her heart-shaped face and delicate features. Her eyes had been aglow with exertion of a stroll along the shore and the brisk sea air.

Today, Nina was the vision of an all-proper lady.

She'd forsaken the mobcap, and her hair had been swept away from her face, styled high yet natural, each curl artful, leaving Damian to admire the tawny color,

equal parts honey and gold and the perfect comple-
ment to her creamy skin.

Her emerald gown was the height of English fashion
with a round neck and stiff *V* front that left a hint of
skin swelling over the frills to tantalize Damian's
imagination. He couldn't remember when he had ever
seen so little reveal so much. The way her breasts rose
and fell on each shallow breath. That pulse in her
throat beating a quick rhythm.

'Twas an effort of will to force his gaze to her face,
lest he find himself staring at the wrong end of Westbury's mood, which appeared as dour as his missive
had suggested. The lord fair bristled with defense,
made no effort to hide his disdain, and stood annoy-
ingly close to his ward, as if expecting Damian to burst
into rut.

He had no ken why this lord should be so disagree-
able. Unless Westbury, like Da, had heard tales about
carryings-on with the Leicesters and feared for his
lovely ward's virtue. For surely naught else would
have earned such open contempt.

But no overprotective lord would thwart Damian's efforts. Not after he'd waited forever to meet the subjects
of "Midnight Magic." 'Twas only left for him to discover what roles they would play in his second chance.

And he wasn't the only one curious . . .

Nina's proper response and cool gaze couldn't conceal her pleasure at seeing him again. That pulse beating low in her throat quickened when he caught her
fingers and lifted her hand to his mouth.

"Good day, milady." He pressed a welcoming kiss
against her satin skin.

"Greetings, Master Hart."

There was no mistaking the whisper of breathlessness in her voice, and to Damian's pleasure, the blood pumped hard through his veins in reply, a much-savored feeling of excitement.

Nina felt the queerest flutterings pool low in her belly as Damian's mouth brushed her skin. Heat swept through her, and she couldn't explain such a reaction to a stranger, except that she was so starved for the physical that she was vulnerable to these men she could touch.

Damian was a handsome man in a very aggressive way. Unlike Gray who felt solid and protective with his endearing smiles and warm eyes, this stranger beset her with the striking beauty of his appearance. The wild red hair. The tall, jutting body and restless strength. He had bold eyes that looked where he pleased with no thought for propriety. He had eyes that savored details. Artist's eyes.

That he savored her struck a chord somewhere inside, made her imagine the way a caress might feel, something to spark those visions that taunted her dark bed, when her body yearned in a way that had no release. She possessed the feelings and longings of a woman full grown, one who had never known pleasure. One who never would.

Not without the miracle of a second chance.

Was that miracle holding her hand?

Nina didn't breathe again until Damian finally released her and fixed his gaze on Gray. "Lord Westbury, I thank you for the honor of painting your ward."

Gray inclined his head but looked grim. "Let's get to it, man. I suppose you'll have all your own ideas about how you want to pose her."

Damian Hart did indeed, and he took Gray's inquiry as consent to begin an interrogation that resembled next to nothing of their interview with Master Verbrugges.

Where did Lord Westbury plan to display the portrait?

Were the walls in the gallery busy or uncramped?

What lighting would be falling upon the portrait?

Natural from the windows or artificial from sconces?

Master Verbrugges had been willing to accommodate Gray's vision of her portrait and hadn't debated his wishes. The master had been an artist hired to please a commissioner. Their art was an exchange of business.

Damian was no businessman. He was all about the art, and that much became evident when he dismissed the very idea of showcasing Nina against a dark background.

"Milady's skin may look creamy, but we can do better than to leave her disembodied on the canvas. Every face painter on two continents would pose her that way. Your beautiful ward deserves a masterpiece. What do you think, milady?"

Nina thought that Damian was much a prima donna, but she appreciated his effort to involve her in the choosing. She *knew* Gray regretted both his birthday gift and his indulgence. No doubt he was silently reciting a rosary for patience.

But 'twas so hard to feel guilty, when Master Hart's enthusiasm for his work caught her firm in its grip.

Props or no props?

Which way to turn—into the warm light of the north window or the cool light of the south?

Unlike Master Verbrugges who'd respected the boundaries of propriety and allowed Gray to direct her, Damian thwarted Gray at every turn, placing his hands freely and moving her all about his studio as he might move a piece of furniture needing a new home in an already-established decor.

Touching seemed to be an intrinsic part of him. He sidestepped Gray, took her hand and led her to the window, slipped strong fingers over her shoulders to position her into the light then away again.

Gray kept attempting to curtail the man's bold freedoms, but his efforts met with no results, leaving Nina to wonder if Damian purposely baited Gray and, if so, to what purpose.

Whatever the reason, a power struggle waged, and fearful Gray would lose his temper and cancel the sitting, she tried to anticipate Damian's requests to carry them out before he needed to touch her.

Of course, Gray soon realized she tried to ease the tension and graciously let Damian have his way. From Gray's expression, 'twas only a battle in what appeared to be turning into a war.

His generosity only added weight to her guilt, for she didn't mind Damian's touches at all. Each casual brush of his fingers made her skin tingle. Each gentle nudge of her shoulders in a new direction sent her insides to trembling, a mad sensation that made her chest tighten around every breath. She was aware of this man in a way she tried never to be aware of Gray.

"I fear your face is simply too lovely to choose sides," Damian finally said.

"Paint her full on then," Gray offered, and Nina heard his rising impatience.

Damian didn't reply but squinted at her for a long while. Then he caught her chin and tilted her face this way and that. That casual grip of work-roughened fingers managed to feel possessive in a way that fired those mad urges inside her. Not guilty urges for a man who mourned the loss of his beloved wife, but forbidden urges for a stranger.

"A mirror." Damian released her to move across the room. "The lighting will be a trick, but no mind . . ."

He dug out a large gilt-edged mirror from a behind a stack of canvases. The man was a bundle of impatient energy, as unlike stately Gray as rain from hail. They were both surely attractive men, yet so entirely different.

What she felt when Gray touched her held only a vague hint of the erotic. Shame for her unholy thoughts had kept her imagination and reactions in check. Her body felt awakened now, as if every sense took a first full breath of life.

When Damian returned and drew close, she could smell the fresh sea tang of his hair as the tight queue he wore swung across his broad shoulders. She caught the hint of freshly scrubbed skin below, a scent she recognized as male as he leaned over her to prop the mirror behind her.

He blocked out the sight of Gray with his broad shoulders, and took even bolder advantage of their concealment.

Nina's whole body poised tensely on the edge of her chair as he held her gaze in the mirror's reflection, trailed his fingertips down her cheek, a slow stroke, a caress.

'Twas a touch so simple, almost reverent . . . or mayhap it only felt that way to Nina for the sensation whispered over her face and down her neck, a feeling she'd only ever imagined.

"There we are." His voice throbbed between them, seductive. "Now we can see both sides of your lovely face."

Tracing the outer curve of her lips, Damian curled his palm under her chin and tipped her face upward. He peered into her face, and for the first time she saw feeling in those dark eyes. A look of approval, a glance that smoldered with admiration. And something else. Something far bolder.

A promise.

"There," he said in that whisky-rich voice. "Now fix your gaze on the door and let milord see what we have wrought."

Damian stepped away and swept a hand toward her in a dramatic gesture. "What say you, Lord Westbury? Will she not grace your gallery to perfection?"

Nina could see Gray in reflection and fought to look cool and composed when her body was on fire. Damian had fashioned a comfortable space well across the room, one that skillfully provided the least amount of view. Or so it had seemed to Nina before the mirror.

Now she felt speared on the edge of Gray's expression, a stern look that faded as wonderment softened his edges. She suspected in that moment he might forgive Damian much of his boldness for the pleasure he'd wrought with this pose.

With Gray, justice bore out over all. He would be fair whether fairness suited his mood or not. 'Twas the promise he'd made to live according to justice, and 'twas a promise he would keep, for he was a man who kept his promises. Always.

"She will indeed, Master Hart." His voice held a velvet-edged concession, and Nina felt the first flickers of hope that all might yet turn out well. "She will indeed."

Damian knew his father had been right about one thing—painting was an addiction. As surely as if he craved a draught from an opium pipe, he craved this artistic release. He had been able to think of nothing but painting Nina in the long hours since she'd left Hart Hill yestermorn.

After carefully arranging the studio for her second sitting, he had transcribed his preliminary notes so as not to lose a single detail. He'd sanded his canvas and readied his supplies, consumed with the idea of capturing her likeness.

Visions of her poised in the mirror's reflection haunted him as he'd forced himself to leave his studio to fulfill his promise not to get behind in his work. But all the while he'd handled tasks in the shipyard, Damian had been preoccupied with those visions of Nina . . .

Still today, he could see her face in his mind's eye, the

expression that was such an intriguing blend of world-weary innocence, as if an old soul stared through molten amber eyes in a beautiful young face, eyes that hinted at having seen so much yet still valiantly remained unaffected by it all.

He would start by painting her eyes to catch that unique manner, an air that struck him as . . . *yearning*.

What did Nina yearn for?

A life filled with intrigues and challenges, or babes at her breast? To be sheltered and safe in the arms of a noble husband or freed from her wary protector?

For a tryst with a stranger.

Damian wanted this woman in a way he didn't remember ever wanting. 'Twas as if they were connected by "Midnight Magic," which erased all the boundaries of propriety.

He had seen her and Westbury inside the painting, but had no ken why they might be involved in his second chance, should he ever decide to take it. He knew only one thing.

Nina was his destiny.

His inspiration.

Suddenly, he could paint. He felt alive.

Whether she had come to rescue him from his spiraling descent into ennui and hopelessness, or to stiffen his spine so he could forsake his vow and avail himself of the unique chance "Midnight Magic" offered, he knew she was his chance for a future.

As often as he'd been tempted by the possibilities that painting offered, Damian hadn't abandoned himself to its fate, no matter how much he'd wanted to.

And he'd wanted to, desperately.

But the memory of his mother stopped him every time. Sometimes when he'd stand inside Master

Verbrugges' gallery, staring at Nina and Westbury's faces, he'd see her face, too.

Not in the painting, but in his mind. He'd hear her voice. She'd believed in him always, had been the only reason his father had financed his training and not pressed him into service at the shipyard with his brothers.

All his family had sacrificed to leave him free to follow his dream, not because they believed in his talent, but because his mother did, and they loved her.

He'd failed them all.

A second chance inside "Midnight Magic" would mean dishonoring his mother's memory, and his father and brothers' sacrifice, no matter what their motives.

So Damian had chosen to repay his debt, but 'twas beyond his ken how to find contentment. Not when life had gone stale so long ago, since long before he'd finally exhausted his funding and been forced to return home to honor his commitments. As the rejection of his talents had pursued him, small successes and renewed hope followed by crushing disappointment, his looming failure had grown to become all consuming.

He couldn't remember the last time he'd felt challenged, *alive* . . . . 'Twasn't until Westbury ushered Nina back inside his studio that he felt hopeful in the face of her loveliness.

And when Nina glanced up at him with her serene smile and wanting eyes, Damian wanted to be warmed by her light.

His inspiration. His salvation.

"Lovely lady Nina." Bowing low, he brought her hand to his lips, unable to resist touching, tasting, convincing himself what he felt right now was real. "Welcome."

"Master Hart."

Her smooth voice chased through him as vibrant as the satin touch of her hand against his mouth, a lustrous sound that had substance as it trailed over his skin as a warm breeze.

"Master Hart." Westbury intruded upon the spell of the moment, an intentional intrusion, Damian guessed when he met the lord's gaze and found displeasure.

"Lord Westbury. Please make yourself comfortable." Damian released Nina, resenting that the man's moods should dictate his actions. "I've taken care of all the preliminary work in your absence, so I'm ready to sketch milady this morn."

Westbury eyed the large canvas Damian had set on an easel. "Master Verbrugges sketched on parchment."

"He prefers to perfect his details by transferring an image onto the canvas. I prefer to capture milady in composition. Allows me a freer hand with my edges and brushwork."

"His way sounds more thorough."

"A matter of preference. Master Verbrugges' gift for face painting is in his ability to make every subject attractive. I tend to capture the true personality of mine."

"Whether good or bad?" Nina asked.

He nodded. "In your case, milady, the result will undoubtedly be bliss."

She gifted him with a smile that transformed her face and snatched at his breath with its beauty.

"I wonder if all your subjects appreciate your candor," Westbury said.

"Only those who possess a solid strength of character," Damian admitted, amused that he even sounded breathless.

Nina laughed, a silvery chime through the chamber, brightening even the darkest corners.

Westbury's gaze fell upon his laughing ward, and his scowl faded. Nina met her guardian's gaze, and their obvious fondness excluded Damian from the moment and made him an outsider to the exchange. A feeling that made the warmth fade from his mood.

Motioning to the area he'd set up for Westbury's leisure, he said, "Please make yourself comfortable, milord. I'll ring my man to bring refreshment."

Westbury did as requested, although Damian sensed the man's gaze as he turned his attention to Nina and settling her into her pose.

With his back to Westbury, Damian caught her gaze for his own, smiled in private greeting. The amber lights in her eyes sparked in warm reply, so motioning her to sit, he waited while she lifted her hoops and arranged her skirts. Then he gave in to the urge to touch her.

"Do you remember the pose, milady?" Catching her chin between thumb and forefinger, he tilted her face toward his.

"Yes."

Her mouth parted around the word, and drawn to the sight, he traced his thumb over her lower lip, a glancing touch that might have been accidental. Or not. "Excellent."

Her chest rose and fell sharply, and Damian guessed she wasn't sure whether his touch had been accidental, either. He dragged his thumb across her lip again, this time a slow, deliberate stroke.

Her gaze grew dewy and soft, a tantalizing look of hesitation and undeniable awareness he intended to capture on canvas. This was how he wanted to paint her—with this look of uncertain arousal on her face.

Tipping her chin to the side, he smiled down at her, reminded, "Keep your gaze on the door."

Then he retreated to his canvas and reached for the charcoal, focusing on his task in that moment, the image he intended to capture, determining his proportions before daring the first stroke.

The feeling of charcoal between his fingers was familiar, his concentration magic. He lost himself in this world again, a world that had called to him since before memory. Indeed, he couldn't remember a time in his life when he hadn't had the urge to take the visions from his head and convey them into life.

Damian had always seen images as visions and gave them over to the canvas, or parchment, or any medium, permanently altered by his view.

A talent, he'd been called, and he'd never argued the term, or savored it, either. Painting was what he did. Could one own pride for breathing?

To paint again was a gift.

With each stroke he reassessed his proportions, outlined the position of each eye, then her nose, her mouth. He glanced up at her often, pleased how she managed to maintain the longing, as if her mind was filled with the promise of intimate touches and she wasn't quite sure if such urges were permitted indulgences or wicked sins that threatened her soul.

But Nina's eyes were a mirror, as her features were a reflection of her heart. Indeed, Damian could suddenly imagine her whole body as a canvas, her long, slender curves terrain he could mold and shape to his will to breathe life into the most striking of visions . . .

His knowing glances would heighten the color in her cheeks until creamy skin glowed with the hue of sunrise . . .

Hot kisses would steal her breath until her lips parted around shallow breaths and her lush mouth grew moist and reddened beneath his . . .

A glancing stroke of his fingers down the slim column of her throat and the pulse beating there would quicken . . .

He could entice her breasts above the ruched bodice, tweak her nipples until they grew as red as her lips.

Damian brought the charcoal over the canvas as his thoughts trailed down a dangerous path, each glance at his lovely subject prompting him to take another step . . .

Suddenly he could see how Nina might look if he pressed her back into the pillows. He would lift her skirts to reveal sleek legs. His imagination filled with the vision of her creamy skin, the feel of his hands parting her bare thighs.

He could stroke her hidden places, with his fingers, with his mouth. He could make her body flush with arousal, make her sigh with pleasure.

His hand trembled, and he was forced to lift the charcoal from the canvas until he managed the sensation, was almost surprised to find that his body had answered the call of his lusty thoughts, his groin uncomfortably hard in his breeches.

A reaction he would do well to control as Westbury remained a looming presence, always there, always watching.

What would the possessive lord think if Damian were to kneel before the lady, wedge his shoulders between her thighs and press tempting kisses over her smooth skin? Would Westbury enjoy seeing desire on his ward's beautiful face or would her desire for another man send him for a pistol?

"Master Verbrugges did not tell me how you came to make his acquaintance." Damian struck up a conversation, wanting to know all he could.

"The lieutenant governor recommended Master Verbrugges' services, claimed he was the best face painter we'd find south of New York."

"So he is."

"Not you?" Nina asked.

He eyed her narrowly around the easel, a silent reminder not to move. "Not me. He was the master and I the apprentice. I don't ply that trade anymore. I work in my family's shipyard."

"So Master Verbrugges mentioned," Westbury said. "He showed us the sketch of what you'd seen in 'Midnight Magic.'"

That brought Damian up short, and he turned to face Westbury. "He didn't tell me. Did you look upon the painting? Were you able to see inside?"

Westbury didn't reply, but Nina had turned to stare at her guardian, a suddenly wary look in her eyes, as if she awaited his next words as eagerly as Damian.

"Milady, did you see 'Midnight Magic,' too?"

She darted her gaze between them, seeking Westbury's guidance and awakening something darkly possessive in Damian.

"Lady Kirkby and I both viewed the painting, Master Hart. We saw the same image."

"The same? 'Tis unusual that. Would I be rude to ask what that image was?"

"You."

The charcoal slipped from his fingers, and Damian leaned back against the table, gripping the edges to steady himself.

"Well, milord." He barely recognized his voice. "I'm curious to know what you make of seeing me inside that painting. You don't seem as a man much given to fancy, and 'Midnight Magic' is the most fanciful notion I've come across in my travels."

"Master Verbrugges claims the painting is a gateway to second chances."

"Aye. But do you believe him?"

"I'm more curious to know how we're connected. You drew our likenesses long before we arrived in the colonies."

"Is that why you sought me out?"

Westbury nodded.

Damian wanted to glance at Nina, to read her reaction in her open expression, but knew Westbury would only perceive the break in eye contact as a threat.

There was much Damian must learn from this man. About Nina, who held the secret to his inspiration, and about how Westbury might assist Damian's designs on the future.

"I do not know how our fates are entwined, milord, but I've been wondering ever since seeing your faces in the painting."

"If you believe Master Verbrugges' claims then why did you not step inside the painting yourself?"

"I have a debt to repay," Damian said simply. "What about you, milord?"

"I do not believe in magic."

"Do you only believe in what you can see and touch?"

"I believe what the Lord has proclaimed as truth."

Damian inclined his head. "Then you are far more accustomed than I to believing without seeing."

" 'Tis called faith, man."

"I'm familiar with the concept."

"Mayhap you should try it."

"I have faith—in what I can see and touch."

No question remained about Westbury's opinion of his declaration, and Damian finally couldn't resist the urge to look at Nina, found her heart-shaped face grim, expression closed, and he wondered if she were reassessing her opinion of him.

The silence lengthened. Dust motes swirled in the light. No one seemed willing to move or disturb the moment.

Finally Nina broke the quiet. "Is that why you've never taken your second chance? You don't believe the magic works?"

"I believe, milady. But I am a man who repays my debts."

"Master Verbrugges explained why you no longer painted." Westbury said. "Did you offer your services to us when we backed out of our arrangement with him to continue our acquaintance?"

"I should have thought my reasoning obvious, given what I saw in the painting. I offered my services to you because I was curious, and . . ." He met Nina's gaze and smiled. "I couldn't resist painting such a lovely subject."

Westbury rose and went to stand with her, resting a hand on her shoulder, a gesture of possession that reminded Damian of how they'd looked when he'd seen them in "Midnight Magic."

She obviously cared deeply for her stoic guardian. 'Twas in her manner. What would Damian have to do to win a special look, a look she would wear only for him?

"So our lives are connected through a magic painting not all of us believe in," Damian said. "Where does that leave us?"

"With you painting my ward's birthday gift," Westbury said with a curt note of finality.

Damian inclined his head in acknowledgment of the reproof. Circling the easel, he reclaimed his subject. "Then if you'll allow me to reposition milady. I will get back to my work."

He and Westbury stood nearly eye to eye, his own slight advantage not enough to withstand the challenge in Westbury's manner. Damian recognized the threat and had his answer. This fiercely protective lord intended Nina for himself.

And he finally understood why he'd seen this man inside "Midnight Magic."

Westbury stood between him and Nina.

CHAPTER 6

After the priest departed the chapel and their hymn faded to silence, Nina genuflected before the altar only to have Gray place his hand on her arm to halt her exit.

"Join me, my dear." He knelt again, and as they were due to leave for her sitting with Damian, she glanced at him, her surprise revealing itself because he said, "Only a few moments."

Arranging her skirts, Nina sank to her knees and waited.

"I have been praying for guidance." He looked grim. "I feel I should mention my concerns."

"Concerns about what?"

"You."

'Twas exactly what Nina did not want to hear, and she squelched a sudden rush of impatience at this delay when she wanted so much to be on her way to Hart Hill.

Clasping her hands before her, she inclined her

head, encouraging him to begin so they could get on with their day.

But he only stared down at her, mayhap contemplating what to say or seeking enlightenment from the Holy Spirit.

He, too, knelt with his hands clasped as if in prayer, a position that suited him. Whenever Gray knelt to pray, silence seemed to settle around him, a transparent veil that bridged the distance between the living world and the divine.

Watching him, she remembered a similar thought about Damian, when she'd first seen him on his boat. His tall, aggressive body had appeared one with the swift-moving vessel, his every movement confident and graceful.

Gray trailed his gaze over her, a gentle look that warmed her with caring. "I want to caution you about Master Hart."

"Why?"

"I have grave misgivings about the man."

That was also not what Nina had expected to hear, so she stared at him, unsure how to reply.

"I don't see how he could know about your ability. Even if Master Verbrugges revealed what he'd witnessed in his studio, I don't think he could understand what was truly happening."

"Why do you think Damian knows?"

"Because he makes free with his hands. I get the sense that he's using his touches to . . . *tempt* you."

"Tempt me to do what?" Nina scoffed. "I am sitting for a portrait, Gray. What can I do?"

"Precisely my point. For a woman without your ability, a portrait sitting would be commonplace, but for you, my dear' 'tis much more. 'Tis a license for this man to touch you, and a place where your thoughts are free to roam."

Nina had the unkind, and rather mutinous thought that Gray didn't like having his position as the only man who could touch her usurped, but why should Gray care? 'Twas not as if he intended to claim her for himself.

Suddenly a vision burst into her mind like a striking fist, an image as provocative, as shocking as those that awoke her from sleep late at night. Nina could see two naked bodies, arms clinging, limbs entwined, a woman and a man exploring each other in passion.

A vision that continued to plague her though she pressed it back time and time again.

Squeezing her eyes shut, she inhaled deeply, willed the image to vanish. 'Twas enough to shame her in the dead of night, but before God's altar . . .

" 'Midnight Magic' tempts you." Gray's voice penetrated her darkness, silken, swaying. "I do not believe in magic, nor do I believe in the need for second chances, but you don't feel that way, do you, my dear? You see what the painting alleges to offer as a chance for a life different from what you have."

For some stupid reason hearing her most private thoughts spoken in his gentle voice made sadness swell inside. Stupid tears sprang to her eyes, though she kept them pressed tightly shut, refused to give way to heartache. Was her every thought so transparent to him?

"Would that be so very wrong?"

Gray understood her conflict and slipped his hand over hers, a simple touch meant to reassure. "Of course not. How you feel is never wrong, but simply how you feel. You walk a path that differs from most.

'Tis not an easy one, I know, but God has granted you such grace for a purpose."

"What purpose? Not even you can say, and all I see is that I've frightened more people than I've helped."

"'Tis God's place to deliver guidance. Not mine, nor any other man's."

He referred to Damian. And to the choices she'd made when they'd left England. "I won't change my mind about using my abilities. I won't subject us to any more judgment or criticism or fear. I only want to live in peace."

"Even if you're the one interfering in God's will?"

"I should suffer condemnation for who I am, for an ability I had no say in and cannot change? What of all your talk of God's love and compassion?"

His hand squeezed tight. "Don't you see how your choice isolates you, leaves you vulnerable to men like Damian Hart—"

"Men like Damian?" Nina found her courage and faced him. "I've never met another man I could touch besides you."

"We haven't made his character yet."

"Isn't that why you accepted his offer to paint me?"

"Yes, but not enough time has passed. 'Tis why I caution you."

Nina knew Gray only sought to keep her from harm, so the anger that welled up inside her shocked her by its heat. The raw, aching feeling made her suspect he wanted to snatch away her only fleeting hope of any happiness.

And that terrible, *terrible* voice inside demanded to know why Gray should be so selfish to keep her to himself when he wasn't prepared to care for her as a man cared for a woman. He above all understood that she would never know the kind of love he'd shared with Juliette. And she accepted that he would never love anyone the way he had his wife.

But would he deny Nina the chance to know the only other man who might care for her in that way? The only other man who might touch her in the way she yearned to be touched?

She couldn't bring herself to ask. Not Gray. Not in God's house. Not even when she wanted so desperately to know.

"You've been graced with a gift, Nina. You alone have the power to help people find their salvation. To covet such a gift when you might help so many . . ."

"Damian has been graced with the gift of his art, yet he uses his hands to cut timbers and build ships."

Gray exhaled a sigh. "There is a difference between the two, I believe."

If there was, Nina was unwilling to concede it. Not now, not when she struggled so hard to beat down this beast inside her. Self-pity had never done her credit. She loathed it so, knew not why it struck at her again and again.

Even if Damian was a devil sent to tempt her, he made her feel things she'd never felt before. How could she ignore the only glimpse of hope she'd seen?

"I will heed your warning." The anger behind the words felt poisonous, profane as it poured from her lips. "'Tis the best I can offer now."

But when they arrived at Hart Hill a while later, Nina knew her best would not be enough. Not when she noticed the area designated for Gray's leisure had moved clear across the room.

Gray turned to Damian, who swept a hand toward the easel where the portrait took shape, a living form that grew before their eyes, then grew again when he worked in their absence.

Flashing a smile, he said, "I will block Lady Nina's face today and thought you would enjoy seeing how she comes to life on the canvas."

A reasonable explanation, and a considerate one, too, Nina thought stubbornly, yet she also couldn't help but notice how this move meant Gray could no longer see her—not where she sat nor reflected in the mirror.

During today's sitting, she and Damian would be able to look upon one another unobserved.

Nina's defiance and selfish anger faded away beneath the knowledge that Gray was right, as always.

"We will have to cancel today's sitting, I fear." Gray informed Nina over breakfast. " 'Tis no help for it. The lieutenant governor can come no other time, and 'twould not do to deny the man when he arrives solely to meet with me."

"You must work, of course," Nina said, mind racing.

She should acquiesce to his wishes and offer to greet the lieutenant governor and usher him inside the office, but the very idea of forsaking today's visit threw her mood.

She did not want to forsake precious time with Damian. Not when her time at Hart Hill would all too soon come to an end.

For after her anger at Gray had burned away, she couldn't deny that he had every right to be concerned about Damian. Nina might be a maid, sheltered in many ways by Gray and her circumstances, but she'd touched more evil in her life than her years should have allowed.

Damian was a temptation. The greatest she'd ever faced.

She also knew Gray would never give more credence to the legend of "Midnight Magic" than as pure fabrication or a lure hell-sent. Either way, he would never agree to surrender himself to the painting for a second chance.

Nina would never leave Gray.

Even if remaining with him meant yearning for a life she would never have and living in fear of discovery. Even if remaining with him meant sacrificing the promise of passion she might know with Damian Hart.

She loved Gray. He loved her.

And while his love was born of commitment and caring, Gray was still her protector, the man who'd willingly forsaken a future for her. She would do the same for him.

But the thought of never seeing Damian again ached. She wanted him. He wanted her. 'Twas in his every bold glance, each secretive touch he dared beneath Gray's nose.

She must accept that he could be no more than a reprieve from her barren life, the man who taught her the beauty of a caress, which meant she must savor her time with him and make the most of chance while it lasted. For she would be left only with a portrait and memories to carry her through a lifetime.

That knowledge bolstered her courage.

"Rather than cancel the sitting, Gray, why can you not simply provide me another escort?" Steeling her spine to meet his gaze, Nina tossed down the suggestion, which would undoubtedly be seen as a gauntlet in light of their discussion in the chapel only days before.

" 'Twill bring us closer to the finish, which I think will suit all the way around."

Not for her, but surely for Gray, and mayhap even Damian. She'd heard enough comment to know her artist-turned-shipwright had kept up his building around his work on her portrait.

While Nina had known the accusation would come, when Gray's expression charged her with straying toward the devil's gate with no cares, she felt his disappointment strike close to her heart.

" 'Twas only a suggestion," she said quickly.

His dark gaze cut through her retreat. Gray knew she wanted to go. He knew *why* she wanted to go.

She should have felt shame for her yearnings, but her conscience couldn't dim the tiny spark of hope inside.

The resignation she saw in Gray's gaze assured her that while he knew she chanced fate, he would indulge her. He had always respected her will, whether he agreed or not.

" 'Tis your choice, of course. Hurst will attend you."

Setting his napkin back on the table, he slid the chair away and stood. He lightly kissed the top of her head, bade her good day then departed the dining room without another word or even a backward glance.

Though there was nothing dramatic about his exit, Nina's chest constricted around a swell of emotion as she stared at the empty doorway, felt the shriek of a silence as though a thousand voices hurling accusations of betrayal.

'Twas only one sitting, she told herself. And with Hurst, no less. No doubt Gray would send their coachman for the very same reason he'd brought Hurst to the colonies; Hurst was a giant. The man literally towered above Gray, weighed an easy three stone more and rarely spoke. Any highwayman or scoundrel would think twice before attempting mischief on Lord Westbury's coach whenever she and Gray traveled.

Would Damian think twice as well?

Nina mulled the question during the ride to Hart Hill, where each passing mile found her guilt ebbing in the wake of excitement. Her sense of danger grew, making her feel eager with the promise of the upcoming encounter, and so incredibly alive.

Damian was a temptation true, but she would not be led astray, would only pause for a quick glimpse down the path. Time enough to make her memories.

When they were escorted into the studio, Nina found him already in front of his easel. He must have heard rather than seen them enter for he never glanced away from his brushstrokes.

"Good day," he said. "Come and see what I have wrought. I am working on milady's reflection. What do you think of the values? I've decided to lighten the image to create distance."

Nina moved inside the room to approach and as she did, Damian turned to her, caught sight of Hurst.

"Lord Westbury?" he asked.

"Was detained with work. Our man Hurst shall sit with me."

Damian nodded to the burly coachman, "Then welcome, Hurst. Portrait sitting is deadly dull business I'm afraid. Make yourself comfortable over there, and I'll see what we can come up with by way of entertainment."

Another servant might have responded with a polite thanks or even an avowal that he needed no entertainment to distract him from his task. Hurst only glared threateningly at Damian to set boundaries, gave a grunt and made his way to the chair.

Nina didn't miss the glint in Damian's eyes or the tug of humor around his mouth, as if amused Gray had thought a man of Hurst's size would deter him from handling Nina as he pleased. And no sooner had Hurst taken his seat than Damian set aside his palette and bowed low over Nina's hand.

"Welcome, milady," he said in the height of graciousness, but he pressed an open-mouthed kiss to her skin, velvet-hot tongue sampling her in a tantalizing lick. "So what say you about the reflection? Do you like what I have done?"

Nina had naught to say at that moment, for her heart stopped entirely, leaving her gaping.

Damian raised his gaze, peering up at her beneath lashes as dark as his eyes, gauging her reaction and missing naught.

The dashing smile that tipped his lips assured her he knew full well how she responded to his daring.

Then he stood, his strong fingers grasping hers in an iron grip before he brought her around to face the portrait.

'Twas indeed a thing of beauty, though she still had trouble believing the image in front of the mirror was her own. Both Gray and Damian had assured her the likeness was commendable, though, so Nina had no choice but to believe.

Damian had sketched the whole scene then painted in sections. "Blocking" was the term he'd used, she recalled. He'd completed her face and hair, and the colors were vibrant, the shadowing masterful, the brushstrokes smooth and expert.

But the expression was what held Nina in amazement.

On her face was an expression of such heartfelt yearning, a curious yearning, and a tentative one. 'Twas as if Damian had seen straight through to her soul, had summed up her whole life in one glance.

"You are so gifted," she exhaled the praise on a sigh, felt her cheeks grow warm as he stared down at her, his pleasure so evident in his handsome face.

"So you approve?"

"Of course. You have made me beautiful."

"'Tis what I see when I look upon you, milady."

She saw no guile in his face, no pretty words designed to flatter, only honesty. Beneath such candor, she felt that wild anticipation again, a feeling as if she might die of pleasure and be thrilled to go in the process, no matter that she knew heaven and hell would be waiting.

Hurst might have been in another town for all the notice he could pay Nina as she sat on her perch in front of the mirror. Damian, temptation he was, set upon taking immediate advantage.

Stepping in front of her, he moved in so close that his knees bumped hers through her skirts. With a few nudges, he directed her to lean away from the mirror then, cupping her shoulders with both hands, he guided her upper body in the opposite direction. The result was a pose that looked relaxed and natural, but left her slightly off-kilter.

"We'll settle you properly today, milady. We were off somehow yestermorn. The north light threw too many shadows." Damian kept up a steady stream of chatter, likely to allay any cause for Hurst's worry, but if her coachman could only see the liberties taken behind that mirror.

Damian leaned over her, so close she could smell

his freshly laundered shirt, see a pinprick scar mar the tanned skin at his neck. After tipping her face toward the door, he dragged his open palm down her throat, his rough skin igniting fire in the wake of his touch, making her swallow hard.

"How's that, milady?"

"Fine."

He rested his palm outstretched on her chest. Her heart beat as if it had sprouted wings and meant to take flight.

"You're comfortable?" he asked.

"Quite."

His dark gaze never strayed from hers as he toyed with the ruching then traced the swell of her breast above her bodice.

Nina could only stare into his face as her body responded to that light brush of skin against skin. Her breasts swelled, suddenly tight within her clothing, and she was so aware of her nipples, achy and confined.

"What about now, milady?"

This time Nina only nodded, not trusting herself to speak.

Gray's caution echoed in memory, a voice of reason far too faint to heed in the face of the awareness pulsing through her. Damian took such liberties with her person, and she dared to let him, had never experienced such heat firing through her veins, sparking her body to life.

He pressed forward even more, and in her periphery, she could see their reflection in the mirror, watched him bend low enough until his nose almost touched the crown of her hair. But he only inhaled deeply as if savoring some glorious scent.

When his queue slipped around his shoulder and dangled heavily between them, Nina could not have resisted a liberty of her own had her life depended upon it. Reaching up, she dragged her fingers along the thick rope of hair. 'Twas as silky and lush as she'd imagined, glossy strands wound into a cool silk rope that inspired thoughts of what 'twould look like unbound, feel like to the touch.

Damian sucked in a hard breath, his chest swelling visibly, and Nina smiled, pleased with herself for invoking such a reaction from this dashing man.

"Remember to look at the door." He stood upright, his hand lingering softly above her breast, his queue trailing through her fingers as he moved away.

Then he was gone to his place at the easel, where she could only make out his motions in her periphery, leaving her with her skin tingling and her thoughts racing.

And waiting. For she knew Damian would never allow this chance from beneath Gray's watchful gaze to pass unheeded and she wondered how he might take advantage of the time.

'Twas the beauty of the man, she decided. His knack for making each moment a thrill. Irreverent, mayhap, a temptation surely. Though she didn't dismiss Gray's concerns, 'twas all too easy to rationalize this excitement, to allow herself this chance to feel something other than fear and that desperate wanting she would never satisfy.

Time passed, and the effects of Damian's touch hadn't yet subsided, and she savored the sensations, the tingling of breasts that had never felt so needy, of heat pooling between her thighs.

"You are unwell today, milady?" Damian asked when he was forced to leave the easel to adjust her pose for the third time.

"Not unwell, just too restless to sit still."

The palette clattered onto the table then the brush beside it. "Come, Hurst." Damian motioned to the coachman. "We're going to take the lady out for a breath of fresh air. She's been cooped up inside this studio for days on end. A stroll will help you walk off your restlessness, milady."

"Yes." Nina popped up off her seat. "I believe you are right. What say you, Hurst? Would you care to see the shipyard?"

Her giant companion flashed a toothy grin, as much enthusiasm as Nina had ever seen him display, which warmed her to the idea of an outing even more.

The devil gleamed in Damian's gaze as he offered his arm. Nina looped hers through and let him escort her from the studio.

"Is your man always so curious?" Damian asked as they strolled through the shipyard.

Of course, he had to speak low so as not to be overheard, which meant leaning close enough to whisper in her ear. And as they'd left the studio so quickly, Nina hadn't retrieved her cloak, which currently left her unhooded and his mouth pressed perilously close to her ear.

His breath gusted in a warm burst that sent shivers straight to her toes.

"In truth, Hurst has spoken more this quarter hour past than I have heard him speak since sailing from London."

Damian only nodded then led them down to a pier that straddled a hull at anchor and a warehouse.

"Tomas," he yelled up to a man on deck. "Where's Blair?"

"In the hold. Ye want me to fetch him, lad?"

"My thanks." Then Damian turned to them and explained. "Blair is my brother between Gordon, the oldest, and me. He oversees the building of this ship for a merchant who has made his fortune with the Triangle Trade."

Hurst gazed up at the towering hull with obvious interest. Nina had heard Gray speak of the three-legged trading route that began in New England, where textiles, grains, and rums were put aboard for a journey to Africa. There, goods were exchanged for slaves that would journey to the Caribbean to be sold to sugar planters for molasses and sugar, which returned to New England for conversion into rum and a new start of the cycle.

When Blair Hart appeared on deck, Nina smiled at the resemblance of these Hart men.

"Permission to board, captain," Damian called out. "My guests would enjoy a tour of your vessel."

"What say you, Hurst?" Nina asked, though the man's answer glowed in a fast nod and quick smile.

She peered up at Damian. "You're sure 'twill be no bother?"

"My brother will be grateful for the distraction." And when Blair called out, "Come aboard," Damian led them to the pier.

'Twas not until they reached the gangplank that they encountered the first real difference between a completed ship and a partially constructed one.

Nina took one look at the narrow plank the shipwrights used to board the vessel and stated flatly, "I cannot walk up *that* in these hoops."

Damian frowned, and Hurst stopped short, glancing at her with sudden uncertainty.

She had no doubt Damian had known she would

never be able to board, and suddenly Nina stood on the crux of a dilemma. Gray's cautions echoed as if he'd taken up residence inside her skull, while Hurst's obvious eagerness to see the inside of the ship and Damian's skillful manipulation to escape her protector combined to pit reason against opportunity.

The disappointment in Hurst's face and the dare in Damian's left Nina feeling as if an angel sat poised on one shoulder and a devil on the other. And the all important question . . .

Did she dare?

"Are ye coming?" Blair called, and Damian motioned him to patience while his gaze caught hers, tempted her with promises of pleasures even a few unescorted moments might bring.

"Hurst, why don't you go?" The ease of the words surprised her. "Master Hart will remain with me until you're through."

"I promised milord—"

"I'll take good care of the lady," Damian prompted. You have my word. We'll stroll the shipyard until she's able to sit again as a proper subject."

Doubt warred over Hurst's face, and Nina felt an uncomfortable tug of guilt at the man's obvious discomfiture. She and Damian were tempting him to play their game, for she well knew Hurst would pay hell to Gray should anything unfortunate happen while she was out of sight.

"We're surrounded by a shipyard filled with people," Damian pointed out. "You've no need to worry."

Hurst looked to Blair, who stood watching them at the other end of the makeshift gangplank then back to her. "Milady?"

"'Twill be fine, Hurst."

"She will not be left out," Damian said. "I plan to show that small vessel moored over there. She should be able to board that one, don't you think?"

Hurst's toothy smile seemed to mock Nina's calm, and she stubbornly tamped down her guilt when the man took off up the gangplank faster than she'd ever seen him move.

"Well done, milady." Damian's gaze openly caressed her.

"You are a bad influence, sir. You encourage me to risk myself and my man, for if anything should happen to me, Gray will skin Hurst alive and I'll roast in hell for my duplicity."

"I encourage you to enjoy the time available to us, milady. No more," he said reasonably. "Say you do not want to, and I shall behave and simply stand sentinel until your man returns."

She scowled.

He laughed, and the rich sound was snatched up on the sea breeze to swirl around them as a living thing, coaxing Nina from her guilt.

Damian extended his arm, and she had only a moment's hesitation before looping hers through it, allowing him to lead her back to shore.

"What do you think will happen to you in my care, Nina?"

"I can only imagine," she admitted. "But given your daring since our acquaintance, those imaginings make me breathless."

"'Tis by design, you know. You are such a vibrant woman it pains me to see you live in such dull shades of gray when there is a rainbow to be had."

She frowned up at him. "What gives you that impression of me?"

He arched an eyebrow. "Impression? 'Tis no impression. You remind me of sandpipers that chase the tide. Instead of riding the surf to great heights and plummeting back to shore, you run away from the breakers and avoid the tide altogether."

'Twas such an apt description of Nina's life that she could think of no worthy reply, only feel sad that this man had so completely summed up her existence. As with the expression on her face in the painting, he seemed to see inside her in ways that no other had.

And even now he must have realized he'd struck close to her heart for he brought her hand up to press a kiss there.

"I did not mean to sadden you. I know not why you avoid life, but 'tis obvious you do. Mayhap the cause is your guardian. He hovers over you closer than a gaoler."

With good reason, Nina thought. "Things are not always as they seem. I beg you not to judge Gray harshly. He has my best interests at heart always."

"Is that why you won't take the chance 'Midnight Magic' offers? Are you so content with your life or are you beholden to Westbury?"

"Neither. Both. Gray believes the painting is some hellish temptation."

"What do you believe?"

That she had been given a chance to lead a normal life at a cost beyond what she was willing to pay. "I believe I have a few stolen moments to enjoy. Please do not press me further. I will not leave Gray, and he does not believe in second chances."

"Then I must be content with a few stolen moments to make you smile." Damian directed her down another pier where the vessel she had first glimpsed him sailing rode at anchor. "Come, let me show you my newest design. I built her for a rather enterprising plantation owner, who'll take delivery as soon as his man arrives to sail her to Cape Fear. I am taking the opportunity to enjoy her while I can."

Nina liked that about Damian. He seized his chances, didn't let them pass by to be regretted later. She liked having the chance to do the same, even for a few stolen moments.

After boarding the craft, he reached for her, his strong hands circling her waist to help her aboard. For that brief instant their bodies drew close, a tantalizing instant where she could feel the heat of him even through the layers of her gown.

He held her until she gained her balance on the gently swaying deck then explained the various features of his design.

"'Tis a marvelous craft, Damian. Much more comfortable than its size would allow. At least from a distance. Your talent shows through in all you do."

He waggled his brows at her comically before directing her to the rail. "A compliment from the lady. I shall steal you away from your guardians more often if it means hearing such rich praise from your lovely lips."

Before Nina knew what he was about, he'd slipped the knot from the mooring rope and the vessel drifted from the pier.

"Damian," she gasped. "What are you about?"

"I'm stealing you. I want to see you ride the crests."

Another choice. 'Twas then Nina had her first inkling temptation wasn't so entirely in her grasp as she'd believed, that a situation could move beyond her control without notice.

Gray's warning sounded in her mind again, along with the realization that Damian dared much by his actions, exposing them all to potentially dangerous consequences.

She opened her mouth to say to him nay. 'Twould be reckless to leave without Hurst, a betrayal of Gray's expectations, but as she watched Damian strip off his shoes and hose and begin to unfurl the rigging, she sensed the challenge in his actions, the presumption that she was bold enough to follow where he led.

Nina supposed he had every right to believe such with the way she'd encouraged his flirtation.

With each foot the boat eased away from the pier, she felt her choices slipping away and own sense of daring grow. She recalled the first time she'd seen him sailing the bay in this very boat, and knew yearning again, the desire to feel the wind on her cheeks, to cut across the waves and outrun fate.

Would she seize this chance or let it pass by?

When the wind caught a sail, snapping it to attention with a crack that made her start, Nina found her courage, hoisted her skirts and took a seat in the stern, determined to enjoy her chance to experience the freedom of riding the waves and not running away from the tide.

Damian brought the vessel about, not toward the bay as she'd expected, but so close to the hull of the larger ship that her mouth went dust dry.

He drew close enough to call up, "Tomas, where are Blair and his guest?"

Within moments, Hurst and his guide peered over the rail.

"I'm taking milady for a ride on the bay, Hurst," Damian explained. "We did not want you to worry. We'll stay where you'll see us from the deck."

Hurst cut a scowl to her, but Nina forced a smile before Damian maneuvered the sail until they slipped slowly away from the larger vessel toward the diamond waters of the bay.

"Hang on," he told her while unfurling another sail that caught the wind and shot them from the piers.

Hurst and Blair Hart disappeared again, and Nina turned into the wind as the boat skimmed smoothly through the swells and the shore fell into the distance.

"'Tis amazing." Even the whistle of wind in her ears couldn't mask the sound of her excitement. "I've sailed before, but never like this."

The wind whipped at her skirts and snapped at her cheeks, but the chill exhilarated her. Damian only smiled as he moved fluidly over the deck, retrieving a blanket from a storage hatch and draping it over her shoulders to protect her from the wind.

She pulled it tight, admired the sight he made working the rigging with the wind whipping his queue to and fro, sneaking inside his collar to puff his shirt at his back and mold his broad chest in the front.

'Twas a sight that captured Nina's imagination, fired thoughts of what his hair would look like unbound, flowing over his body. She'd touched him once before, would she seize the opportunity to touch him again if one should arise?

Could she ever be bold as he?

"I should like to paint as I see you now," he said. "You look even more beautiful with the color in your cheeks and excitement in your eyes."

Her cheeks grew hot at the silk in his voice, a tone that brought to mind what his hand had felt like against her skin.

"Your guardian talks of faith, Nina, yet he would

have you on your knees in prayer. Here is God, all around in the waves, in the wind, in birds circling our heads. Do you see him?"

Nina nodded, savoring the beauty of the moment and the truth of Damian's words, but the mention of Gray made her notice the shipyard fading in the distance. "Where are you taking me?"

"A special place. Do not fear. Hurst will still see us from the deck."

Scanning the horizon, she spotted what appeared to be tiny isles clustered ahead. Sure enough, Damian made into the cove of one, and a glance revealed she could still see the ships riding anchor below Hart Hill.

"Clever man. You set the boundaries then push them as far as they will stretch."

He must have deemed that high praise for he caught her gaze around the rigging and winked.

"Now hang on tight to the rail or I'll lose you overboard. I must run aground lest I risk getting your skirts wet, but I do not want to get us stuck."

Nina realized the trouble as the boat skidded into the sand and Damian hoisted himself overboard, splashing to the shore to moor their vessel against the tide.

She appreciated his caution, tucked the blanket close around her to protect her gown. "I'd rather not be forced to make excuses, either."

When Damian reappeared at the stern, he took her measure in a glance and frowned. "I was going to tell you to contain your gown so I can carry you ashore, but I fear your hoops will be our undoing."

The bell-shaped hoopskirt was pliable, but when she compressed one side, the other popped up in the balance. "What do you suggest? For I know you have a plan."

"Do you now?"

She nodded.

"Leave the hoops aboard."

"To do that I would need assistance removing them."

"Are you asking me to help you remove your undergarments?"

"Damian."

"My pleasure, milady. Truly."

Laughing, he hoisted himself back onto the deck. His bare feet dripped, and she stepped away to avoid getting wet, turning her back to him and maneuvering her skirts up so he could reach the fastenings at her waist.

The scoundrel made the most of the moment, too, pressing close to rest his chin atop her head. He was obviously familiar with the workings of a lady's undergarments, for he quickly freed the ties and the whole skirt fell to the deck with a hiss. Catching one end, he motioned her to step out from the circle of boning while keeping it from the puddle growing beneath him.

Bundling her skirts, Nina did as he bade, feeling caught up in the moment, the daring of shedding any part of her clothing for this man and their adventure.

"There." He eyed the thing narrowly while setting it on the bench out of harm's way.

Then he disembarked again, this time reaching for her. "Put your arms around my neck."

Damian scooped her up against him and carried her ashore, and without her hoops swelling between them, her body felt bared to his strong embrace.

"Now come and see this island gem. 'Tis a favored place of mine. Tell me if you see God's hand in its making."

Nina wondered if 'twas his wont to spirit maidens away from their guardians and bring them here, but didn't ask. She'd rather leave her whimsical notions intact and believe that this man was so caught up in stealing moments with her that she drove him to such daring.

Had it not been for the trees, Nina might have seen from one end to the other of this tiny paradise. The sandy shore inclined a hilly bank into a wooded glade and cut off the sight of the bay yet still filled with the rhythm of the surf.

She could hear wildlife in the underbrush and gulls crying, and when Damian led her over the rise, Nina saw the treasure of this island—a small lagoon complete with a rock ledge.

" 'Tis a place from heaven," she said.

He glanced down to her face, his fingers seeking hers and drawing her close. "This place doesn't touch your beauty, Nina. I want to kiss you. Will you say me yea or nay?"

Her breath caught as she recognized the intent in his dark gaze, and she found no words of protest or permission. Instinct claimed her and she swayed forward in reply, a thrill rippling through her when he lowered his face to hers.

He urged her lips apart, and she did not resist, though he stole the very breath from her lungs as he made her acquaintance with a shocking thrust of his tongue.

Nina wasn't entirely sure what she'd expected, but this . . . *possession* was not what she'd imagined. Suddenly her wildest fantasies seemed all too missish against the reality of his mouth slanting across hers with such forceful deliberation.

She felt hot and cold all at once, as if her body burned and thawed in turns. A brilliant tension gathered deep inside and she clung to him, awed. She'd never known the simplest caress, yet now feasted on abundance. 'Twas the awe, surprise, and effortless pleasure that led Nina to kiss him back.

Tangling her tongue with his, she sampled his mouth, the intimate caress of his tongue, the breaths he stole only to return in equal measure. She knew not whether she was too tentative or too bold until tasting his reply, a growl that rumbled low in his throat.

Damian brought his arms around her, pulled her hard against him as he braced his legs apart to steady them. Suddenly, she could feel all of him, the iron-thewed wall of chest, lean stomach, solid shaft of flesh between his thighs.

He arched his hips forward, pressing so close, so hungrily, an act that told her clearly of his hard-won restraint. Mayhap she should worry for his control, yet Nina felt only excitement. For once in her life she would know the thrill of being touched.

'Twas pure selfishness, she knew, yet when his hands trailed down her back and pressed her impossibly closer, she understood that this pleasure was meant for feeling, not for questioning. 'Twas its magic. Its peril.

Pleasure . . . a blessing and a curse.

Nina understood this concept so well she could only surrender herself to sensation. A tingling tension spread inside her with each lush stroke of Damian's tongue, its counterpart below with his moving hips.

He devoured her mouth, conquering any hesitation beneath an awareness so potent her heart swooped end over end as she tested her own limits, met his demand eagerly.

Suddenly his hands were everywhere, gliding down her throat, rounding her shoulders, touching her breasts.

Nina gasped at his boldness, and the whisky-rich sound of his laughter burst against her mouth, mocked her surprise, carried away on the sea breeze.

"I knew kissing you would be a fantasy come to life." He molded his hands over her breasts. "Do you deny it, Nina sweet?"

This time she could feel the pressure through the layers of her bodice and trembled.

"Nay."

'Twas all the permission Damian needed for he trailed his mouth from hers and nibbled kisses toward her ear.

Molten sensation poured through her, a thick wave that stole the strength from her limbs and spurred heat to every place in between. He held her steady, so close to block out the view of their paradise with his broad shoulders. He sucked a moist path from her ear down her throat, and she arched against him, savored the forbidden feel of taut muscles, the friction of their clothing, the heat of their bodies.

Touch . . .'twas better than she'd dared dream, and she felt sad and angry all at once, *denied*. Others lived their lives to the call of their passions, to this tender tension mounting between her thighs. Most were so used to touch that they took the beauty for granted, never grasping the special gift they'd been given, never understanding how barren life would be when one feared the slightest contact.

This moment was hers.

When the blanket slipped from her shoulders, Nina felt no chill. Indeed, how could she feel anything but their bodies locked together, this need soaring inside?

She *felt*.

The sheer thrill of the thought spurred her to tip her

head back as Damian devoured her throat, to make demands of her own. Catching his queue in her hands, she tugged the binding away.

"Nina." Her name burst from his mouth, a sound that was half groan, half laugh.

"Your hair." She forced steel into her voice. "I wondered how 'twould look unbound."

Turning, he presented his back, and she rose up on tiptoes to reach the binding at his nape. "Whatever milady wishes."

She wished they had more than a few stolen moments. She wished Gray wasn't looming at the back of her thoughts. She wished for the courage to make this moment hers in every way.

Her fingers trembled as she unfastened the leather tie, and determined to seize the moment, she threaded her fingers through the silken strands, loosed the bright cascade down his back.

His hair reached nearly to his waist, all heavy silk, thick and cool to the touch. She smoothed away the creases left from the bindings, thinking she'd never seen a more erotic sight than this man and his hair. Each simple caress moved her, aroused feelings she didn't quite know what to make of.

But Damian did, and he spun toward her, hair whipping out in a burnished arc as he caught her and sank to the ground.

She came down on top, pinned inside her voluminous skirts. His glorious hair fanned out behind him. His dark eyes smiled.

"You make me feel beautiful, Nina."

"You are." She trailed her fingers along the jut of his jaw, traced the mouth that had ravished hers.

"You humble me." Turning his face, he pressed his

mouth to her palm. His lashes fluttered shut, as if he needed to block out the sight of her to regain himself.

"Why does feeling humble bother you?"

He inhaled deeply, and when he opened his eyes again, the shadows had passed. "I know not. What I do know is I have the loveliest woman in my arms, and we're wasting time talking."

'Twas an evasion, she knew, but he also made a fine point. They could waste no time. Their stolen moments were fleeting.

"Kiss me." He challenged her with a glance and worked his hands under her skirts and over her bottom.

She gasped at his daring, but he only laughed.

"Kiss me."

Nina meant to show him she could give as good as she got, but her kiss proved another missish effort, hindered in part by his laughter, and her own distraction as the chemise did naught to shield her backside from his roving hands.

He kneaded his fingers into her bottom, bringing her sharply against that hard ridge between his thighs. Then he rode her, touching her in a secret place that made her grow hot and dizzy with his each thrust. Shimmering heat built inside, spurring her to move against him to let the sensation build.

Damian moaned, low and thick, as if her motion affected him, too, and suddenly he gave a groan that must have startled the wildlife for the way it made her jump. His arms tightened around her, his leg locked around hers, and he hoisted himself up, twisting her onto her back in the process.

The weight of his body pressed her into the blanketed earth as it yielded beneath their weight. His hair cascaded around them, blocking out the sun and cocooning them in a private place that felt intimate and inviting.

"I prefer the contest of making you swoon, lovely Nina. Not the other way around."

She might have relished the knowledge that she affected him, too, but before reason allowed her a moment to gloat, Damian seized his advantage and pressed down her bodice. Stays bit into her middle, compromising her ability to breathe even further. Then her skin swelled above the ruches and her breasts popped out, exposing her in a wanton display.

A protest tumbled out as a desperate bid for air, but catching her breath was a lost cause for Damian took her nipples between his thumbs and forefingers and squeezed.

Pleasure speared her as if a finely honed blade, and he squeezed again, his dark gaze holding hers purposefully, as if cautioning this was only a prelude of what was to come.

A moist heat mounted between her thighs, made her feel clammy and achy, made her move beneath him in growing arousal. And when he bowed low over her breasts, taking a rosy nipple in his mouth in a slow, wet pull, Nina came off the blanket.

He kneaded and savored her sensitive flesh, and she could only let her eyes drift closed as unimagined heat washed through her. She clawed his silky hair, a boneless effort to hang on.

Her pleasure was so complete she didn't realize he'd worked a hand beneath her gown until his fingers touched her private places. His rough hand shocked her delicate skin, and she cried out, clenching to bar his way, suddenly unsure what to expect.

Damian hushed her with whispers and kisses,

touched a secret spot that made heat pour through her, blinding her to anything but the spiking need that made her raise her hips to increase the friction.

He eased a finger into her wetness, a wholly unfamiliar sensation. A cry escaped her lips. But 'twas the push she needed. The tension inside gathered taut to bursting. Then sweet, shivering spasms poured through her.

Nina had felt lust while touching others' souls. But she'd never understood the temptation that caused one to risk salvation for a fleeting brush with unholy desire.

Until now.

Nina clung as though she might never let go, her face buried against Damian's neck as she came apart in his arms. He held her, whispered encouragements into her hair, staggered by the tenderness he felt toward this maid.

The feeling came from a lifetime past, from a time when he'd behaved as a man who possessed the ability to care.

As he held Nina in his arms, struggling to contain his own need to allow her recovery, content for the pleasure he'd wrought from her body, Damian remembered the feeling and tried to recall exactly when he'd lost it.

He couldn't. 'Twas no defining moment, but a journey through life's rejections and disappointments that had led him to the place he was now.

Hidden away to steal a lady's virtue.

He'd schemed to seduce Nina, and now when he finally held her in his arms, her soft breasts crushing his chest and his cock so hard he ached with every throb of his suddenly feeling heart, he regretted sacrificing all for a few stolen moments.

He wanted to feel her stretched out full against him, her lush curves naked. He wanted to hear her laughter as he introduced to her to a world of carnal bliss that would earn more delighted tremors and breathless sighs.

Damian did not understand why Nina had been so ripe for the picking save Westbury overly sheltered her. Indeed, why the lord hadn't pleasured her himself was beyond Damian's ken, for she was a woman grown, a beautiful, spirited lass with an abundance of healthy curiosity and desires.

Westbury had desires of his own. No surprise. Nina was the loveliest of women, even lovelier in her passion.

And now as she lay beneath him, ripe and willing to be tutored in pleasure, he wanted to take her at his leisure, delight her with more erotic education, teach her to delight him, but he had no right to anything but stolen moments . . . in truth he had not the right to even those.

The ongoing tale of his life.

Too late. Too provincial. Too talented.

By rights Damian should bundle her up and send her back to her guardian, maidenhead intact and head filled with fantasies to keep her blushing until Westbury got around to the task.

"I feel . . . amazing." Her words gusted against his neck, soft warm breaths that made him shiver.

He should roll away from her naive wonder, tempting curves, and willing arms. He should kiss her soundly and get her back to the boat while he could still look himself in the mirror.

His choices were suddenly so clear in his mind,

along with the truth that he'd taken advantage of her, whisked her out from beneath Westbury's trusting eyes with no thought but for himself and his desires, his future and his inspiration.

Nina claimed she wouldn't leave Westbury.

Should he believe her?

Could he blame her?

Westbury was a titled lord, Damian a failed artist and a grudging craftsman. Aye, he could do naught else but believe her. He had to wonder if he'd known all along, had been just desperate and dissolute enough to bid for her anyway.

The question shocked him with such simple clarity and the knowledge he still possessed the freedom to choose.

She threaded her fingers through his hair and brought the weight down around them, pressing a tentative kiss to his throat, daring to drag her tongue along his skin.

His cock surged in his breeches. He wanted to savor her shy exploration without recriminations, but such freedom was not his. Not when he'd truly sunk so low to care for naught but this moment, for the magic they shared together.

He'd intended to seduce Nina and steal her away to "Midnight Magic," yet now she told him nay, mocked the one glimmer of hope he'd had since his return from Europe.

A wave of hot defiance swelled inside him, and Damian rolled to his side and urged her up from the blanket. Her breasts swayed enticingly as he shoved up her skirts to expose thighs as sleek as he'd envisioned.

If he faced the muzzle of Westbury's pistol on the morrow, so be it. Death might be a relief to this life he'd been leading. Right now he would take these moments as his and tomorrow be damned.

He would pleasure Nina, sink deep inside her, feel her tight wet heat. He would turn her gasps of surprise into sighs of ecstasy that would make her every ache a memory to haunt her in the loneliness of her bed.

Dragging his fingers along her smooth skin, Damian guided her to straddle him. With her arms around his neck, she did as he bade, her mouth parted around excited breaths, her nipples round and tight and begging for attention, her thighs parted provocatively, her manner trusting.

Curling his fingers inside her sex, he sought and found the tiny bud of her desire and pressed his thumb until she squirmed.

Her arousal acted as a balm to his soul, and he toyed with her idly, lowered his face to her breasts, laved the tips with swirling strokes of his tongue.

She trembled and closed her eyes, threaded her fingers into his hair to hang on. Damian nipped and suckled and tasted. He unleashed his greedy cock, arching his hips until he could drag the head through the wet folds of her heat.

Nina may be a maiden, but she was a woman whose passions ran deep. Her bottom swayed against him in erotic rhythm, instinctively sensing a greater pleasure to come, arousing him to a fury that made him sink a hand into her hip to lengthen the tender torture of each stroke.

She pressed sweet kisses into his hair, along his temple, daringly swirled her tongue inside his ear then laughed when he shuddered. She played the game with her innocence, and her instinct, passion, and eagerness undid him.

Damian burned for her, could barely contain his groans as his cock swelled against her, gliding through her dampness, pressing inside just enough to torture him with wanting more.

He told himself 'twould be good for her; he would make it so. He told himself this moment was theirs. She wanted him. He wanted her. That bound them, made this moment their right.

And with defiance fueling his thoughts and the lure of her moist depths fueling his ardor, Damian eased upward, pressing inside her, forcing himself to go slow to ease his passage.

She stiffened then tried to scramble away, her panic sharp.

"Shh, Nina sweet." He caught her around the waist and locked her against him. Then he thrust up to finish the deed.

She cried out, a sound that echoed off the waves, through him. Burying her face in the crook of his neck, she muffled the sound against his throat, her tears dampening his skin.

And fool he . . . his eyes stung with a burn wrought of tenderness, of concern, of affection. All tender feelings he hadn't remembered he could feel. All tender feelings he had no business feeling for Nina.

He stroked her face to calm her, cradled her close, waited until she stilled against him.

"Nina, sweet," he breathed into her ear, swirled his tongue inside the delicate shell, was rewarded with a shiver.

Dragging his mouth down her cheek, he coaxed her face up with feathery kisses, nibbled at her lips when she faced him.

Her amber eyes glinted. Tears streaked her cheeks, and he kissed them away, paid homage to her beauty and the trust she'd gifted him with.

His cock fair ached with the waiting, but he dragged his hands down her throat, coaxed her back into the game with seductive caresses and gentle kisses.

Her body relaxed by degrees, and when he finally made his way back to her breasts, beautiful breasts that seemed a touchstone for her arousal, he felt her spasm around him.

Then he pushed in deeper and felt her tremble.

Suckling her nipples as distraction, he began to rock beneath her, enough to torture himself by pressing inside her, enough to coax tiny gasps from her lips as he drove away her breath with each slow thrust.

'Twas Nina who began to move in earnest. Nina, who speared her fingers inside his hair and dragged his head back so she could reach his mouth for fiery kisses. Nina, whose passion unleashed until he could do naught but drive his hips upward, plunging deep, championing the white heat of passion until he felt her tightness clench around him in pulsing bursts.

She cried out his name along with her kisses, and her surrender fueled his until their moans mingled together. He exploded inside her, hips arching, thighs trembling violently, a welter of shimmering sensation unlike anything he'd ever known.

Reality intruded. The awkward untangling of their bodies. The clumsy adjustments to their appearance.

Damian foolishly wanted tenderness and laughter when prudence demanded they return to the shipyard.

His time had come and gone.

He made to tame his hair, to conceal all hints of their tryst, but Nina stopped him.

Brushing his hands away, she smoothed the stands with her fingers. He remembered her earlier boldness, knew his imagination would conjure visions of her hair unbound, the honeyed tresses flowing over her naked body, visions that would taunt him until his dying breath.

Visions he would never realize as truth.

Gathering the weighty mass of his hair into a queue, she fastened the binding at his nape, another at the bottom.

"Many thanks, milady."

She met his gaze with a look of such shy confusion that he was forced to turn away, to stare at the lush branches overhead, the glimmers of sea sparkling through the leaves. *Anywhere,* rather than face the conviction he saw shining in those amber depths, the belief that no matter how sordid the circumstances of his seduction, no matter what the consequences might yield, she had been right to trust where he led.

'Twas a look that shamed Damian to the core.

They returned to the boat in silence. He helped Nina slip back inside her hoops. Then they were underway, returning to the shipyard as if life hadn't twisted unexpectedly during their absence, hadn't changed everything.

Any desire to break the silence was lost beneath the weight of emotion and the irony that he had been chasing any and all reminders of a beating heart within his breast, and now he knew. Now he knew.

A small crowd awaited them on shore, and he steeled himself for the anticipated scene, cursed himself for not stealing one last kiss.

"Damian," Nina said, a hint of urgency in her voice. "I will not be able again—"

"I know." He caressed her with a gaze, captured her image as his own, unwilling yet to accept' 'twould be the only part of her he would truly possess.

Then their stolen moment was over.

There was naught left to speak, naught to do but steer into the moorings and help Nina disembark, put on a casual smile when Hurst and Blair hurried toward them, meeting them before they even stepped off the pier.

His brother stood with arms folded disapprovingly, but Damian cut him off from any reprimand by turning to Hurst.

"I showed Lady Kirkby the islets," he said. "You should have been able to see us."

Hurst scowled. "I saw your boat."

Nina gifted him with a smile of reassurance, but Damian noticed her gaze cut across the yard to where her coach stood waiting.

"Shall we return to the studio?" He glanced up at the sun. "Refreshment, I think, after this outing. We still have time before Lord Westbury will expect your return."

"Milady," Hurst said. "I brought the coach around."

Hurst would never deign to suggest Nina bid her farewells, but he radiated irritation that she'd given him the slip. The choice became Nina's, and Damian sensed her conflict between putting on a performance that all was normal and guilt for her recklessness.

In an effort to sway her toward the performance, he extended his hand and moved in. "Milady, shall we?"

She moved toward him, but Hurst stepped forward to cut Damian off, growling as he came between them, sheltering his lady behind his bulk. Nina looked surprised and caught a heel on the wooden slats of the pier. Her hoops swayed wildly as she stumbled, off balance.

"Milady," Damian called in warning, reaching for her, but as Hurst, as large as a mountain, stood between them . . .

Hurst grasped Nina's arm to steady her.

Damian exhaled a sigh of mixed relief at the near accident and annoyance at the servant's effrontery, but had no chance to react, so stunned was he by the sight before him.

Nina jerked upright as though her slim body had been impaled on a captain's mast.

Her eyes shot open, and in the spate of a heartbeat, the expression fell away from her face, all color, too, leaving her skin suddenly bleached as a shell on the sand, lips that had been reddened from his kisses ghostly pale.

Her chest heaved on a ragged breath, and she swayed wildly, not as though she would swoon, but as if battered to and fro by unseen hands.

The hairs at the back of Damian's neck prickled, and by his side, he heard Blair say, "Sweet Jesus."

WHOOSH.

Images crowded Nina, forcing her to gasp for breath. She couldn't break free from the press of visions pelting her, one on the heels of another . . .

Hurst as he'd once been, a boy of no more than twelve, cowering in the hay. The thick smell of earth and manure. Horses whinnying as a sneering man brought down a lash, shredding fabric and laying open skin in a foaming red line.

Hurst's need to defend himself, almost irresistible. Raising a hand to strike back. Fear making his fingers clench into a fist, over and over. Not fear of his abuser, but of losing all control and having murder on his conscience.

Don't give sway to the anger . . .

Two men at fisticuffs. Hurst, a man full grown. Another man nearly equal in size. Pummeling blows thudding against flesh. Muscles straining. Sweat. Blood.

Shrieks of excitement urging on the violence, as people jammed tight to form a circle. Anticipation shuddered through the crowd, alive. A cheering onlooker tossed down a handful of shillings that rained over the combatants as tears.

Stop, stop, stop.

Hurst as Nina knew him. Indomitable. Silent. Unwavering. He stood with Gray, whose hand was outstretched in greeting. An offer of friendship.

Trust your heart, believe.

Nina saw him older, as he would grow to be, passing by a waterside tavern. The urge to step inside ached through him. The taste of ale on his tongue biting. His mind said nay, even as his footsteps moved toward the door.

No, no, no . . . Stay strong. Resist.

Need. Despair.

The door creaked open. She saw faces. Heard laughter. The cool liquid over a parched tongue. Then the scene shifted. Sudden. Stark. A dagger thrust between his ribs, searing through flesh and organ.

The sudden violence of the attack shocked. The burn of Hurst's lifeblood as it poured out, not onto the scarred wood floor but inside him.

Nina felt his confusion when he touched the spot where he'd been stabbed. The big hand he pulled away, fingers smeared with blood. Disbelief mingled with weakness as he sank to the floor.

Death claimed him before he knew it would come, before he could accept.

Then shadows clashed against a glaring brilliance . . .

*   *   *

Damian watched as Hurst stared in horror then seemed to regain his senses and snatch his hand off Nina. Staggering backward, he abandoned her to whatever this fit that beset her, murmuring over and over, "Milady, I am sorry."

The loss of his touch won another violent reaction, for Nina jerked upright again, her body shocked into stillness, her gaze unfocused, her mouth moving in some silent chant.

Then she collapsed boneless.

Damian rushed forward to catch her, dragging her against him and lowering her to the ground.

Nearby workers, noticing the commotion, drew around, muttering questions and offering help, looking to Blair for guidance.

Their father came running from the office. After taking in the situation, he barked orders that Damian heard as if from a distance. He cradled Nina against him, fanned her face to no effect, silently willed her to awaken, knew whatever affliction held her in its thrall wasn't natural or right.

Peering around, he caught Hurst's stricken expression and demanded, "What's happening, man? What do I do to help her?"

"I cannot touch her. No one can. Only the master. Please. Take her to the coach. I must take her to the master."

Damian lifted Nina into his arms and rose to his feet. "Clear away," he commanded the onlookers. "Get back."

He didn't ken what was happening, but Nina's fit had started with the man's touch, so there was no dispute. As he held Nina close, he could hear her ragged words, talk of darkness and light. Of eternal salvation and damnation. Of choices to be made and paths to be avoided, of the battle that would wage for Hurst's soul at his death.

Damian had the wild urge to shake her, to stop the mad mutterings from tumbling off her lips, but he resisted, paralyzed into inaction, frightened that Nina might die in his arms while he was powerless to help her.

And deep inside, pulsing through him like venom, was the notion that he wrought some hurt upon her with his actions this day. The staggering enormity of what he'd done hit him hard, and he could only wonder if making love to Nina had somehow brought this unholy spell upon her.

"*I cannot touch her. No one can. Only the master.*"

Why had Hurst's touch brought on this fit? And why could Westbury touch her?

Why could Damian?

Cradling her in his lap, he stroked her face, caressed cheeks that were as cool as marble, whispered, "Nina."

He half expected her to bolt upright in that strange fit again, but he felt her pause . . .

"Nina. Nina, sweet, come back."

He whispered her name over and over as the coach rambled through the lanes of St. Michaels, feeling fearful and useless and so horribly guilty. That he should sprout a conscience now could only be God's judgment against his sins.

Yet Damian continued to whisper her name and stroke her face, fearful to stop though her manner finally eased and her mutterings faded to silence. She relaxed against him, falling into an exhausted slumber.

When the coach ground to a halt, he found that Hurst had delivered them to Westbury's office. Nina only stirred restlessly when he lifted her from the coach.

"Not through the front," Hurst said when Damian headed down the entryway. "Milord is with the lieutenant governor."

"I don't care if Christ Jesus himself is inside. I want Westbury, and I want him now."

As he bellowed the last words, Damian wasn't surprised when the office door flung wide and Westbury appeared, along with a man Damian recognized as a Maryland official behind him.

Westbury took in the sight of them in a glance, but his expression revealed no surprise when he said, "Hurst, show Master Hart to the back chamber."

As Damian followed the servant across a reception area and into a hall, he overheard Westbury tell his guest, "My ward is given to fainting spells. I must see to her needs."

"Go then, Gray. I shall be in touch."

The back chamber turned out to be comfortable sitting area set up for entertaining. Westbury appeared as Damian settled Nina onto a settee and Hurst brought a blanket from an armoire.

He didn't acknowledge Damian but asked his man, "What happened, Hurst?"

The servant began a recitation of the day's offenses, and Damian was forced to retreat from the settee, so Westbury could kneel beside Nina. He stood aside, not offering defense, simply watching as Westbury caressed Nina's temple, tested the pulse in her throat, brushed errant strands of hair from her cheeks with a tenderness that was wrenching to watch.

"She will recover, Hurst. Have no fear. You may go."

Hurst backed out of the chamber without another word, looking contrite and shaken.

"What the hell happened?" Damian demanded of Westbury when the door had shut.

Westbury appeared intent upon ignoring him, for he stood without reply.

Damian braced himself, feeling the full weight of his actions that had wrought this mess. Just as he'd had no right to pursue Nina, he had no right to make demands of her guardian now. He was surprised when Westbury finally retreated to a sidebar to pour two snifters of port.

"You took my ward sailing?"

"I did."

"Without her companion."

"Yes."

Westbury just inclined his head, seeming content to draw his own conclusions. Then he turned, and his fist flew so fast Damian had no chance to recoil before the blow sent him staggering backward. His face exploded in crushing agony, but he managed to catch himself at the last possible instant before toppling over a chair.

Breathing heavily, he righted himself and faced Westbury, rubbing the ache in his jaw, obliged to offer a defense where no defense would exonerate him. "She was fine until your man touched her."

"I imagine what happened came as a shock."

"'Twas no swoon, I assure you, but some sort of fit."

"No. 'Twas no swoon." Westbury exhaled a breath heavy with resignation and motioned to a chair. "Sit, Master Hart. We have much to discuss."

Damian was surprised by the civility, but he did as requested. Westbury handed him a snifter then sat in a winged chair opposite, his gaze darting back to Nina, whose beautiful face looked almost peaceful now, that terrible grip that had claimed her replaced by even breathing.

"She seems more restful," Damian said.

"She'll sleep a while longer."

"This has happened before." Not a question. Westbury had the look of a man who has seen and survived such trials.

Westbury nodded.

"Your man believed he caused her ailment," Damian said. "He said he couldn't touch her."

"He cannot. Nor can anyone else."

Damian had no ken what to make of that statement, so he just waited while Westbury brought the glass to his lips.

Finally he said, "Nina has a rather unique ability, Master Hart. Whenever she touches someone, or is touched, she can see that person's death."

Damian shook his head as if to clear it, unsure if he'd heard correctly. "You speak of deviltry when you claim to believe in the Lord?"

"Deviltry?" Westbury frowned. "Nay. 'Tis God's grace. Nina has the ability to see the choices people make over a lifetime, the choices that lead to their salvation, or their condemnation. She can influence people with this gift, to help them make the choices to save their souls."

Gooseflesh prickled as Damian tried to consider Westbury's claim, tried to imagine the effects of an ability that made a chill ice along his spine. "*Everyone* she touches?"

"Except me. For some reason Nina cannot touch my death."

Then Damian remembered their initial meeting on

the pier at the shipyard, and the significance of her surprise when he'd taken her hand. She'd been visibly shocked; Westbury, too. "Or me. She cannot touch my death either."

"No, she cannot."

"Why?"

Westbury shrugged. "Until you, only I held the distinction. We have never understood, but the why has bound us together."

"'Tis why you accepted my offer to paint her. You wanted to understand why she could touch me, too."

Westbury raised his glass in salute.

While Damian did not ken what would have earned him such a place beside this titled lord, he did understand Nina's vulnerability to his seduction and why he had seen her and Westbury inside "Midnight Magic."

They were all bound together in a fashion Damian would never have been able to guess, and as the implications of Westbury's claims sank in, Damian also thought he understood something else, too—Westbury's anger.

Until days ago, Gray Talbot had been the only man who could touch Nina, yet she had remained a maid. The why to that question wasn't so hard to divine anymore and cast Damian in such a dim light he could barely meet the man's gaze.

"Damn you," he demanded. "Why did you allow her to come to me today?"

"'Twas Nina's choice."

"And you let her go? Why? You want her."

"I was arrogant, Master Hart. I believed we had all the time in the world." Westbury stared into his glass as if he might find answers inside. "My ward and I are at cross purposes over her ability. I believe she has been blessed. She views her blessing as a curse. I only lost my wife little more than a year past, and Nina is still young. I'd hoped she would find peace and settle into our new life."

"Why has she not?"

Westbury raised his gaze and glanced to Nina, expression thoughtful. "I fear many do not understand her gift, and she has been much vilified. 'Tis the reason we fled England."

This revelation helped Damian understand why Nina might feel so beholden to her guardian, why she'd been so tempted by the escape "Midnight Magic" offered. And why she wouldn't take her second chance. Like Damian, she had a debt to repay.

"You and Nina are also at cross purposes over 'Midnight Magic,' " he said.

"Nina believes the painting is the means to living the normal life she has been denied."

"Yet you deny her?"

Westbury frowned. "Nay, Master Hart, I deny her naught, though I fear for her soul should she involve herself with that painting. Nina has been blessed with a gift that can bring many into glory—including herself."

"That *gift* could see her burned at the stake for witchery."

"We all walk our paths. Nina's may be more difficult, but I believe 'tis because she has the grace to do greater good."

Damian found no reply. He didn't know if he held such a puritanical view of Nina's situation, but when he saw the peace on her beautiful face, he knew that he wished for her to find that peace waking as well as in slumber.

"I want to be a part of her life. I want to help." When

Damian turned back around, he found Westbury had followed his gaze and watched Nina, too, his expression unreadable.

"That choice will be Nina's, of course. She possesses the will to choose her own path."

"You will respect her wishes?" Somehow Damian already knew the answer.

Gray inclined his head. "Always."

'Twas the dead of night, but Nina made her way inside Gray's study, the lantern she held bright enough only to keep her from stumbling over the furniture and alerting the whole household to her presence downstairs.

She would be hard-pressed to explain why she wandered around at this late hour dressed in her riding garb. After today's happenings with Damian, every one of their servants would have roused Gray from his bed to alert him that his wayward ward was up to her antics again.

She'd jeopardized everything with her escape today, and she reaped the results of that daring.

The beauty she'd found in Damian's arms.

Her shame in the shipyard.

Her utter humiliation to awaken in Gray's work chamber to discover he'd sent Damian away and consoled an anguished Hurst, leaving her to face him, and though he tried nobly to hide it, his disappointment.

"Please forgive me," she'd told him.

"You have done naught for me to forgive, my dear. You followed your heart, and I would never begrudge you that. Not when you have so graciously allowed me to follow mine in all these long months since Juliette's death."

"I have made a spectacle of myself—in front of a shipyard filled with onlookers and the lieutenant governor. 'Twill start up the talk and begin the questions all over again and spoil everything you've worked so hard for."

"As I said, there is naught for me to forgive." He stroked her cheek, smiled softly. *"You must forgive yourself."*

Nina would carry the memory of Gray's smile locked tight in her heart for whenever she grew lonely or fearful. She would remember that Gray prayed for her, believed in her always, even when she did not believe in herself.

Lifting the quill pen from the case, Nina dragged the inkwell to her, firm in her resolve that for once today she had made the right choice. Gray did not deserve to be burdened by her—no man did. Not even Damian who threw caution to the four winds and decried every convention and propriety.

But especially not her noble guardian who had sacrificed all and had loved her in his fashion.

Pressing her pen to the parchment, she wrote:

My beloved Gray,
I will forgive myself only when I no longer weigh as a burden upon those whom I love above all else. If 'twas only my future that looked so bleak, I would willingly bear the expense, but, alas, 'tis not the way of things.

Juliette would want you to find love and happiness again and 'tis what I wish for you, too. Live your life, my darling, live to the fullest for you deserve nothing less. Pray for me as I shall pray for you.

Always,

N.

Sanding the ink, Nina set the letter on the desk and prayed Gray would understand and forgive her. She returned the pen to the case, retrieved the lantern, and left the study.

Making her way out the kitchen door, she dimmed the lantern and crossed the grounds to the stables under the light of the waxing moon. She would not allow fear or uncertainty to deter her, firm in her resolve that 'twas time to accept that the future was hers to make *alone.*

Short of death, there was only one place she might do that.

Dawn broke in pastel shades of crimson and gold when Damian banged on Westbury's front door, demanding entry of the startled footman who stood blinking as if the guest on his stoop had been wrought of his imagination.

"Come on, man, wake up," he prodded. "'Tis urgent. Where is your lord?"

Without further delay, the footman led Damian to a study in the well-appointed manor, where he found Westbury standing behind the desk, hands clasped behind his back, staring out at the paling dawn through an unshuttered window.

"Milord, you've a guest," the footman announced.

Westbury turned, looking genuinely surprised. "Why are you here?"

"Do you not know? Nina took her second chance. She went to Master Verbrugges during the night. The master came to Hart Hill to inform me only an hour past."

Westbury grimaced as though pained, and Damian realized he held a letter clenched in his fist.

"From Nina?"

Westbury nodded. The man was clearly in agony, and Damian wished he could find compassion, wished to find some emotion that would do him more credit than the envy he felt at all Westbury possessed by right. The man had earned Nina's unswerving gratitude and affection.

Damian had squandered the precious time he'd had with her on selfishness.

"Why have you not gone after her?" Damian demanded.

Westbury leaned over the desk and offered the letter. Damian scanned the missive, and again bit back the sharp edge of a jealousy he had no right to feel.

Nina and Gray had developed the closeness they shared over years. Damian was new to their lives. He had thought only of swaying Nina to his side, hadn't made an effort to understand her situation, had grossly underestimated the power of the love she possessed for the man who now stood before him.

He'd thought only of himself and his desires.

Only now did he understand Gray's fierce protectiveness, and the true harm he himself had wrought by making Nina yearn. Only now, after she'd flown, did he try to fashion a way for her to live the peaceful life she longed for.

"I am going after her," Damian said.

"What of your debt?"

"I am going."

"I thought you would have gone already," Westbury admitted. "I'd thought you would have stolen off into the painting to claim her for yourself."

"I wanted to."

"Then why are you here?"

Damian inhaled deeply, steeled himself to admit a truth he still didn't fully understand, knew Westbury wouldn't believe. "This is not about me."

" 'Twas all about you yesterday, man. You paid no heed to what was best for Nina. You might not have known the truth, but you knew she was tempted by your seduction."

"I stand by my actions and feel shame."

Westbury held his gaze for a long moment before inclining his head in acknowledgment of that hard truth, and in doing made Damian feel the depravity of his own actions all the more keenly. "So, are you here to offer me to take your place?"

"You credit me with too much nobility, milord. I want to be a part of Nina's life if she'll allow me. But understanding her situation, I respect she'll never be whole without you. I would not have her choose between us."

Westbury's brows rose in surprise. "You would have us both follow her inside that painting?"

Damian nodded.

Westbury turned to the window and didn't turn back again. He revealed naught to give the impression he considered the choice, or was even shocked by it. Damian had no way of knowing what demons Westbury faced, if he had dismissed the suggestion outright or entertained the compromise, but the man cared deeply for

Nina, so Damian stood there silently, waiting as the sky beyond the window brightened past dawn into morning.

When Westbury finally turned around, dark eyes haunted but determined, he inclined his head, and Damian knew, for the first time in recent memory, the choice he'd made was right.

EPILOGUE

2006, St. Michaels, Maryland

Roman Barrymore steered his Mercedes sedan off the thruway and down the exit ramp leading to the scenic route along Chesapeake Bay. This detour would buy him additional time to clear his thoughts before arriving at the White House for a two o'clock briefing with the president.

On the surface, his reaction to the latest terrorism threat plaguing the nation might seem a knee-jerk reaction to a growing global problem, but the president was about to learn that the terrorist cell with the highest death toll in the contiguous United States had another foothold—in eight states.

This threat was a ticking bomb. As acting director of a covert national antiterrorism agency, Roman needed to defuse the threat before winding up with a replay of 9/11 proportions.

Steering through St. Michaels, a picturesque town on Maryland's Eastern Shore, he mentally reviewed the intel he would present in only a few hours.

He'd intentionally overestimated the time of the drive from the country safehouse where he'd debriefed a defector for the past several days. Roman hadn't slept in more than forty-eight hours and needed to decompress before the president and his advisers started firing off rounds of questions to justify the political muscle he wanted to put a fast end to this threat.

As he decelerated to turn into a public parking lot, he spotted a business sign that read Second Chance Gallery. Someone had clearly given a second chance to a former auto repair center. One glimpse of the renovated antique shop convinced him the cool quiet of antiquities would better suit his mood today than the sweltering heat of the shore.

Lush greenery and the smell of coffee welcomed Roman into a surprisingly upscale place housing an array of objets d'art in partitioned rooms, and a gallery that displayed a wide variety of art. A good choice because art happened to be an interest.

His role as acting director demanded the vast majority of his time be spent inside Command, where overhead satellite arrays allowed him and high-clearance operatives to monitor active missions around the globe and assess potential threats that could impact the United States or her allies.

Roman had made it a point since early in his career to fill his life with reminders of the world he'd devoted himself to protecting. Those reminders included art on the walls of his office and inside the home he all-too-infrequently inhabited, along with visits into the real world beyond the maximum security compound north of Washington, D.C., that housed his agency headquarters.

Spotting a Lekinff, he moved inside a gallery much more high-caliber than he'd expected to find in this small Eastern Shore community.

The oil painting turned out to be an original, but even more impressive was an unfinished portrait hanging nearby. The canvas depicted a young woman with honeyed hair and creamy skin reflected in a gilt mirror.

Her face was innocent, almost uncertain at first glance, but her expression ached with a yearning so compelling that Roman could only marvel at the skill of the artist who'd filled gold-flecked amber eyes with a living emotion.

The whole scene had been sketched in charcoal on the canvas, but only the center had been painted. Expert brushstrokes brought the woman's beautiful face to life, the colors vibrant against the faded charcoal background.

"She's lovely, isn't she?" A feminine voice asked, and Roman turned to find a slim blond woman dressed in a stylish summer ensemble approaching.

"Very."

"Sara Tripplehorn." She extended her hand and they shook. "Welcome to Second Chance Gallery. I heard the bell, but it took a few moments to end my call."

"Giving me time to admire your collection."

She inclined her head, a wave of blond hair slicing across her shoulders. "Straight to the art. What drew you in here?"

"The Lekinff."

"It didn't keep your eye though."

"No. This did. Do you know why the artist never finished her portrait?"

Sara followed his gaze to the beautiful face, a thoughtful expression on her own. "Afraid not. The portrait is unsigned, but through the years there's been a good bit of speculation about the artist. Lots of opinions but no concrete proof."

"Do you have an opinion?"

"I believe it's a Damian Hart. He was a local painter who gained renown back in the early eighteen hundreds. He painted some true masterpieces. I recognize the technique as his, although there are many who have other ideas."

Roman nodded.

"Have you seen 'Midnight Magic' yet?"

"No. Show me."

Sara led him toward the rear of the gallery, and Roman observed how her gaze skimmed dotingly over each painting they passed, as if each was a cherished family member.

"A place of honor," he commented as she led him to the turret-like alcove where this particular painting was displayed.

"A special painting deserves a special setting."

Alcove or not, this painting had a special setting, Roman decided. Sara Tripplehorn had a gift for showcasing rare treasures in unexpected places, judging by his impression of her acquisitions. That was Roman's gift—judging people.

"Take a look," she suggested. "Tell me what you see."

At first glance "Midnight Magic" seemed an unusual part of her collection. Tiny dots of thick oil paint in vibrant colors filled the canvas, and Roman recognized the abstract technique—pointillism—and looked closely as the colorful dots blended together to create an image.

The effect could be almost disorienting—"Midnight Magic" apparently more than most. But Roman kept his gaze fixed on the painting, made out the images materializing through the slashes of living color.

"The woman from the unfinished portrait," he said.

"Really?"

"You sound surprised."

"Does she look the same?"

"Older. Not by much. She's sitting for another portrait. With two men."

The unfinished woman's companions stood behind her, each with a hand on her shoulder, a stately dark-haired man on her right and a striking man with long red hair on her left. She held a hand over each of the men's, but unlike the yearning he'd seen in her unfinished portrait, her expression in "Midnight Magic" seemed contented, complete.

But as Roman stared into the faces, so lifelike in the seductive colors of "Midnight Magic," he had to wonder if some trick of his imagination made their expressions change, almost as if they were beckoning him . . .